"Five y
from m...

Lani looked at him with worry in her eyes.

He pulled her close. Five years! he thought. If there had been a reason, if he had done something wrong, he could have handled it. But to be jailed for a cover-up...

He felt Lani's full breasts softly pressing against his body, and all at once his anger exploded into frustrated passion. He was tired of waiting, waiting and more waiting. He wanted to make love to his wife.

Lani was startled, then reluctantly excited as Bryan tilted her face up and kissed her with all the pent-up passion of five wasted years. Without missing a beat he scooped her up, carried her into the bedroom and placed her on top of the bedspread. As he greedily lowered his head, she saw that his passion-filled eyes were almost black. He reminded her of a pirate, and she knew that she was the booty to be plundered....

Dear Reader,

Among the stellar authors in our January lineup is Lynda Trent, well-known for her weighty historical novels. What keeps her coming back to Silhouette **Special Edition**? Here's how she explains it:

*"I write for Silhouette **Special Edition** to share a romantic fantasy with my readers, an emotional adventure in which a woman might be an heiress, a commoner or a Mata Hari... and still be loved by the perfect man. Within the broad scope of a **Special Edition**, she might dare to love a dangerous man; she might chance everything for a noble cause. I want to weave a tapestry of romance blossoming, of dreams fulfilled, and I want to share it with other dreamers."*

Like the piratical hero of Lynda Trent's *Like Strangers*, the authors and editors of Silhouette **Special Edition** want to knock on the door to your heart... and open it to all the possibilities life and love have to offer.

Share your tastes and preferences with us. Each and every month we strive to offer you something new, something *special*. Let us know how we're doing!

Happy new year,

Leslie Kazanjian, Senior Editor
Silhouette Books
300 East 42nd Street
New York, N.Y. 10017

LYNDA TRENT
Like Strangers

Published by Silhouette Books New York

America's Publisher of Contemporary Romance

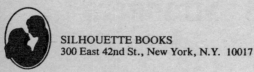

SILHOUETTE BOOKS
300 East 42nd St., New York, N.Y. 10017

Copyright © 1989 by Dan and Lynda Trent

All rights reserved. Except for use in any review, the reproduction or utilization of this work in whole or in part in any form by any electronic, mechanical or other means, now known or hereafter invented, including xerography, photocopying and recording, or in any information storage or retrieval system, is forbidden without the permission of Silhouette Books, 300 E. 42nd St., New York, N.Y. 10017

ISBN: 0-373-09504-X

First Silhouette Books printing January 1989

All the characters in this book are fictitious. Any resemblance to actual persons, living or dead, is purely coincidental.

®: Trademark used under license and registered in the United States Patent and Trademark Office and in other countries.

Printed in the U.S.A.

Books by Lynda Trent

Silhouette Intimate Moments

Designs #36
Taking Chances #68
Castles in the Sand #134

Silhouette Desire

The Enchantment #201
Simple Pleasures #223

Silhouette Special Edition

High Society #378
A Certain Smile #409
Heat Lightning #443
Beguiling Ways #457
Like Strangers #504

LYNDA TRENT

started writing romances at the insistence of a friend, but it was her husband who provided moral support whenever her resolve flagged. Now husband and wife are both full-time writers of contemporary and historical novels, and despite the ups and downs of this demanding career, they love every—well, *almost* every—minute of it.

Chapter One

The hot south Texas wind tousled her short coppery hair as she built a pyre around the clay god. She struck a match, and as she shielded the flame with her cupped hand she coaxed the twigs into a crackling blaze. As the fire leaped eagerly around the reddish clay figure, Lani moved upwind and sat down on the powdery dirt of her backyard to watch. She hoped that this time she had used the correct grade of cinnabar in her latest creation, because she wanted her hearth gods to each be a rich red-brown. Only in time would she know.

Carefully she added kindling to keep the fire constant around the statue. Firing the clay properly was the most important part of the process.

When the clay breastplate of the god began to deepen to the shade Lani was trying for, she relaxed. She continued tending the fire until all the moisture had been baked from the clay, and she remained sitting cross-legged on the ground until the flames died down. The squat statue, with its alert expression and folded arms, watched back. It was relatively small, just over fourteen inches high, and was topped with an elaborate headdress with curling ear covers. This was one of her most popular designs.

When she was certain the fire was out, Lani left the statue to cool and went back into her studio. The air-conditioned interior of her shop felt good after the heat of the summer sun and the fire. Lani splashed her face with water from the utility sink, then patted herself dry on a towel. She hoped there would be time to finish the other two statues before Jay Harmond came to pick them up the following week. The process couldn't be rushed, not with the authenticity he demanded.

Resuming her work, she checked the temperature reading on the conventional kiln on the far side of the large room. While most of her income came from her Mayan gods, Lani also produced a line of pottery that she sold through some gift shops in nearby Laredo. In her spare time, what little she had, she worked on what she considered to be her most important pieces—sculptures that spilled cascades of water in a fluid music that was as important as the shape of the sculpture. She called them her waterfalls.

Lani narrowed her green eyes and looked out the window at the Mayan god, squatting there like a time traveler, his expression promising safety to whatever hearth he was destined to guard. As were all her clay gods, this sculpture was entirely of her own invention, though the materials, patina and method of creation duplicated that of the ancient Mayans as closely as she could manage. The end result looked quite authentic. Although she signed her clay gods with a small triangle on the base, the pottery made for the gift shops and the waterfalls she hoped to one day exhibit were signed with her name, Lani Cameron, and the date.

She went to a shelf of jars and sacks and measured out some cement, fresh lime and ammonia, and mixed them into the hot sugar water from the top of her portable stove. As she continued stirring the mixture with a brush, she went back out to the statue. Kneeling, she painted the still-hot surface to give it the proper patina. As a sealer she used a mixture of a Mexican glue and dirt.

Lani stood and dusted the knees of her jeans as she went back inside. The hearth god was finished. As soon as it was cool, she could pack it in a bed of sawdust. When Jay arrived she would show it to him for his approval, then seal the crate for shipment.

She had been fortunate to find Jay Harmond—or rather that he had found her. She couldn't possibly have supported herself these past five years on her pottery alone. Most tourists passing through Laredo wanted Mexican crafts and keepsakes, not American-made pottery. Once again she told herself she should establish a contact farther from the border, say in Austin, but Jay had always dissuaded her, and his orders for the Mayan gods kept food on her table. Even though Bryan had been doubling up on their house payments before he left on that cursed flight, she had had to refinance the house to get the payments down to something she could afford.

Lani lifted a blue-and-green bowl into place on one of her waterfalls and aligned it so that it was in line with the lotus-shaped cups that spiraled above it. She filled the reservoir with water and turned on the pump. A trickle of silvery water filled the top lotus, then spilled into the next, and then the next. The melody of falling water filled the studio. It worked.

As Lani disassembled the fountain, she wistfully thought of Bryan. Handsome and gentle, he had been her perfect mate. For three years they had enjoyed a marriage with few of the traumas that could have beset a relationship in which the husband was gone so often. Bryan had owned a small air cargo business—one plane, which he piloted himself—and had been on the verge of buying another when he disappeared.

The trip had been purely routine. He was to fly a shipment to Mexico City and return home empty. Although he had hoped for a return cargo, no arrangements had been made before his departure on the relatively short flight. But he never returned.

For a while she thought he might have had to make an emergency landing in a town too small and remote to have telephone service. As the days became weeks, then months, she had had to accept the fact he wouldn't be coming home. Mexico was big, and if he had crashed in one of the many remote, unpopulated areas, his plane might never be found.

Back in the good days, she had been happy as a housewife with her pottery as a hobby. She had sold bowls and jugs whenever she felt like it, but the sole provider had been Bryan. In time, as soon as the cargo business had become successful, they had planned to have children. The small farm they lived on was perfect for raising a family, and their wood-frame house—not fancy but spacious—had several extra bedrooms. But Bryan had flown away and never returned, and the hopes of children had vanished just as completely. Her family suggested she obtain a divorce on the grounds of desertion and start a new life, but she only wanted Bryan. He was the only man she had ever really wanted. He was the only one she had ever loved.

In two more years he could be declared legally dead. Lani looked down at the narrow gold wedding band she still wore. He had been gone longer than they had been together, but she still missed him. By now the agony had subsided into dull loneliness. She had had chances to date. Jay Harmond had made passes at her more often than she preferred, but she had refused his advances with no regrets. She still felt as though she was Bryan Cameron's wife.

At her clay-smudged workbench, Lani unwrapped the wet cloth from a rain goddess. She had no names for her creations; she spoke almost no Spanish. Idly she wondered if Jay gave them names when he sold them, but she decided that was fanciful. Why bother to name Mayan look-alikes?

At first she had been skeptical about creating them at all. Art forgery was something she wanted no part of. But Jay had explained that his interior decorating company had a number of clients who wanted to collect pre-Columbian art but were reluctant to pay the price for genuine artifacts. Some preferred the art replicas as they did faux jewelry because of the fear of being burglarized. Lani could understand this—money was frequently scarce around her own home. So, she had studied pre-Columbian art and how it had been made, designed a series of gods and goddesses and went to work.

The rain goddesses were Lani's favorite designs. She had given them fanciful headdresses of stylized lightning bolts, clouds and slanting streaks of rain. Lani never made two statues identically, and allowed herself more creative freedom with the rain goddess than, say, the hearth god, who was supposed to stay put and take care of the home.

As Lani worked, the shadows lengthened and the crickets began to sing in the sweltering twilight. She took time to eat a sandwich as she watched the evening news, then went out to bring in the cooled hearth god. The setting sun emblazoned the western sky with reds and golds, while the opposite horizon was darkening from purple into night. Already a few faint stars could be seen just above the treetops.

With precise, careful movements Lani dusted the clay figure. Evenings were difficult for her because, traditionally, families drew together at this time for supper after a day of work. But the worst time for her was bedtime, and most nights the bed still seemed vast and empty. Lani usually worked long into the night, tiring herself so she would go to sleep quickly. She knew after all this time that Bryan must be dead, but it was the lack of evidence that kept the issue alive. She still felt as if he was a part of her, and it kept her from going on with the business of forgetting and making a new life.

She took the statue inside and carefully examined it under a bright light. There were tiny imperfections and blemishes that made the new statue appear to be ages old. Jay would be pleased. Her latest pieces looked as authentic as the real thing. Lani put the statue in the crate of sawdust and fitted the top loosely in place to protect it. There was no point in securing it until Jay gave it his approval.

For the next several hours she immersed herself in the job of preparing the clay for the next day's sculpting. As usual the hours passed slowly, but she was accustomed to that. Living alone had at least taught her patience. She thought she heard a faint noise, and she paused in the act of working moisture into the lump of stiff clay to listen. She heard only the usual night sounds, so she resumed her work. It was getting late, but she still wasn't sleepy. Restlessly she again opened the crate that contained the hearth god. The clay could crack if it were jostled in shipment, so she again checked to be sure the sawdust cushioned it properly. When she was satisfied the statue couldn't break by accident, Lani put the box back with the two others she had finished, and perched on her stool to examine the mound of clay she had been working on. She was particular about her clay, buying only that which matched the consistency and coloring of the Mexican clay she was trying to duplicate. Once she added the cinnabar, even an expert would have trouble determining whether the clay was American or Mexican.

Again she heard a noise and looked up sharply. She had no dog or cat, but then this wasn't the sort of noise an animal would make. Instead it sounded as though someone were trying to open the front door.

Lani slid off the stool and armed herself with one of the mallets she used to pound pigment into the clay. Her heart beat faster as she heard the sound again.

Not bothering to turn on the lights in the rest of the house, Lani made her way through the darkness. The front and side doors were shut and securely locked as she had expected them to be. She frowned, wondering whether she ought to call the sheriff. Since she lived several miles out of town, she had no close neighbors. Normally she enjoyed the solitude, but tonight she felt distinctly uneasy.

As she went back toward the studio, she heard a rustle and scrape as if something—someone—had stumbled against the cast-iron barbecue grill. A deep dread suddenly filled her. She had been out back to bring in the hearth god, but had she locked the studio door?

Her steps quickened along with her pulse. She couldn't remember turning the dead bolt! It was such an automatic act that she could have forgotten it. In all the years she had lived in the farmhouse, she had never once had a prowler and had become less cautious than when she was first alone.

As she reached the studio, she heard the unmistakable sound of footsteps on the brick patio out back and could see a man's shadowy bulk outside the window. She bit back a cry of fear and ran toward the door. Even from across the room she could tell the bolt wasn't in place.

Before she reached it, the knob turned and the door opened. Lani lurched to a halt as a large man loomed into the room. For a moment she stared at him as her hands knotted around the mallet's handle. He stared back.

Then slowly her fingers relaxed their grip, and the mallet clattered to the floor. "Bryan?" she gasped.

He wasn't easily recognizable, and for a minute she had thought she must be mistaken, for his dark brown hair was long and shaggy, and a dark beard covered most of his face. Only his brown eyes were familiar.

He pushed himself farther into the room, and Lani retreated several steps. This couldn't be Bryan! This man was too thin, and his clothing was little more than rags. He looked as if he hadn't had a bath in quite a while, though his pant legs were damp as if he had forded a stretch of water. Under one arm he carried a bundle wrapped in a ragged jacket that still bore the faded emblem of Cameron Cargo Service.

Again she looked into his eyes and felt even more doubt. Had Bryan, with all his cocky self-assurance, ever looked so lost and miserable? She took another step back.

"Lani?" he asked in a familiar voice. "Don't you know me?"

"Bryan?" she repeated in a whisper. "It can't be!"

He tossed the bundle onto the worktable and swayed as if he were about to fall.

"Bryan!" She ran to him and stopped just inches from him. "It *is* you!"

He put out his arms and drew her to him. As he embraced her, he breathed deeply taking in the smell of her clean-scented hair. "Oh, God, Lani! I've missed you!"

Lani's eyes were open wide and filled with apprehension as he held her tightly. This couldn't be Bryan—he was dead! Yet somehow, by some miracle, it was!

There were no words to form all the questions in her mind; she was speechless. Slowly she put her arms around him. He was thin and he was dirty, but he was indeed Bryan.

After a moment she pulled back and again looked into his eyes. They were moist with emotion and filled with love for her. "How..." she began. "Where..." No words were adequate for what she was feeling. "You're supposed to be dead!"

"Dead! No, I'm not dead, but I'm awfully tired."

She thought how strange it was to hear Bryan's voice coming out of this stranger's face. "Where have you been? What happened to you!"

He gave her a steady look as if he couldn't believe she had no idea where he had been. "I assumed that... It's a long story, Lani. I..." He swayed again, and she put her arm around him.

"Come sit down. I'll fix you something to eat."

"What I really want is a bath." He looped his arm around her shoulders. "Then food. And lots of it."

She walked him to the bathroom and felt a twinge of shyness as she saw him staring at her panty hose looped over the towel rod to dry. Quickly she scooped them up and wadded them in her hand as she avoided his eyes. This was silly, her rational mind said. This was her husband, not some stranger! But he looked like a stranger, and a very disreputable one at that.

Awkwardly she opened the linen closet and got out a towel and washcloth. She put them on the vanity and noticed that he was staring at himself in the mirror, as if he hadn't seen himself in a long time. As he touched his face and beard, a haunted look came into his eyes.

"Soap is in the dish," she said with a quick wave of her hand. "I'll try to find you some clothes."

His eyes met hers in the mirror, and he silently nodded.

Lani backed out of the bathroom, her panty hose still knotted in her hand, and closed the door. Part of her brain was screaming that this couldn't be her beloved Bryan, another part was assuring her that none of this was happening at all.

For a long moment she stood in the middle of her bedroom, staring at the closet door. After five years Lani no longer had any of his clothes hanging there. She had given away most of them after it became evident that he would never return. Fortunately she had kept a few of his favorite things, the ones that most reminded her of him. She pulled the cardboard box out of the storage closet and sorted through it until she found a pair of jeans and a short-sleeved pullover. There was no underwear, no socks, but she unearthed a pair of tennis shoes from the depths of the box. They had been almost new, and she had hesitated to throw them out.

She carried the clothes back to the bathroom and stopped. She could hear the bath water running, and knew he must be undressing. He might be her husband, but she couldn't possibly walk in as if there hadn't been five years of absence that was now standing between them. She put the shoes on the floor just outside the closed door, folded the clothes neatly on top of them, then backed away.

Food. He wanted food. She hurried to the kitchen and flicked on the light. Panic threatened to overwhelm her. What if that wasn't Bryan, her doubts demanded of her. Except for his eyes, this man bore only a passing resemblance to her husband. Surely many men had the same coloring and a voice the same pitch and cadence! That could be a stranger in there, bent on doing lord knew what!

She tried to force herself to be calm. Of course that was Bryan; incredible as it might seem. After five years she looked different, too. Her hair had been longer, her body had been more rounded, she had been far more shy and dependent. Where had he been? He looked as if he had been living in hell.

With trembling hands she cooked the first thing she found in the refrigerator—bacon and eggs. Incongruously she remembered Bryan had always liked her home-baked bread. But she hadn't baked bread in five years. There was no joy in cooking special food when she was the only one to eat it.

While the bacon was frying, Lani tiptoed back to the bathroom door and listened. He was definitely in there; she hadn't imagined it. She could hear him sluicing water over himself as he bathed. She put her fingertips to the door. As if he had heard her silent movements, he paused. Was he listening? she wondered. Slowly Lani backed away.

As the fried bacon drained on a paper towel, she cracked eggs in the skillet. She put in two, then after a moment's consideration, added two more. He was so thin! She put two slices of bread in the toaster and pressed down the lever. Where had he been? Who was supposed to have notified her, and about what?

As she was putting the eggs on the plate with the bacon, she saw a movement in the doorway and jumped. Bryan stood there in the clothes she had found for him. For a long moment their eyes met. Suddenly the toast popped up, breaking the spell. She put it on the plate and pushed it onto the table.

Bryan sat down and began to eat. She had the impression that he was struggling not to wolf it all down in one gulp. "Where have you been?" she asked as she cautiously sat opposite him.

"In a Mexican jail." He downed the glass of milk she had poured him, and she quickly got to her feet to pour him some more.

"What were you doing in there? Why didn't you let me know?" she asked as she put the refilled glass back on the table.

"I thought someone had contacted you. I wrote you regularly."

"I never got a letter!"

He stared over at her. "You didn't?"

"Don't you think I would have written you if I had? I would have moved heaven and earth to get you back!"

"I assumed they were keeping your letters to me. The bastards must not have even mailed the ones I wrote you." Although his voice was level, Lani detected an undertone of resigned anger and could see the exasperation in his eyes.

"Bryan," she said, forcing herself to speak more calmly. "What happened?"

"I flew a cargo to Mexico City, but didn't want to come back empty. No profit in that. But even before I put the word out that I was looking for a load going back to the States, a man hired me to fly to southern Mexico and pick up a shipment for a company named IOTA. He said it was flower pots and piñatas and things such as that. He wanted them delivered to Brownsville.

"I followed his directions to a little village near the coast that had a runway that was so small and in such bad shape it would have given any pilot nightmares. Right after I landed, a handful of men started loading the cargo. All at once there were people running up with guns, yelling at me in Spanish."

"Why!"

"Damned if I know. At the time I couldn't speak any more Spanish than was necessary to conduct business and talk to the Mexican air traffic controllers. Anyway, they hauled me off to a little adobe jail. I don't know what happened to all the men loading the plane, but as I was being taken away, I heard gunfire and I saw some of them fall and not get up. Most of them seemed to get away though. All I can figure is that those 'flower pots and piñatas' must have been filled with drugs, because later I was told I had been arrested for smuggling."

"Smuggling!" She stared at him. He hadn't shaved his beard, but had clipped it shorter. He still didn't look like Bryan. She couldn't become accustomed to seeing him, and this story he was telling seemed too unreal for comprehension. "What about your trial? You're an American citizen! Surely..."

"There was no trial. I'm not at all sure the Mexican authorities have any idea what happened. This town is in the back of nowhere. I don't think the local police ever reported to anyone that I was in jail. After I learned more Spanish, I found out I was being used as an example of what would happen to other outsiders who tried to interfere. I don't know what interference they were referring to unless the locals, including the police, were smuggling drugs and didn't want any outsiders to horn in on their business."

Lani could only stare at him. "You've been in jail for five years? Without a trial?"

He nodded as he finished eating.

"Why didn't you call when they released you? I would have flown down to get you."

"I wasn't released."

"You mean you broke out!"

"That's as confusing as all the rest of it. I woke up one day and the door to my cell was unlocked. At first I thought it was a trick so they could shoot me as I tried to escape. But the jail was empty! I just walked out! I cut across country until I came to a road, then hitched a ride north. I'm amazed anyone would give me a ride with me looking the way I did, but I didn't have a penny to my name."

"How did you eat?"

He avoided her eyes. "Some food I stole from gardens at night, some I was able to work for. Some I had to beg for."

Lani felt her heart constrict. She couldn't imagine her Bryan, with his pride and honesty, either stealing food or begging. She reached out and covered his hand with hers.

"I finally got to Nuevo Laredo, but the Mexican border guards wouldn't let me cross. They started looking at me very suspiciously, and I was afraid I was about to be arrested again. After all, I'm still not sure if I broke out or was released. So I went away. I walked a long way up the river until I came to a shallow part and waded across—luckily we haven't had much rain this year. Then I walked home."

After a long time Lani said, "That's the most incredible story I've ever heard."

"It's all true." He looked at her warily as if he didn't expect her to believe a word of it.

"I believe you, but it's still incredible."

He gave her a steady gaze. "All those years I thought about you. I've missed you more than I can ever say."

"I can't even tell you how much I've worried about you and wondered what happened to you. I finally had to assume you had crashed and were dead."

"So you had me declared dead?"

She shook her head. "No. I couldn't do that. Even if there had been proof, I couldn't have. But I had to believe it. There was no other alternative."

"In my fantasies our reunion was rather different," he said dryly. "It was a great deal more physical, and you were much more affectionate."

She stared at him, wondering if he had intended that to be a veiled accusation. Defensively she responded, "Bryan, you don't seem to understand what a shock this has been to me! You're supposed to be dead!"

He looked tired as he stood up. "It's just as well. I'm exhausted."

Lani hastily got to her feet. Automatically she said, "The bedroom is through that door..."

"I know where the bedroom is," Bryan said in a clipped voice. Without waiting for her to reply, he went through the dining room and into the bedroom.

Lani couldn't move; she could hardly think. She wanted to run after him and throw her arms around him and shower him with kisses and caresses, but she couldn't. This man wasn't the gentle and vulnerable Bryan she remembered. He had a steely shell about him that almost frightened her. Besides, she had lived alone as a widow for a long time. She couldn't shuck off the past five years and act as if he had only been gone overnight.

After several minutes she went to the bathroom and found the dirty clothes he had left on the floor. Gingerly she picked them up and carried them out toward the back of the house. As she passed through the studio she noticed the bundle he had carried in. More clothes?

Cautiously she poked at it, and the ragged jacket fell away exposing a jumbled stack of papers. She picked up the top sheet and began to read Bryan's cramped handwriting. It seemed to be a diary or journal of some sort. She set aside the pages, and carried the jacket outside with the shirt and pants. There was no point in washing any of them; they were little more than rags. She tossed them in the barrel she used for burning trash and set fire to them.

The flames licking the cloth cast gold highlights over her hair and across her cheeks. Lani gazed into the fire as if she were mesmerized. Bryan was home. She still couldn't believe it. After all these years he had come walking through the back door as big as life.

She turned back toward the house and looked at her dark bedroom window. She had pictured a far different reunion, too. But that had been so long ago.

His smile, she thought suddenly. That's what was so different. Bryan had smiled easily and often. This Bryan had not smiled at all. He looked as if he hadn't smiled in a long, long time.

A night breeze caused the flames to blaze, then gutter, as Lani wondered what she should do next. Was there anyone she should call? All Bryan's family were dead now, and her parents had long since gone to bed. For some reason it seemed logical to wait for morning and not to awaken them. Lani wondered if she were in shock or whether she had gone crazy.

She put the lid on the barrel as the last of the clothing was consumed, then went back into the house. It was quiet—as quiet as if she were alone. With a silent tread Lani went to the bedroom and pushed open the door.

Bryan was asleep on her pink-flowered sheets, his clothes in a pile by the bed.

Quietly she picked up his clothes and laid them over the arm of the chair across the room. For a long time she stood there and watched him, trying to convince herself this was real and that he was actually there.

As if he felt her eyes upon him, Bryan moved in his sleep. She lifted her head as if the motion startled her, then slipped out of the room.

She went into the kitchen and methodically washed and dried the dishes. Afterward she made a cup of coffee and tried to tell herself she wasn't stalling.

By the time the mantel clock struck one, she knew she could postpone it no longer. She had to go to bed. She went to the door of the bedroom, but stopped. She couldn't do it. There was no way she could go into that room, undress and lie down beside a man who was like a stranger to her.

Lani turned away and went down the hall. For tonight she would use the guest room. As for the nights to follow, well, she would just have to wait and see.

Chapter Two

When Bryan awoke he was instantly alert, and his muscles were tensed for action as his dark eyes darted around the room. Instead of the grimy walls and barred window and door he had so long been accustomed to seeing, he saw white-and-pink dimity curtains that billowed on a breeze. Sunshine streamed through the open window. Outside a mockingbird sang lustily. So he hadn't dreamed it! Bryan wasn't sure he could have stayed sane if the past week had been a dream.

He sat up and the soft, pink-flowered sheets pooled about his naked body. The room was vaguely familiar, with the doors and windows in the right place, but instead of blue, the walls were papered in a cream with stripes of pink and coral flowers. The scuffed furniture he and Lani had bought for very little from an auction right after they married had been painted white, and a white rattan headboard had been added to the bed. The room was so utterly feminine, he felt awkward being there.

With a quick movement Bryan looked at the other side of the bed. It was empty, and judging by the angle of the covers and the pillow, it hadn't been used last night.

With lithe grace he got out of bed, and the golden sunlight touched the ivory of his lean body. There had been little sunlight in his cell—though there had been more than enough heat in the summers—and his normally tanned body had paled. Thanks to his self-imposed regimen of push-ups and other exercises, his muscles were taut and well-conditioned. If he hadn't been in such good shape, he knew he would never have been able to make his way home.

He picked up his clothes from the chair. So she had been in. The night before he had been too exhausted to do more than step out of his clothes, and had left them piled on the floor. As he held them, he paid particular attention to the feel of clean jeans and soft cotton. Where was she? he wondered. He supposed he understood her not falling into bed with him. It had been a long time, and it must have been a terrific shock to see him—especially since she thought he was dead. But where had she slept? And how did she feel about his return?

Bryan frowned. He had never once considered that she might think he was dead. Obviously Lani had made a new life for herself. Not only had she repapered this room, but she had also turned his workshop into some sort of studio. He had hazy memories of clay and bowls and things. At the time, he hadn't been too interested in Lani's hobby—he'd been far more interested in her.

The night before she hadn't kissed him or even hugged him, he remembered with a pang, at least not of her own volition. He recalled the clean scent of her hair and how soft and warm she had felt during their brief embrace. True, he had looked like a derelict when he stumbled in, and it must have been very unsettling. Still, he thought, she should have hugged him.

He ran his fingers through his hair. It felt tousled and too long. Maybe he still looked too disreputable. He put his clothes under his arm and went back to the bathroom. Another bath and thorough shampoo would be great. Then he could trim his hair to a more respectable length and smooth the shape of his beard as well. Lani had always been a late sleeper, and he figured if he hurried he could get himself much more presentable by the time she got up.

Although Lani had been awake for the past hour, she was still in bed, her mind racing. She could hardly believe all that had happened the night before. Bryan was alive! In the clear morning light she realized there might be problems that he obviously had never considered. Was he wanted for jailbreaking, for instance. Would he be sent back to Mexico? No! She didn't know how she could manage to hide him, but somehow she would. Her heart ached when she thought of how he had looked when he stumbled through the door.

When she heard the sound of the shower running, she sat up in bed. It was strange to hear someone else in the house.

Lani got up and went to her bedroom and tapped lightly on the door. When there was no answer, she went in. Bryan was in the shower as she had thought. She could hear him closing the shower curtain and adjusting the water. For a minute she looked down at the rumpled bed, then tentatively touched the place where he had lain. The sheets were already cool, but she felt a tug on her heart as if she had touched his essence.

Moving quickly, Lani dressed and pulled on her sandals. As usual she wore jeans but, out of deference to the heat, she put on a white eyelet blouse that looked as cool as it felt.

She couldn't get her hairbrush out of the bathroom as long as Bryan was in there, so she used the one in her purse, then put on a pale coppery lip gloss. As a rule, Lani wore very little makeup, especially in the summer, and she was thankful for this. The rest of her makeup was also in the bathroom and inaccessible to her.

When the shower stopped, Lani hastily left the room. She felt foolish, but she wasn't sure if Bryan would come through with or without clothes, and she still felt quite awkward about him being there.

When she reached the sunny kitchen, she leaned on the countertop to steady herself. This was ridiculous! Bryan was home and she was acting as if he were not only a stranger, but one who might be dangerous!

To have something to do, she put some bacon on to cook and mixed some pancake batter. Bryan had always liked pancakes. Nervously she glanced around the kitchen, wishing she had taken the time to repaint it or to scrub the baseboards as she had intended. And the refrigerator! She had been meaning to use up all the odds and ends of leftovers in there.

She drew in a steadying breath as she put the bacon aside to drain and spooned out a circle of pancake batter. Her house was cleaner than most, and even if it wasn't, Bryan wasn't likely to notice. He had always been absentminded about such things. Nevertheless, she dusted the already clean canisters and straightened the spice jars so that all the labels faced forward.

"Good morning."

With a start she turned to see Bryan standing there. He had trimmed his beard short and had cut his hair before blowing it dry. He wore the same clothes she had given him the night before. "Good morning."

"Did I frighten you?"

"I didn't hear you come in." Lani turned back to the griddle and scooped up the golden pancakes. "Your timing is perfect." She handed him the plate.

For a long moment their eyes met and held. Lani felt a stirring awakening deep inside her. Bryan was home! She wanted to throw her arms around him, but she felt oddly shy. "The syrup and butter are on the table."

Bryan took the dish and lowered himself into a chair where he could watch her. Lani found herself staring at him. He looked different with a beard, but apparently he planned to keep it. Usually she didn't care for beards, but on Bryan it looked good. He reminded her of a Saracen warrior or maybe a pirate. His eyes did nothing to contradict that impression. They held a veiled ruthlessness that had never been there before.

Hastily she turned back to the griddle. "Eat while they're hot. Don't wait for me." She poured additional batter on the hot surface, making more pancakes than was necessary in order to be sure Bryan had enough.

When she sat opposite him, she noticed he had eaten most of the ones she had given him and had stopped. "There're plenty more," she said as she pushed the platter nearer. "Help yourself."

"This is plenty. I'm not used to sweets these days."

"Oh. Would you rather have an egg? I didn't think..."

"No, no. This is fine. I'm just full."

Lani nodded, not knowing what to say. She felt unbearably awkward and shy.

"You've made a lot of changes," he said, his dark eyes studying her.

"That's right, the kitchen wasn't this color when you left, was it? I had forgotten. I've been meaning to paint it again."

"I was thinking about your hair. You used to wear it long."

Lani reached up to touch her coppery cap of hair. "I cut it. It's less trouble this way." She looked at him and added, "I can let it grow again."

"I like it the way it is."

There was an uneasy silence. Finally Lani pushed her plate away. She had no appetite. "I should call Mom and Dad and tell them you're home."

He nodded. "I need to call my father, too."

Lani looked at him quickly and drew in her breath. "What's wrong?"

"Bryan, I don't know how to tell you. He's... It happened three years ago. A heart attack."

"He's dead?" Bryan looked stunned.

Lani covered his hand with hers. "I'm sorry, Bryan. It happened so long ago that I forgot you didn't know."

"He's dead," he repeated. "A heart attack?"

"It was very sudden. He didn't suffer."

Bryan nodded. "He never was happy after Mama died."

Lani saw no reason to tell Bryan that his father had put his life back together, and had been dating a widow who lived near him. She started to get up from the table, but he caught her wrist and stopped her.

"What else do I need to know?"

Lani tried to read his expression, but couldn't. She thought back. So much had happened in five years. How could she tell him all of it? "Mom and Dad still live where they always have. Bob and Harriet got a divorce, and he married a woman named Helen. Harriet moved to Tennessee."

"I never thought Bob and Harriet would split up! They seemed so good together."

"I guess they didn't share that opinion. Bob and Helen are expecting their first baby around Thanksgiving. The Birney house sold to a woman named Monica Denton."

"The Birneys moved?"

"He was transferred to Oregon. The house was vacant quite a while."

Bryan was silent for several minutes. "I wonder if I'll ever get caught up."

"Sure you will."

"What about us?" His eyes pinned her with their demanding gaze.

"I don't know what you mean," she said in an effort to evade the inevitable.

"Yes, you do."

After a pause Lani said, "Five years is a long time. It's especially a long time if you think you're a widow."

"Then you've found someone else." His tone was flat, and his words were more of a statement than a question.

"No. No, I haven't found anyone else."

He sat there quietly, waiting for her to elaborate.

"I haven't wanted anyone. No one could ever take your place."

"You're young and beautiful, Lani. I can't believe no one has asked you out and that you've sat home alone for five years."

"I didn't say that. I said I don't have anyone that I see regularly. I have friends and some of them are single men, but none of them are special to me."

"I see."

His words sounded accusatory, so she abruptly stood. "You aren't being fair! I thought you were dead!"

When he rose, he towered over her. "That still doesn't answer my question. What about us? Don't turn away from me! You act as if I'm a stranger!"

"You are!" When he pulled back, she added, "Bryan, you can't expect either of us to pretend the last five years never happened. We've both changed. If you'd just think about it, you'll have to admit that I'm a stranger to you, too."

His brow was furrowed. "Are you saying you want to live in the guest room until we become reacquainted?"

"I don't know!" She turned away and gripped the back of the chair. "I don't know what to say or what to think. I never considered something like this would ever happen! Do you want me to stay in there?"

"Personally I think that's the sorriest idea I ever heard of." He sighed and ran his fingers through his hair. "But if that's what you want, I won't argue with you. I guess you should take our room, I mean your room, and I'll sleep in the guest room."

"No! I mean, I'm not saying I want that." Her eyes pleaded with him to understand. "Bryan, can't you see my problem? I love you, and I've never forgotten you. But in time I learned to live alone. I cut off all my emotional switches, all my yearnings for you. I can't just flip them back on again!"

A smile turned up the corners of his mouth, and for the first time she saw the Bryan she had known. "You still love me?"

Without hesitation Lani went to him and put her arms around him. She buried her face against his broad chest and breathed in the fragrance of his scent. "Yes, I love you. Don't talk to me about sleeping in guest rooms. Just give me a chance to get over the shock of you being home, alive and well."

Bryan sighed with relief and held her close. She could have sworn he trembled as if he were on the verge of tears, but he said nothing, and she decided she was mistaken.

"I guess you ought to drive me down to the courthouse," he said after a long pause. "I need to get another driver's license."

"You can't go there!" she exclaimed. "Someone will see you."

"So?"

"What if you're in trouble for breaking out of jail? No, you should stay here."

He laughed softly. "Honey, you can't hide me forever. There's only one thing to do. I'll call the sheriff and ask him. If I am, we'll fight it. After all, I was an innocent party to all this." He went to the phone and picked up the directory. "Is Armbruster still sheriff?"

"Yes. Bryan, do you think you should do this? We could leave here and go where no one knows us. We could start over."

"Wherever we went, I would need a driver's license. Since my plane was confiscated, I'm out of a job. That's something else I need to check into."

"You'd go back to cargo flying? After all this?"

After a long pause, Bryan said, "Lani, I'm not trained to do anything else."

She watched as he dialed the number of the sheriff's office. Without his plane his business was gone. She hadn't thought of that. She listened as he told his story to Sheriff Armbruster and breathed a sigh of relief when the sheriff didn't have a warrant for him on his desk.

After Bryan hung up, he said, "So far, so good. If they want me, they aren't advertising. Armbruster is going to call the Mexican authorities and see what he can find out."

"Should he do that? Isn't that looking for trouble?"

"If there is going to be trouble, we have to find out and meet it squarely."

She knew he was right, but a part of her was still frightened. "I guess I'd better call my parents and tell them you're back before they hear it from Della Macom down at the sheriff's office."

As she dialed the number, she watched Bryan pour himself a cup of coffee. He drank it black now, she noticed. "Hello, Mom? I think you had better sit down. I have something to tell you that's going to be quite a shock." After she told the story twice to her mother, she had to repeat it again for her father. "Dad wants to talk to you," she said, holding the receiver out to Bryan. As she watched, Bryan patiently went over all of it again.

When he handed the phone back, Lani's mother was on the other end. "Yes, Mom. I know. I can hardly believe it myself. How does he look? Well, he's thinner. He has a beard. Yes, I guess he plans to keep it, I haven't asked." She smiled at Bryan. "No, it looks very dashing. Scars? No, none that I know of." She put her hand over the mouthpiece. "Mom wants to know if you've had malaria." When Bryan laughed and shook his head, Lani said, "No malaria, Mom." Then she said, "Mom and Dad want to give you a welcome-home party. Is it okay?"

He shrugged. "I suppose."

"That's fine, Mom," she said into the phone. "Saturday? All right. Yes, we'll drive over this afternoon and let you see him for yourselves. Okay, Mom. 'Bye." After she hung up Lani said, "Mom thinks you've been in darkest Africa, I guess. She also asked about beriberi."

"Even if I didn't have to get a current FAA physical anyway, a checkup would be a good idea. There's no telling what I was fed. Most of the time it was unrecognizable."

She drove him to the Department of Public Safety office near the courthouse where he was able to renew his driver's license without having to be retested, then on to their family doctor who was willing to work him in without an appointment.

"Your mother will be pleased," he said when he rejoined her. "No beriberi."

Several of the patients in the waiting room heard him and glanced up. Lani smiled mischievously. "Then I guess we should go home."

As they drove out of town, Bryan said, "I don't suppose I have a business even on paper anymore?"

She shook her head. "There was no reason to keep paying rent at the hangar. I had to sell your tools and equipment to one of the other pilots in order to pay off your business loan at the bank."

"Then we're back where we started from—with nothing at all."

"Not quite. You see, I've been supporting myself all this time. I sell pottery through a couple of gift shops, and I make clay statues for Jay Harmond's interior decorating company."

"Jay Harmond? Didn't I meet him once?"

"Sure you did. He talked to me about doing some Mayan artifact look-alikes."

"I remember. At the time you said you didn't think you should."

"I know I did, but after you disappeared I needed the money. The pottery doesn't bring in nearly enough for me to get by on."

"What about all the insurance I was carrying?"

"You wouldn't have been legally dead for another two years. Without proof, they wouldn't pay anything."

"They didn't!"

"I had to cancel the policy anyway. I couldn't afford the premiums."

Bryan frowned. "It must have been very difficult for you."

"I managed, thanks to my little clay gods. You see, I don't make duplicates. These are all my own designs, and I sign them with a tiny pyramid mark on the base. Only the style and the firing and so forth are authentic. I'm not doing anything wrong." She turned off the highway onto the narrow road that led to their house. "Besides, I'm doing some other clay sculpting that I think will get me some recognition in the art world. At least I think they're good enough."

When Bryan didn't respond, she glanced over at him. "Are you okay?"

"Lani, I can't have you supporting me, and until I can get my pilot's license paperwork squared away and scrounge up money for a down payment on another plane, there's not a damned thing I can do to earn a living."

"You shouldn't go straight to work. You need time to get over your ordeal."

"I need to be useful more than I need rest. Hell, I haven't done much but rest for five years!"

She pulled into the driveway and turned off the engine. "Don't worry about it. I don't make a lot of money, but we can get by. Give yourself some time."

"I suppose I could. I don't know." He didn't sound convinced.

As they walked around to the back door, Lani's heart went out to him. He was a proud man, and this readjustment was going to be even harder because of it. Hoping to get his mind off the plane he had lost, she said, "Come see my sculptures. I want your opinion."

Obligingly he went into the studio and was surprised to find so many projects in their various stages of completion. The pottery was appealing, and the waterfalls showed a lot of creativity. The gods and goddesses were curious little creatures with age marks in their colorings and tiny flaws as if they were very old indeed. He knew little about Mayan art, but they looked authentic to him. Everything she showed him was good, and he told her so. Lani beamed from his praise, and he found himself wondering if he had done enough of that before.

As they went into the living room, the phone rang and Lani picked it up. Her face paled. "It's for you. Sheriff Armbruster."

A knot clenched in Bryan's stomach, but he took the phone. "Hello." He heard the sheriff's scratchy voice drawling in a monotone through the line. "No records of me at all? They never heard of me? What about the IOTA Company?" He reached out and reassuringly stroked Lani's cold hands. "Okay, Sheriff. I guess no news is good news in this case." After he hung up, he said to Lani, "There's no record of my ever having been imprisoned."

"None at all?"

"I guess the village did take the law into its own hands as I had thought. It also explains why I was able to leave the way I did. Since they never officially arrested me, they couldn't officially release me." Anger hardened inside him. "Five years of my life were stolen from me!"

"Bryan?"

He looked into her worried eyes and pulled her close. Five years! If there had been a reason, if he had done something wrong and had had to serve a sentence for it, he could have handled it. But it seemed his jailers may have been covering up something.

As Lani embraced him, Bryan felt her full breasts softly pressing against his body. Five years that he could have spent with her! He nestled his face into her hair and felt its softness. All at once his anger exploded into frustrated passion. He was tired of waiting, waiting and more waiting. He wanted to make love to his wife, and he wasn't in the mood to wait a day or two until she was used to having him around. Almost roughly he tilted her face up and kissed her with all the pent-up passions of five wasted years.

At first Lani was startled and she tried to pull away, but his lips were hot and familiar over hers, though his soft black beard was a novelty. His hand found her breast and its heat seared her. His fingers caressed her as her body responded eagerly.

Without hesitation Bryan bent and scooped her up. Again Lani pulled back as excitement akin to fear washed through her. She and Bryan had always had a satisfying love life, but she had never seen him like this. She had a feeling he wouldn't stop even if she asked him to. Surprisingly, since this was indeed Bryan and not really a stranger, this excited her a great deal.

He carried her into the bedroom and laid her on top of the bedspread, unlike the old Bryan who would have turned back the covers. When Lani tried to roll away and do just that, he caught her and pulled her back.

Joining her on the bed, he kissed her again, demanding that her passion meet his. Lani made an ineffectual effort to push him away, but he held her tighter, not hurting her but showing her that he was in command.

As his hand released the buttons of her blouse, his lips silenced hers. He opened the blouse and covered her breast with his hand, molding it to his palm. Beneath the sheer lace of her bra, she felt her nipple bead to an aching pout. She wanted him desperately, and all her inhibitions fell away as she arched her back toward him.

Bryan tugged off her blouse, then fumbled with the fastener of her bra. Just when Lani thought the hook and eye would surely snap, it came open. He pulled the bra away and raised himself up to look at her, his large hands imprisoning her slender wrists.

Silently he gazed down at her, and Lani felt her excitement building. Bryan's passion-filled eyes were almost black, and a lock of his thick hair had fallen over his forehead. Once more his new look reminded her of a pirate, and this time she was the booty to be plundered. He lowered his head and greedily drew one of her nipples into his mouth.

As he toyed with first one, then the other, Lani heard a moan of pleasure and realized it had come from her.

Bryan released her wrists as he straddled her, supporting his weight on his knees. Without taking his eyes away from her, he shucked off his pullover shirt. His muscles ridged and rippled as he opened the fly of his jeans. Lani felt a tremble of excitement rush through her. She had never been ravished before, and she found herself thoroughly enjoying it.

She moved to let him reach the fastener of her own jeans, but he seemed to think she was trying to escape him because he again caught her wrists and pinned them against the bed as he kissed her, his tongue tasting all the pleasures of her mouth. Keeping her pinned, he rolled to one side, kicked off his tennis shoes and removed his jeans and shorts. When he unbuttoned her jeans and parted the zipper, Lani hastily pushed off her sandals. Bryan obviously meant business, and she didn't want to get tangled in her jeans.

He stripped jeans and panties away in quick movements. Lani felt astonishingly naked as he stared down at her, still not speaking. Holding both her wrists in one hand, he caressed her trembling body with the other. Even if she hadn't wanted him so badly, she couldn't have stopped him if her life depended upon it.

When his fingers slipped between her thighs, Lani murmured and opened herself to him. She was ready for him and eager, and when he entered her she moaned with the pleasure of feeling Bryan inside her again.

Moving with him, she felt her ecstasy rise, and all her senses seemed to concentrate on the center of her body. Her hardened nipples brushed against his chest as he raised a bit to push deeper into her. His eyes were filled with raw hunger. Again she sensed the ragged edge of danger that she had felt in him the night before. He was Bryan, but he was somehow more intense, more demanding—and undeniably in command of her. After years of answering to no one, Lani found this irresistible.

All at once she reached her peak, and great shattering waves of blissful satisfaction roared through her. He released her hands, and she embraced him as she felt the answering culmination rock him.

For a long time they lay still, each holding on to their togetherness. At last Lani whispered, "I love you."

Bryan lifted his head and studied her face as if he were afraid she might not have meant it. "There won't be any talk of separate rooms," he said at last.

With a smile, she shook her head in agreement.

"I love you," he said almost gruffly. He rolled to one side and watched her as if he expected her to leap up and run away.

Instead Lani rolled with him and put her arms around him. "Welcome home, Bryan. God, I've missed you!"

He took her in his arms, and she laid her head on his shoulder. Gently she stroked his body, and her face glowed with a satisfied smile. He hadn't loved her with the gentleness she remembered nor the sweet words, but she had also changed. In time the gentleness might return, but she had a feeling a trace of the roughness would always remain. Although it had frightened her a little, she would be foolish not to admit to herself that it also thrilled her.

Chapter Three

"Relax, Bryan. It's a party, not a hanging."

"I am relaxed." He sat beside her, his shoulders bunched as he stared broodingly at the scenery outside the car window.

"Would you rather drive? You used to be nervous when I drove."

"I'm not nervous," he said in what he felt was a convincing manner. He didn't want her to know he was, because that would be an admission of weakness. Over the past five years he had learned never to show his vulnerability, and now that survival instinct was a part of him. For so long, he had lived in almost complete isolation, interacting with only a half dozen men during all that time of confinement, that the idea of attending a party seemed overwhelming to him. "How many did your mother invite?"

"Not many. Maybe ten or twelve. The Edwards are coming and Monica Denton and the Goldmans."

"I don't know anyone named Goldman."

"Sure you do. Frank and Debbie? She's one of my best friends."

"When did you meet them?"

"I don't remember exactly, but it was before the space shuttle explosion."

"What explosion?" He looked at her in surprise.

"I guess you don't know the Goldmans." She told him she and Debbie had watched the news coverage of the shuttle disaster in January of 1986 for days as NASA had tried to determine the cause. As a strong supporter of the space program, Bryan had many questions, which Lani answered to the best of her ability. As she was finishing, they pulled into her parents' driveway.

Edna and Charles Keyes lived in a small house in a quiet residential development. Lani and Bryan went through the side gate into the backyard. Unlike the barren front yard where the grass was scorched from the blazing summer sun, the small area out back was a veritable jungle of tropical vegetation. Orange and grapefruit trees vied with rattling palms. Huge leaves of devil's ivy made lush pools of green beneath the heavy shade. Bougainvilleas in coral and pink draped the trellis of the open porch. And everywhere Bryan looked, there seemed to be people. He realized quickly that the Goldmans weren't the only guests he didn't know.

He shook hands with Lani's father and gave her mother his customary hug. Lani's family was affectionate, and Bryan had always felt that they considered him more a son than a son-in-law. Since his return, however, he detected a strain between the older couple and himself. They seemed to be trying a bit too hard to pretend everything was normal.

Lani slipped her hand into Bryan's, and he was glad for her support. He felt almost agoraphobic, though this sort of party had been a treat for him before. She introduced him to Frank and Debbie Goldman, a couple who he could have easily mistaken for brother and sister because of their remarkable resemblance. Quickly he understood how Debbie and Lani would be friends, for Debbie was the sort of person who made everyone around her feel welcome and accepted. Under different circumstances, he knew he would have felt quite at ease around her.

As Bryan and Lani mingled, he recognized Albert Richey, a pilot he had often worked with at the airport. Albert had divorced his wife and was with a girlfriend who seemed determined to be more streetwise than friendly. Bryan and Albert set a date to get together the following week, and Bryan let the crowd separate them. He liked Albert's former wife much better than the new girlfriend.

Charles came up with two glasses of lemonade and handed one to Bryan. "Lani, your mother wants you in the kitchen. Something about whether the sugar cookies and pound cake should be served from the same tray. That's all beyond me, so I told her I'd send you in."

Lani smiled up at Bryan. They had often teased her parents about not being able to make minor decisions while having no difficulty at all with the ones that impacted their lives.

When Bryan sipped his lemonade, the taste startled him. He glanced at Charles, who winked back.

"I juice it up a little these days. What Edna doesn't know won't hurt her."

Bryan grinned. Edna was a strict teetotaler; Charles was not.

"Having a good time?" Charles asked.

"Sure. Sure, I am. It's a good party."

"Well, we like having young people about. Now that Lani is grown, we don't see many young faces around here. I've been thinking about coaching a Little League team, just to be around kids."

"Sounds like a good idea."

"What about you? Want to be my assistant manager?"

"Maybe. First I have to find a job and get a salary coming in."

"Yeah, we all need that." Charles took a drink of the potent lemonade. "I guess you've seen Lani's antique statues."

"Yes, I have."

"Can't see why anybody would want that stuff. Looks like a kid did most of it. Supposed to be Mayan, she said. I don't know. I'd rather look at a Russell or a Remington, personally. She says they bring in money, though. I guess that's what counts. We tried to help her out, with money I mean. But she hasn't taken a penny from us. Said she wanted to do it all herself. You'd have been real proud of her."

"I am proud of her."

An uncomfortable silence ensued as each tried to think of something to say.

"Yeah," Charles said finally, "I may sign up for a baseball team. Say, who do you think will win the pennant this year?"

"I have no idea."

Charles looked blank, then embarrassed. "Yeah, I guess you haven't been keeping up with the teams."

Bryan found himself feeling ill at ease as Charles looked even more embarrassed. "There's Bob Edwards! I haven't had a chance to speak to him yet. Will you excuse me?"

"Sure, sure. You go ahead. I'll go help Lani and Edna with the food."

Bryan threaded his way to where his best friend stood. "Bob!"

"Bryan! Good to see you, man!"

"I've tried to call you, but you're always gone. Life treating you okay?"

Bob nodded. "I can't complain. What's been going on with you?" Mild panic rose in the man's eyes as he realized his blunder. "I mean..."

"Other than walking out of prison and hiking across Mexico, not much," Bryan said in a jovial manner to put his friend at ease.

Instead Bob looked more uncomfortable. Bryan wondered for the first time if his prison stay would prejudice his friends against him. Other than himself, Bryan had never known anyone who had been imprisoned.

"Yeah, I know. Albert called me the other day. I sure was sorry to hear it. I mean, I'm glad you're not dead, but it was a real shocker to find out you'd been in prison all this time."

"My return's been a pretty big shock to everyone, it seems."

"No, no. I'm really sorry it happened. It must have been awful."

Bryan looked at him closely. Bob was definitely self-conscious. "Hey, don't let it get you down. I'm here now. It's all over." He clapped his friend's shoulder.

"Sure it is."

"You can't imagine how bored I've been. Have you heard of any job openings around here?"

"You mean a flying job?"

"What else would I mean?" Bryan grinned at him. "That's what I am, remember?"

"I don't know. The Jimisons hire crop dusters about this time of year. So do the Boyds."

"Crop dusting? I'm no crop duster." Bryan gave his friend a searching look.

"I know you weren't, but with the prison record, well, you may not even be able to get your license back."

"I've already checked. I got my physical, and the only thing I have left to do is get my biannual flight review." Suddenly his friend's words sank in. "And I don't have a *record*. Sheriff Armbruster checked, and there is no record of me in the Mexican prison system."

Bob shifted uncomfortably.

"Hey, you don't think I was really mixed up in smuggling, do you?"

Bob grinned disarmingly. "Hell, no. Not you. I wouldn't believe a thing like that."

Despite Bob's words, Bryan saw his gaze waver. Bryan's smile grew stiff. It had never occurred to him that anyone might believe he was guilty.

A woman with close-cropped brown hair and a rounding middle came up and stood next to them as if she wanted to be a part of their conversation.

Bryan smiled at her, though her face was unfamiliar to him. To Bob he said, "Why don't you and Harriet come over one night? We've always had a great time together. She's a barrel of laughs. Where is Harriet, anyway? I don't think I've seen her yet."

Bob's smile froze, then melted. "Haven't you heard? We got a divorce. This is my wife, Helen." He reached out his hand for the pregnant woman at his side.

"Oh." Bryan vaguely remembered that Lani had told him. "I'm sorry to hear that—about Harriet, I mean," he amended hastily as Bob's new wife shot daggers at him. "That is, congratulations."

"We're having our first baby in November," Helen said coolly. "Bob always wanted children."

Bryan cleared his throat uneasily. As far as he knew, Bob and Harriet had never wanted to raise a family. "That's nice," he said lamely.

"We're going to have to be running along," Bob said abruptly. "It's not good for Helen to be on her feet too much. Nice seeing you."

"Right. Good seeing you." Bryan then added, "A pleasure meeting you, Helen."

She barely acknowledged him as she turned with her husband to leave.

Bryan sighed. What had happened? He and Bob had been best friends, just as Lani and Harriet had been. That, he supposed, explained it. Helen must have resented Lani's friendship with Bob's ex-wife and didn't want Bob to renew his relationship with them. Why they were at the party at all seemed a mystery.

"Having a good time?" he heard someone beside him ask.

The woman who had spoken was a tall brunette with dazzling blue eyes. "Sure," he lied. "Have we met?"

"Not yet. I'm Monica Denton."

"Didn't you buy the Birney house?"

"That's right. That seems to be my claim to fame in the neighborhood."

"I knew the Birneys."

"Everyone seems to have." Monica's voice was as smooth and sultry as a fine bourbon. Her eyes swept over his body as if she were judging him sexually. "Lani's a lucky woman."

"Thank you. Is your husband here?"

"I'm not married. My divorce was final six months ago."

"I'm sorry."

"I'm not."

Bryan felt definitely awkward. He had seldom encountered such a blatant come-on. True, Monica's words were innocent, but the way she said them, and the way she edged closer as she did, was pure sex. "Are you one of Lani's friends?" he asked. He couldn't picture Lani having anything to do with a woman like this.

"Only in a professional sense. I own two of the shops where Lani sells her pottery."

"I see." As the woman eased closer, one of her breasts grazed his elbow. Bryan stepped back. Even if he didn't have Lani, he wouldn't be interested in such an obvious woman. "If you'll excuse me, I should go see if Lani needs my help."

"She doesn't. Debbie Goldman is with her." Monica raised her glass of lemonade to her lips and took a sip as if the experience itself were provocative. Bryan wondered if Charles had also spiked her drink. "Lani tells me that you were in a Mexican prison all this time. What was it like?"

"It wasn't a prison. It was a local jail. It was hot and unpleasant."

"Sometimes being hot can be quite pleasant."

Bryan glanced around for a means of escape. "Not in this case."

"Were you mistreated?" Her blue eyes sparkled with anticipation.

"I really don't want to talk about it. If you'll excuse me, I really..."

"Were you celibate all the time?"

Bryan stared at her, not believing his ears. "What?"

"Were there women there?"

"No!"

"Lucky Lani!" Monica's eyes raked over him as though she were a tigress sensing her next meal.

"Maybe I should get something straight," Bryan said, matter-of-factly. "I love my wife and would be faithful to her, even if I were imprisoned in a bordello!"

"That could be exciting," Monica purred.

Deciding that straightforward bluntness was the best course to take in this situation, Bryan said, "I don't understand why you were invited to this party, since you're so obviously not Lani's friend, but lay off. I'm not interested."

"But Lani is my friend. Not a close one, of course, but more than an acquaintance. That's why she sells through my shops."

"Then why are you coming on to me?"

"Is that how you see it? What exactly have I said to make you think that?" Monica's eyes dared him to play her game.

"Things haven't changed *that* much in five years."

Monica's blue gaze swept the crowd. "I imagine everyone here knows you as Lani's husband, except me. All the time I've known Lani, she has been—or thought she was—a widow. Now you show up. And you are about the best-looking thing I've ever seen. People change a lot in five years. You two may not hit it off after having been separated for so long, and I'm right here and available."

Bryan stared at her, too shocked to speak.

"I just wanted you to know. Just in case. After five years, you must have a lot of catching up to do." She smiled in a way that sent a chill through him.

"Even if I were looking for sex, which I'm not, and even if I weren't in love with my wife, which I am, you aren't my type." He turned and left, but the sultry sound of her laughter followed him.

He saw Lani taking an empty tray back to the kitchen and followed her. After he assured himself they were alone, he said, "You won't believe what that Monica Denton said to me."

"What?" she asked, as she put the tray on the countertop and started putting more cookies onto it.

"She all but propositioned me!"

"Oh, honey, she couldn't have. I know Monica, and that's just the way she talks."

"Lani, I tell you she practically asked me to have an affair with her!"

Lani glanced up at him. He really did seem upset, but she couldn't believe Monica would do such a thing—especially not at a time and place such as this. "Will you hand me that knife? I need to cut more pound cake."

"Don't you care that she is coming on to me?" he demanded as he shoved the knife within her reach.

"Of course I would, if I thought she had that in mind. Monica always talks as if her motor's running. That's just the way she is. You're reading too much into it." Again she glanced at Bryan. Had he assumed Monica was making a sexual advance to him because he wanted to think that? Monica was a beautiful woman. "What did she say, exactly?"

"Never mind. As you say, it must have been my imagination." He glared at her.

Uneasiness stirred in Lani. What if he was right and Monica was flirting with him? Lani didn't really know the woman all that well. "What *did* she say?"

"Skip it. I can take care of myself."

As she watched him stride out of the kitchen, her discomfort grew. Bryan was a handsome and sexy man. It wasn't at all unlikely that a woman would be attracted to him, nor that a direct woman like Monica might tell him so. She decided to keep an eye on Monica.

Debbie Goldman entered the kitchen with the empty lemonade pitcher. "They're like a pack of hungry wolves out there," she said with a laugh. "I don't know what it is about this lemonade, but nobody seems to get enough of it."

"Dad makes it from scratch," Lani said. "Debbie, have you noticed anything odd about Monica today?"

"No more so than usual. Frank is avoiding her, as are all the other happily married men. I saw your father all but run from her a few minutes ago. Why? Is she after blood?"

"Bryan seems to think so."

With a shrug, Debbie refilled the pitcher from the crock on the counter. "I think she's all bluff. If one of our men ever took her up on all her heavy breathing and syrupy glances, I'd bet she'd turn tail and run."

"That's always been my guess."

"How did she get invited, anyway?"

"My mom did it. Ever since Monica moved in as a single woman, Mom has invited her places. She says Monica comes on too strong because she's lonely."

With a laugh, Debbie tilted the crock to get the last of the lemonade. "Your mother is a darling, but a tad naive. This is the last of the lemonade. Should I ask your father to make more?"

"The party's almost over. Let's serve this last bit and go mingle."

Lani saw her mother crossing the yard and stopped her. "This is the last of the lemonade. Don't you want any?"

"No, thanks. I've never cared for it. That's your dad's specialty. Everyone seems to be having a good time, don't you think?"

"I'm sure they are."

"Monica's alone again. The poor thing. I think she must be shy. I should go talk to her."

"Okay," Lani said with a smile. "I'll go find Bryan."

She strolled through the yard searching for Bryan, and finally found him alone in the enclosed side yard on the opposite side of the house where Edna hid her clothesline and tiny vegetable garden. For a moment she watched him, thinking about the white-hot passion he had stirred in her each time they had made love since his return. He seemed more virile now than she remembered, yet he had clearly felt threatened by Monica Denton's conversation earlier. This new husband of hers was certainly an enigma.

"Bryan? Why are you in here?"

He looked around in surprise, then shrugged. "I needed to be alone."

"I'm sorry," she said awkwardly as she turned to leave.

"Don't go. I'd rather have you with me."

She came nearer and stood beside him. "I didn't mean to upset you about Monica."

"As you said, I don't know her. I also insulted her."

"Oh? What did you say to her?"

"I said she isn't now and never could be my type."

"You did?" Lani smiled despite herself. "She's awfully pretty."

"Not unless you like predators." With the toe of his shoe, he nudged the hairy, fibrous leaves of the yellow squash that was taking over the tiny garden. "I won't apologize, Lani. I know I didn't misunderstand what she had in mind."

"I wasn't asking you to apologize."

"Will it affect your ability to sell through her shops?"

"No, my relationship with her is purely business, and Monica loves money too much to let her feelings get in the way of a profit." She hoped she was right. At the moment, they couldn't afford a cut in their income.

"I also insulted Bob and his wife."

"You've had a busy day. How did you do that?"

"I forgot he and Harriet are divorced."

"That would do it. Helen is about as jealous as anyone I've ever seen. She wants to know where he is and who he's with every minute of the day. I'm not very fond of her. Since the divorce, I almost never see him."

"I think he believes that I actually was involved in the smuggling!"

"He said that?" Lani stared up at him in disbelief.

"Not in so many words, but he seemed to imply it."

"I'm sorry, Bryan. I guess we have to expect that, but I'm surprised at Bob. He's changed since the divorce."

"He must have if he'd rather have Helen than Harriet. And where did Albert meet that woman he's with? She seems to be daring everyone to offend her."

"She's just a date. They aren't serious."

"I think the world has turned upside down. No one is the way they were before."

"Mom and Dad are."

"Are they? Every time I try to talk to them, they seem to freeze up like people do at a funeral. I feel like the corpse that no one is supposed to mention. I don't want to go into great detail telling people about my imprisonment or privations, but they treat me as though I might go berserk if I even hear the word 'Mexico.' Did you know your mother actually avoided saying 'enchilada' in front of me?"

"She didn't!" Lani exclaimed with a laugh.

"Yes, she did. And every time your father brings up anything that I don't already know about, he gets embarrassed, and that always embarrasses me."

"They are only trying not to hurt your feelings."

"I know, but their obliqueness is driving me crazy."

"I'll talk to them."

Bryan sighed and frowned down at the garden. "Lani, I don't fit in here anymore."

She stared at him as dread spread through her. "What do you mean?"

"I don't fit in. Everybody has changed, and we've all changed in different directions. You fit with them, but I don't."

"So? What did you have in mind?" Lani clasped her palms together and interlaced her fingers to stop them from trembling. For such a hot day, she suddenly felt quite cold.

"I don't know."

Again the silence strung tight between them. "As I understand it, that's more or less what Harriet said just before she left for Tennessee. Are you planning on going to Tennessee, Bryan?"

He managed to smile at her. "No. I'm not saying that."

"Then what are you saying, exactly?"

He shook his head as he shifted his weight and shoved his fingers into the back pockets of his jeans. "Everybody I've talked to has told me how great you're doing with your pottery. Bob seems to think I can't even get a job as a pilot."

"What does one thing have to do with the other?"

"I'm not cut out to be a house husband."

"I wasn't suggesting that you should be. Bob is no expert. He isn't working as a pilot anymore. Helen saw to it that he got a desk job."

"He suggested I try crop dusting."

Lani tried to swallow her flash of anger at Bob's insensitivity. "Don't put so much stock in what Bob says. He's clearly no longer your friend."

"I want to find a job so you can quit work, and we can go back to the way we were before."

After a pause, Lani said, "I don't want to quit work, Bryan. I enjoy my sculpting."

"I wasn't suggesting you never touch it again, only that you let me support you."

"I don't want to be supported." She stepped nearer and put her hand on his arm. "I like knowing that I'm independent and can do more than just pull my share of the load."

"You used to like being a housewife. Don't you think I can take care of you again?"

"It's not a matter of me being taken care of. My clay work is important to me. I like knowing no one else can do exactly what I do. I liked being a housewife, and if nothing had changed, I would probably have been happy in that role forever. Someday, especially if we have children, I may go back to it for periods of time, but not now, and not permanently."

"What you're saying is that you don't need me," he said in a tight voice.

"I'm saying I *want* you. I doubt anyone really needs another person so long as he's healthy and able to fend for himself."

"You're different, too." He studied her face as if he were trying to find the Lani he had once known. "I can handle knowing everyone else has changed, but I never thought you would."

"People are supposed to change, Bryan. You've changed, too. That's part of living."

He looked away. "Philosophy I don't need."

"So what do you intend to do?"

"I don't know."

"I can't turn back the clock for you."

"I know that."

She could feel a great chasm between them, though she stood by his side. Against her will, she felt the protective emotional wall begin to surround her, the wall that had buffered her from hurts and feelings too intense to bear for all those years he was gone. "I'll leave you alone, then. Obviously you need time to yourself to think this through. I'll go back to our guests."

"Your guests," he corrected quietly.

Lani gave him a long look, then turned and left. Her heart was beating tattoos. Was he about to leave her? To ask for a divorce? Many of her friends were divorced. She had never considered that she might join their ranks.

"You look pale," Debbie said when Lani joined her.

"Must be the heat," Lani said quickly.

"Could be your father's lemonade," Debbie said in an undertone. "I tasted some, and now I know what all the fervor was about. He can make lemonade for me anytime."

Lani wasn't listening. All she could think of was Bryan and what he might be considering.

"Lani? Are you sure you're okay?"

"I'm fine. Debbie, would you and Frank like to come over for supper next Tuesday?" Maybe if she found him some new friends, Bryan wouldn't feel so lost.

"Tuesday? Sure. We don't have any special plans."

"Great. I'll make that zucchini casserole you like so well."

"That would be wonderful. What can I bring? Wine?"

"Fine. Come about seven."

"Are you sure you're all right? Maybe you should go in and lie down."

Lani saw Bryan come back into the yard, and their eyes met. She couldn't tell what he was thinking or feeling, but he didn't look as if he were on the verge of packing. "I'm okay," she said to Debbie. She could ask Albert over one night, too, if she could think of a way not to ask his militant girlfriend. Albert was very levelheaded, and he would be good for Bryan.

Debbie was also watching Bryan mix with the crowd. "I wonder if he should get some counseling," she mused.

"Always the wife of a shrink, aren't you?" Lani teased.

"He wouldn't have to see Frank. There are other psychotherapists in his office. I was just thinking he might need to talk about what he's gone through."

"The old Bryan would do it. This one I'm not so sure about. I think what he really needs is a friend." It hurt her to admit it because before, she had always considered herself to be his closest friend. Now he seemed to shut her out.

"You know, I seem to always be categorizing everything in terms of 'before' and 'now.' It's as if I'm beginning a new life."

"Are things all right between you two?"

She shrugged. "I don't know. I thought they would be, but every time I relax and try to get back into our life together, I find another way he's changed or that I've changed. We can't possibly go back to the way we were."

"No one can."

"He wants to."

"Maybe. I'll bet what he really wants is to recapture the same old feelings."

"I think you should hang your shingle up with Frank's. You're a pretty good shrink yourself," Lani said with a sad smile.

"And give up the thrill of teaching? Not a chance," Debbie said in mock horror. "I really do enjoy it."

"I know. I feel the same way about my work. I finished that waterfall. When you come over, I'll show it to you. Next week I'm sending it and two others to a show in Abilene."

"You're going to do it?" Debbie asked with excitement. "I'm so glad! Those waterfalls are much too good not to show them. Is Bryan excited?"

"I haven't told him. Bryan doesn't like to hear about my work."

"Have you given him a chance? You have to coax him into understanding."

Lani shifted uncomfortably. "I may not have given it my best effort. He seems so defensive whenever I bring it up."

"He's barely had time to settle in. Don't expect him to adjust overnight."

"I know you're right. Debbie, I love him, but everything is so different! I'm not used to sharing a house twenty-four hours a day, especially with someone who is so different from before."

"That's only to be expected."

"Surely *I* haven't changed that much. I'm still me."

"Since I didn't know you when you were together before, I can't say, but I'll bet you have. People don't notice it when they're with someone every day. Give it time, Lani. It'll work out."

"I hope you are right." She looked across the yard to where Bryan was talking to Albert. She hoped she would have enough time to make it work out right.

Chapter Four

Bryan sat in a lawn chair in the shade, his feet propped against the trunk of the enormous cottonwood tree in their backyard. Clouds piled high above the house in a promise of approaching rain. He breathed in the fresh scent and sighed. It was good to be home.

Whenever possible Bryan sat outside. He couldn't get enough of the small freedoms of life everyone seemed to take for granted—being able to come and go as he wished, hot tap water, electric lights that he could control. But as much as he appreciated these things, he knew they all had a price. And that reminded him that he still had not found a job. Albert had given him several leads, but none of them had panned out. No one in the area needed a pilot, certainly not one who hadn't flown in five years. Getting his license renewed wasn't going to be as difficult as finding a place to use it. But then he wasn't positive he really did want to fly again. Five years away from his profession had given him time to look more objectively at the risks, and for the first time he had been able to understand Lani's concerns. Still, he wasn't trained to do anything else.

Bryan was beginning to worry. True, he had been home only a couple of weeks, but he saw no changes looming in the future. Life in Laredo was fairly slow paced. If there were no jobs today, there would likely be no jobs tomorrow, either.

As he slouched lower into the lawn chair, he tried to think of something else he could do to earn a living; it was either that or move, and neither of them wanted to leave their home. He could probably work at one of the nearby farms or ranches as a handyman, but that wouldn't bring in much money. He wanted to make enough to take care of Lani when she decided to quit work. She had never wanted a job before, and he was pretty sure she would tire of the grind of production now that he was home and could provide for her.

But Lani had changed. She was no longer dependent on him, and had said she didn't want to be. He had always admired her gumption and feisty spirit, and her independent thinking, but the family's money was a different matter. Bryan came from a long line of paternal providers whose women had never worked, and he felt uncomfortable knowing that Lani not only worked, but was their sole support at the moment.

As thunder began to rumble in the distance, Bryan's thoughts turned to his other concerns. He had been unable to decide whether he should go back to the sheriff's office and pursue the matter of his false arrest. Armbruster had counseled him to let it go and try to forget about it, but Armbruster hadn't spent five years in a Mexican jail. Then Bryan had tried the FBI, but the agent he spoke with said it was out of their jurisdiction, and the man at the

State Department advised him that since the Mexican government seemed unaware of the incident, trying to prove it had happened at all would only strain the international relations between the two countries. Bryan had no grievance with the Mexican government—he just wanted to get back at whomever had been responsible for him being jailed. Without the support of the American authorities, he felt he had no choice but to back down.

With frustration, Bryan kicked at the tree trunk, sending a spray of bark onto the sun-scorched grass. No one seemed to understand. Frank Goldman had suggested that Bryan come in for counseling, but Bryan was reluctant. He liked Frank a lot and was sure they would be friends, but he couldn't afford the sessions and was too proud to ask Frank to reduce his price. Lani's clay work paid the bills and bought groceries, but there was little left over for extras.

Bryan's train of thought was interrupted as fat drops of rain began spattering the arid ground. He watched in fascination as the dry grass seemed to soak up the rain as quickly as it fell. He was reluctant to go inside, even for rain. On the other hand he knew it worried Lani when he did things that weren't considered normal. Slowly he swung his feet down and stood as the rain began to fall in earnest. Taking his time, he crossed the yard and let himself into the studio.

Lani looked up and smiled. "I'm glad to see the rain. We need it."

"We sure do." As he watched her deft fingers move over the clay, he pensively wondered if they had been reduced to talking only about the weather? There was so much he wanted to know—such as what the world had been up to these past five years. People kept dropping words and phrases like Chernobyl and Black Monday, and he hadn't any idea what they were talking about. At first he had asked, but soon felt self-conscious that the answers were apparently obvious to everyone but him.

After quietly watching her work for a while, he asked, "What are you making?"

"A rain goddess. Pretty appropriate, right?" She added a straplike strip of clay to the elaborate headdress. "This one is going to Atlanta, I hear."

"That's good. I guess Atlanta could use some rain, too." Intently eyeing one of the completed statues, he said, "I really admire what you're doing with these, but I can't help thinking how reluctant you were at first about doing this sort of thing. Lani, are you sure you can't get into trouble making these?"

"Of course. I'm not doing anything wrong. These are all my own designs."

He didn't look convinced. "Sometimes a person can get in trouble when he hasn't done anything wrong at all." When he saw the concern in her sea-green eyes, he said stiffly, "I'm sorry. I didn't mean to bring that up again."

"It's not that. I just don't want you to worry."

"Okay. If you say there's nothing to worry about, then there's nothing to worry about." He made his lips smile. He felt as if he and Lani had grown far apart.

She went back to her work. "I saw those papers you brought home with you, and I read a few. I hope you don't mind."

"No, why should I?"

"What is it? Your journal?"

"I guess you could call it that. I didn't have that in mind at the time, but it turned into one." For some reason his jailers hadn't refused his requests for pens and paper and had allowed him to keep what he'd written. And with nothing else to do, Bryan had written a great deal. He had documented his ordeal day by day. An idea sprang to his mind. "I wonder if I could sell it?" he said aloud. "My journal, I mean."

Lani looked up blankly as if her mind had moved on to something else. "Maybe you could. I don't know anything about selling books. Wouldn't you need an agent or something?"

"Search me."

"Do you really want to sell it? Some of it must be very personal—your innermost feelings and all."

"I want to tell my story. Lani, you don't understand how important it is for me to know those five years haven't just vanished! I was alive! I felt things! It's not that I want people to know what happened to me as much as I need to reassure myself that I *was*!"

"How about television?"

"What do you mean?"

"You know, the talk shows, like Oprah Winfrey."

"Who?"

"Phil Donahue, Johnny Carson."

Bryan's face brightened. "I never considered a talk show. Somebody might be interested in hearing my story. At least on a local level. I'm not sure Carson would jump at the chance, but the local station might."

"You never know. That's one thing Jay told me. You have to aim high. That's why I tried the waterfalls I sent to that Abilene exhibit."

Jealousy touched him. "You mention Jay Harmond pretty often."

"Do I? I guess it's because I've been working on these Mayan figures quite a bit lately. He should be by in a day or two to pick up his last order."

With a frown Bryan turned away. "I might write up a synopsis of my story and send it to a few TV stations."

"It can't hurt."

He watched her resume her work, her face reflecting her concentration. Why didn't she ever see his need to talk and put her work aside for a few minutes? The old Lani would have. With a sigh he went to the back room to set up the typewriter.

Lani glanced up at his retreating back. He was so self-contained since his return. Most of the time she felt as if he didn't need her at all. She never knew whether it was all right to talk about his unpleasant experiences. Sometimes he opened up, but at other times he withdrew as if she were intruding. She didn't understand him at all these days.

The rain pattering against the window would normally have given her a feeling of coziness and security, but today she felt edgy. Perhaps it was the increasing volume of thunder. She tried to lose herself in the idea of incorporating the essence of rain into the goddess she was sculpting.

When the knock sounded on the door, she looked up with a start. She hadn't heard anyone drive up. Jay Harmond stood beneath the overhang on the back steps, his sleek black car parked in the driveway.

Lani hurried to open the door before he got any wetter. "Come in," she said with a smile. "I expected you to call first."

"I was passing by the turnoff and thought I would take a chance on finding you at home." Jay was rather tall, with sandy brown hair and pale blue eyes. Lani had always thought he just missed being handsome. Though each of his features was good-looking, somehow together they left something lacking. He was a big man who was beginning to edge toward being overweight.

"I've finished the statues. There they are on the bottom shelf. Be careful when you lift them; the tops of the boxes aren't nailed down." She went to the hot plate. "Coffee?"

"No, thanks." He took out the hearth god and examined it critically. "Very good. If I didn't know better, I'd swear this came from a Mayan ruin."

"It's all in the type of clay and the patina and how it's fired. None of them is a reproduction."

"Fine, fine." He looked at them one by one, then replaced them in the crates.

Lani filled each of the boxes with sawdust, then tapped the covers down. "Send them to good homes. I'm beginning to like these little fellows."

"I will." Jay's pale eyes followed her movements carefully. "You know, you should move away from here," he said. "Come to Houston and get out of the boonies."

"No way. I like my boonies," she said with a laugh.

"You must be lonely here. There isn't another sculptress in town that I know of. In Houston there are many."

"All the more reason for me to stay here. Besides, I'm not lonely anymore. Jay, you'll never believe—"

"Don't tell me there's another man in your life. I can't bear it!"

"Actually, I was going to say—"

"You don't deny it? Good lord, Lani! Don't tell me you've taken up with a farmer! Come with me to Houston before you end up as a wife and mother."

"You make it sound like a death sentence," she protested as she skillfully avoided his arm. Jay was harmless, but he was a groper. She was accustomed to fielding his passes.

"For you it would be. You have talent, Lani. Don't throw it away."

"Then you're interested in the rest of my work as well? Such as my waterfalls?"

"They're just fine, but they don't suit my clientele."

"I never knew interior decorators specialized the way you do. I never dreamed there would be such a demand for southwestern interiors."

"It's the newest rage."

"I see." As he tried to edge her into a corner, Lani stepped adroitly to one side. "Have you seen my rain goddess? She's for the Atlanta client."

"Very nice. Very good indeed. I like her helmet." He eased closer.

"Jay, for heaven's sake behave yourself," Lani said as she slid away. "Go get yourself a girlfriend."

"I thought you'd never ask."

"Not me."

"Now, Lani, we've been all through this. You're a beautiful woman, and I find you very attractive. You and I can have something special together."

"Jay, I've been trying to tell you—"

"Don't talk, just come here."

Lani glanced toward the door to the kitchen. Had she heard Bryan's footsteps? "Jay, stop it this minute."

"I'm not trying to do anything you would object to. I'll tell you what—come with me to Houston, and I'll set you up in a studio apartment. You'll have everything you could possibly want. What do you say?"

Before Lani could say anything, Bryan burst through the door. She had never seen Bryan like this. Anger flashed in his dark eyes, and his fists were clenched, ready to do battle. He grabbed Jay by the collar and yanked him around so that he and Jay were nose to nose.

"What in the hell are you saying to my wife!" he growled menacingly.

"Wife! What..."

Lani tried to get between them. "Turn him loose, Bryan! Jay, that's what I was trying to tell you! Bryan has come home. He wasn't dead after all."

Jay looked more closely at the bearded man and paled. Beads of sweat dotted his forehead. "Bryan Cameron?"

"That's right," Bryan said as he finally let Lani separate them. "And I sure as hell don't like you propositioning my wife!"

"I had no idea you'd...I mean, I thought you were dead!"

"I thought so, too," Lani said, "but he wasn't. He was in a Mexican jail and only now came home."

Jay quickly backed away. "I see." He was visibly trembling. "I never expected—"

"Well, you know about me now," Bryan growled, "and you had better steer clear of my wife or I'll tear you into little pieces." He looked as if he not only could, but would enjoy doing it.

Jay hastily handed Lani a check from his coat pocket and scooped up all the boxes at once. "I see, I see. Sorry, Lani. I never...I see." He backed up to the door as Lani hurried to open it.

"Do you want me to help you?" she asked. "If you drop one it'll break."

Jay pushed through the door. He was clearly more anxious to get out of there than to preserve the statues. As he ran across the yard, he splashed through the shallow puddles rather than running around them.

Lani watched as he struggled to get his car door open, deposited the boxes and dashed around to the driver's side. He had never struck Lani as being particularly macho, but the haste of his flight seemed rather odd. After all, Bryan had not actually tried to hit him.

"He runs fast for a big man," Bryan observed.

"You scared him half out of his wits." She turned away and shut the door. "At least he remembered to leave the check."

"I doubt that he'll ever come back here."

"Don't be silly, Bryan. Of course he will. He has to. I can't trust these statues to the mail, and I can't afford a special courier."

"I'm telling you, I don't want him out here! I heard what he was saying to you! He was asking you to be his mistress!"

"That's just his way of flirting."

"Is that supposed to reassure me? I don't want someone flirting with my wife!"

"I don't belong to you, Bryan," she snapped. "People don't belong to people!"

"You belong to me!"

"I belong *with* you! There's a big difference."

"How long has this been going on between you?" Bryan demanded.

"There's nothing going on at all."

"No? You knew I was in the house, but he didn't. Maybe if I hadn't been here you might have welcomed his advances!"

"Bryan!" She stared up at him in shock. "I can't believe you said that!"

"Why? Do you think my being gone has made me blind and stupid? I saw him trying to put his arms around you."

"And you saw me move away!"

"He must have had some reason to think it was all right, or he wouldn't have kept pressing the issue."

"I can't believe this! What are you accusing me of?"

"Are you having an affair with Harmond?"

Lani glared at him speechlessly. Finally she managed to say, "If I thought you believed that, I'd throw something at you!"

"Why shouldn't I believe it?"

"Because it's ridiculous!"

"You're one hell of a sexy woman, and I've been gone five years. Are you trying to tell me you've never been to bed with a man in all that time?" he roared at her, at last verbalizing his greatest fear.

"I wouldn't go to bed with Jay Harmond if the future of human existence depended upon it!" she yelled back. "And I'm disgusted at you for even thinking such a thing. Jay Harmond! Good lord, Bryan, give me some credit!"

"Then why was he coming on to you? Why won't you tell him to stay away?"

"This is why!" She grabbed up the check and waved it under Bryan's nose. "His business is our main source of income! I can't afford to offend him. Jay likes to flirt, and he makes outrageous propositions, but I ignore them."

"Then this isn't the first time?"

"Of course not. Jay comes on to every woman he sees. It doesn't mean a thing. Not to me, and least of all to him."

"I can't believe that."

"It's true. I just hope you didn't scare him into withdrawing his order for more of these statues. When he has had time to reach his hotel, I'll call and smooth things over."

"No, you won't." Bryan's eyes narrowed. "How do you know where he's staying?"

"He always stays at the same place. That should prove to you that there's nothing between us. If there were, he would stay here." She glared up at him, her hands balled on her hips.

That made sense to him, but Bryan continued to frown down at her. "I still don't trust him."

"It's up to you whether you believe me or not, but don't chase away our paycheck!"

Bryan took the check from her and read it. "This is awfully generous for four clay statues."

"I happen to be good," she said in a strained voice.

"It's still a lot of money."

"It's supply and demand. I'm the only sculptress he knows who will take the time to make them using authentic procedures. He's paying me not only for my expertise, but to keep me from selling to another decorating firm."

"Is there that much demand for clay gods?"

Lani shrugged. "I guess so. He says this is the latest look in home decorating."

"I guess so?"

"Look, I know you don't like Mayan and southwestern styles, but that doesn't mean no one else does. I really am good at this, and I'm being paid handsomely as a result. Besides, this check has to last us a long time. They don't come regularly, you know."

"You don't have to rub it in!" Bryan turned away angrily.

"What are you mad about now?" Lani went around to stand in front of him.

"You have to tell me that you are earning money and I'm not."

"I wasn't!"

"No? Then why did you say it like that? 'This check has to last us a long time. They don't come regularly, you know.'"

"I didn't mean—"

"Look, Lani. I earned a damned good living for us at one time, and I'm going to do it again! It's not my fault there are no flying jobs here."

"Do you want to move?" she asked almost fearfully. "Leave our home?"

"I didn't suggest that."

"I don't want to leave our home," she said as if he hadn't spoken. She looked around her studio with its fine layer of red clay dust. "I have everything just the way I like it here. We bought this place just after we married."

"Thank goodness it's paid for," he added.

"Almost paid for," she amended. When he looked puzzled, she said, "I couldn't afford the payments, so I extended the mortgage." In response to his frown she added, "With both of us working, it will soon be all ours. At least we own the land free and clear."

Lani went to him and put her arms around him. "I know it's as hard on you as it is on me—readjusting, I mean. But we love each other. We can work it out."

"I do love you, Lani," he said as he embraced her. "It's just that sometimes it's as if I stepped into the twilight zone. Nothing is quite the same, yet everything is familiar, then I turn around and it's not familiar at all."

She laid her cheek against his chest and listened to the steady beat of his heart. "It seems like that to me, too. You look like Bryan, you sound like Bryan, but the Bryan I know would never take a swing at someone for a harmless flirtation."

"I didn't swing at him, and it wasn't harmless," he snapped defensively.

"Yes, it was. I learned how to handle Jay years ago. He knows the limits."

"He didn't sound as if there were any."

"Don't start in all over again," she warned. "We're making up, remember?"

"Sorry," he said, then added, "Does that mean I've changed, too?"

"You're so... well... intense. I never knew you to get uptight about anything."

"I had to learn how to take care of myself physically. If I hadn't, I probably wouldn't be here."

As she maneuvered him toward the door, she reminded him, "We always made love when we made up before."

"I remember." A smile lit his eyes.

"I think we should keep the tradition intact." Arm in arm she led him through the kitchen and down the hall to their bedroom. As they stood beside the bed, Bryan studied her for a moment, then said, "At times when we make love I get the feeling that you're half scared of me."

"You make love differently than you used to. I never know what to expect. But scared? No. Just excited." She unbuttoned her blouse and slipped it off. Keeping her eyes on his, she reached behind her and released the fastener of her bra.

His eyes widened with desire as she let him gaze at her breasts. Slowly she unfastened her skintight jeans. Stepping out of jeans and shoes, she stood before him in her lacy bikini panties. "You seem to be overdressed for the occasion," she said.

As she stretched out on the bed, he shucked off his clothes and laid down beside her. Bracing himself on his strong arms, he gazed down at her. "I dreamed of you like this," he said in a low voice. "Day and night I saw you lying naked beneath me. The only memory that tormented me more was the remembrance of your laugh, and how you'd move, and all the little things we did together."

"I'm sorry I was a torment." She stroked the hard muscles of his chest and sides.

"You gave me a reason not to give up. I knew somehow I would get back to you."

"If I had known you were alive, I would have done whatever was necessary to free you."

"I know. Thank goodness I didn't know at the time you had given me up for dead. That would have driven me mad."

"I'm glad it's over."

He didn't correct her, but he wondered if it would ever really be over. Their enforced separation seemed to color every minute of their lives.

He lowered himself over her, shifting his weight so that one of his hips and elbows supported most of his body, yet he could feel her warm flesh pressed hard against his. He bent to kiss her as his hand found the tantalizing curve of her breast. He covered it, feeling the nipple grow harder against his palm. Gently he began to stroke the velvety skin as his tongue tasted the sweetness of her mouth.

Lani writhed beneath him, her silken legs moving over his, her small hands caressing his body and making his flesh tingle with desire. She was a woman who thoroughly enjoyed making love. At least this hadn't changed. In bed they were totally compatible.

Bryan ran his hand over her side and slipped his fingers under the lacy edge of her panties. They were so small and feminine, so sheer they might rip apart with a strong tug. Carefully Bryan pulled them down over her hips and past her thighs so that Lani could kick them aside.

She lay naked and eager beneath him. Bryan's gaze ran the length of her ivory-and-apricot body with its nest of russet curls a hand's length beneath her navel that were only a shade darker than the hair on her head. Her coloring had always reminded him of a Rembrandt or a Titian, though her body was much more slender than those artists' models. She was a work of art, a composition of desirable loveliness, and she was all his. When they were together like this, with love shining in her green eyes, he had no doubts at all.

He lowered his head and gently pulled her nipple into his mouth, bathing it with his tongue and teasing it with a gentle suckling. Lani moaned with delight and moved against him, her legs pulling him toward her. He knew what she wanted, but he wasn't yet willing to comply—not until he had satisfied his need to lick and kiss and caress her. After all the times she had haunted his dreams he wasn't about to rush matters.

As he lathed her nipple with his tongue, his fingers explored the warm wetness of her femininity. She was ready and eager for him, and that excited him even more. Gently at first, then more demandingly, his fingers stroked her.

Lani murmured his name as if it came from the depths of her being. She closed her eyes and arched toward him as his fingers pleasured her. Bryan lifted his head to watch as ecstasy lit her face. Knowingly he probed and urged her to greater passion, then suddenly she cried out as her culmination was reached. Quickly his flesh joined hers, and he held her close as the rhythmic waves of her body stroked him from deep within her.

When she drew a deep breath and sighed in satisfaction, Bryan smiled. Slowly he began the dance of love, forcing her to match his pace in order to extend their pleasure as long as possible.

Lani tried to hurry him with fevered words and passionate caresses, but he loved her at his own pace, gauging how to give them both the most enjoyment. Sweat slicked their bodies, turning Lani's skin from velvet to satin. Her hair was tousled around her head like tongues of flame, and she moaned with her desire for him.

Bryan could prolong the exquisite pleasure no longer, and he moved quicker, triggering their mutual release. Lani cried out and tightly embraced him as the purest of ecstasies poured through him. He buried his face in the hot hollow of her neck and inhaled the clean scent of her skin and hair. She was his woman, his mate, and he was hers. He found it deeply satisfying to know he could please her so well.

For a long time Lani clung to him, unwilling to let the world reclaim them. As much as she had cared for Bryan before, her feelings for him now were even stronger. When they made love, she not only knew he was in command, but that he had the love and the expertise to fulfill every need and desire of her mind and body. There was a primitiveness to his lovemaking that made her feel like a bawdy wench and a lady, somehow all at the same time. She didn't quite know how he did that, but she loved it. The old Bryan had loved her well, but always as though she were a lady—desirable, but always a lady. With the new Bryan, Lani felt free to experiment, to let herself go.

When he started to roll away from her, Lani looped her leg over his thigh and pulled him back. With a seductive smile she put her arms around his neck and drew him down for her kiss. As she did, she began to undulate her hips against his. Gratifyingly she felt him grow ready again.

Lani ran the tip of her tongue over his lips, tasting the faint saltiness of the sweat from his upper lip. His eyes were dark and sultry as desire for her quickened again. Lani felt the tensing and releasing of his smooth muscles as he moved. His buttocks rounded under her palms, and she ran her hands over the slight indentation of his spine.

She rolled so that they lay side by side, her head cradled on his arm and his other hand free to toy with her breast. Closing her eyes, she enjoyed him and let him enjoy her with kisses and hot touches that left her wanting more.

After a while she felt his pace change. Again he was the lusty pirate, and she was the willing plunder. She moved with him, letting him take command of her senses, carrying her to heights she could never have reached alone. Lani felt the world dissolve in an explosion of delight, and moments later she knew he, too, had reached ecstasy's summit. Their senses intertwined, mingled and shimmered as their bodies surrendered to love.

Several minutes later, she opened her eyes to find that he was watching her. With a satisfied smile she stroked his cheek, feeling the now-familiar texture of his beard. "You're terrific," she whispered.

"Lady, so are you."

"I love you, Bryan."

"I love you. We'll work it out."

Lani nodded and closed her eyes again. They had to work it out somehow. She loved him too much to ever give him up again.

Chapter Five

"Do you want to ride with me to Monica Denton's?" Lani asked as she passed a hairbrush through her short hair.

"Not particularly. Why are you going?"

"I have to take more pottery to her. She had two tour buses come through yesterday, and she called to say she needs more bowls and jugs."

"Those boxes are heavy. I'll go with you to help."

"It's not necessary. I've been delivering them by myself for years." Instantly she regretted her choice of words. She had been trying to avoid references to their separation, hoping that would help bridge the gap between them.

Bryan smiled at her. "That was then and this is now. You shouldn't have to lift such heavy boxes."

"Okay." Lani was relieved that he hadn't taken offense this time, and was glad for the second chance to take him up on his offer to help her. "Besides, if you're with me, I'll have an excuse not to linger and talk. I know Monica must be lonely, but she's not my choice for a friend."

"Speaking of friends," he said as he pulled on his socks and put on his new top-siders, "I called Frank a few minutes ago and asked them to come over at seven tonight instead of eight. Did you get the hamburger meat out of the freezer?"

"It's thawing even as we speak," she said lightly. "I'm glad you like Frank and Debbie. They're fun to be with."

"After that fiasco with Bob at your parents' house, I needed a new friend."

Lani applied her lip gloss, then put on her sandals. "I saw Bob and Helen at the store yesterday, and they scarcely spoke. Too bad. Bob was so nice before Helen got her hooks into him."

"People change. You and I are living proof of it."

Lani glanced at him. He didn't look unhappy, but some subtlety about him often reminded her that they weren't the same. Again she felt a niggling fear. "I'm ready if you are," she said with bright cheerfulness.

Bryan easily loaded the boxes that Lani would have had to struggle with. She truly appreciated his help, but having to fend for herself had created a fierce independence in her that kept getting between them. She enjoyed his companionship, but having someone doing things for her felt odd. As Bryan drove, Lani tried to sit back and enjoy it, but after having driven herself for so long she found it difficult to surrender even this responsibility to someone else. "It's this next corner," she said.

"I know where The Outpost is." He turned at the corner and pulled into the parking area. "Why did Monica choose such Western names for her stores when she's so sophisticated?"

"She thought Outpost and South of the Border would attract the tourist trade. She was right. Monica's pretty sharp when it comes to business. I have to give her that." Lani got out of the car and went around to the trunk to help Bryan unload.

They carried the boxes through the side door into the storeroom. The jumble of merchandise, some packed and some unpacked, that filled the back room shelves was a great contrast to the well organized and neatly arranged sales floor out front. In one corner of the back room a woman sat on a stool amidst a large assortment of wrapping paper making the elaborate bows that Monica put on all her gift-wrapped boxes. Lani nodded to her and turned as Monica breezed into the room.

"Hello," she said throatily as she saw Bryan. Then, "Hello, Lani. What have you brought me?" Her blue eyes traveled over Bryan as if she hoped he were part of the delivery.

"There are four large bowls, three medium ones and eight small ones." Lani ticked off the items on her fingers, not noticing the predatory look Monica had fixed upon Bryan. "This box has two water jugs, that one has three smaller ones that could double as vases. I also included three platters. I know you said they haven't been moving as well, but I'm using a new glaze that may make a difference." She glanced up. "Monica?"

"Oh, certainly. Whatever you say. I'm sure they will do nicely." To Bryan she said, "Lani's work is quite popular with my tourist trade. She has such a ... rustic ... touch."

Bryan narrowed his eyes and a muscle tightened in his jaw.

Lani shrugged. "I never thought of it as rustic, but if it sells, who am I to argue? Do you want me to leave all the pottery here, or should I take some of it to the other store?"

"Just leave it here. I'll sort through it and send over whatever I need." Monica ran her tongue over her lips as she met Bryan's eyes. "It's hot. I would have thought that rain yesterday would have cooled things off."

Bryan looked at Lani and gave her a sexy smile. "Not necessarily. Sometimes rain just makes it hotter."

Lani blushed and said hastily, "If you don't want me to unpack, I guess we'll be going."

"If you must," Monica replied, her voice barely masking her displeasure at Bryan's obvious double entendre to Lani. "I have to work late tonight. I usually do on Thursdays." She shot Bryan a glance to be certain he had heard. "I can unpack them then."

"Whatever." Lani went to the door and opened it to the sunlight. "I'll be talking to you." She waved goodbye to the silent employee.

As Bryan shut the door behind them, he said, "That woman is a shark!"

"I know you don't like her, but she probably means well."

"Like hell."

"Assertive women are in style now," she said with a smile, as she automatically opened the door on the driver's side and got in behind the wheel. Suddenly remembering Bryan wanted to drive, she slid to the other side.

With an appreciative nod, Bryan said, "There's a big difference between assertive and aggressive. Monica is definitely aggressive."

Lani watched Bryan go around the car to get in. He mentioned Monica's blatant sexuality every time her name came up. She wasn't entirely comfortable with his linking Monica and sex. Bryan was a sensual man, and while he always spoke of Monica in a disparaging tone, the relationship between Lani and Bryan didn't feel secure enough for her to laugh it off.

Taking a few minutes to familiarize himself with the changes to the area during his absence, Bryan drove through downtown Laredo, then out to a nearby residential area. When he came to a small park, he slowed and parked by the curb. A dozen or more children were running and playing on the grass beneath the sheltering mesquite trees. The children tumbled and raced around like puppies.

"Aren't they something?" Bryan said in a voice as gentle as the one she remembered from the first time she ever saw him. "Look at them. Not a care in the world."

She followed his gaze and nodded. "All children are beautiful. Sometimes I come here and sit on a bench and just watch them."

"We ought to have one that age," he said in a tighter voice. "If things had been different, we would have had one about the size of that boy in the red shirt."

"There's still time. We aren't exactly over-the-hill yet."

"It's a waste that bothers me." The frustration was back in his voice. "All the damned waste!"

"Things didn't happen the way we planned, but we can't do anything about that. All we can do is start from here."

"Start from scratch, you mean. Hell, Lani, we're right back where we started. No airplane, no cargo company, no savings."

"We aren't quite back where we were. We have the farm and our home, and I earn a living."

Judging by the look of displeasure on his face, she figured she had made a mistake by mentioning her income again.

"I've looked all over town, and there's nothing for me to do. Not even any jobs that *don't* involve flying or planes. Nobody is hiring." With a forced grin he said, "Maybe I could work for Monica. What do you think?"

"Forget it. I don't trust her *that* far."

"What do you suggest?"

"Say, what about that journal you wrote? You said once you might try to get it published."

"Who would want to read it? I'm not anybody special. No one even knew I was gone except for you and a handful of people around here. Anyway, it's depressing."

"I read some of it, and I thought it was good. Sure, it depressed me, but that's because I love you and I want only good things to happen to you."

"No, I'm not a writer. Nobody is interested. I never even heard from any of those talk shows I wrote to."

"Maybe there hasn't been time yet. I don't know how long these things take." She watched two girls each trying to swing higher than the other. "Let's give it more time."

Bryan's expression hardened as he said, "What about us, Lani?"

A knot formed in her throat, and she found it difficult to breathe. At last she managed to say, "I think we should give that more time, too."

He nodded, not trusting himself to speak. He had hoped she would say she was still happy as his wife and that she didn't want to leave him. Evidently she was still trying to decide whether or not they could make it. His muscles were stiff as he maneuvered the car back into traffic. What would he do if Lani decided she would rather keep her life of freedom? He knew he wasn't easy to live with these days, but his lack of a job kept him on edge. He *had* to find work of some sort. Maybe trying to turn his journal into a book wasn't such a bad idea. At least it would fill his hours and might give him some sense of accomplishment.

He glanced at Lani's small, trim figure, and his train of thought switched to a more pleasurable track. She looked damned good in jeans—even better than she had in the dresses she used to prefer. He liked the way the tight denim molded her legs and bottom and tucked in at her waist. Although he preferred her hair longer than it was now, he was becoming accustomed to its present length and even thought that it suited her personality better. He enjoyed running his fingers through it and watching it fall back into place.

He was even becoming accustomed to having Lani's clay gods sitting around in odd places. Lani said she was experimenting with different ways to season the statues—using everything from fireplace ashes to talcum powder. She had one hearth goddess standing between the burners on the stove to catch whatever might spatter from a pot or skillet and another stacked among moldering wood left over from last year's wood pile. Lani was very creative when it came to the addition of a patina of age to her Mayan figures.

Her waterfall sculptures were another matter. He really liked them. She had devised a glaze that made them shimmer with opalescent hues, the colors shifting subtly as the piece was viewed from different angles. Bryan had encouraged her to do more of these and less of the gods and pottery, but Lani had only smiled at his suggestion. The pottery and statues were their bread and butter, whereas the waterfalls had yet to sell at all. Bryan decided he didn't know enough about art to advise her.

When they reached the house, Bryan left Lani in the studio and went in the back room and hauled out his journal. It had seemed awfully bulky when he was carrying it across Mexico, but it really wasn't all that thick. During his confinement he hadn't known if his supply of paper would be canceled, so he had taught himself to write in a minute hand and to cover the entire page. It was amazing, he thought, that Lani could decipher it at all.

Armed with only rudimentary typing skills from a course he had taken in high school, Bryan began the laborious process of making his story legible and readable. The effort of reliving the years of his imprisonment soon pressed upon him like a physical weight, but he continued. Along with the depression, he hoped would come a catharsis; he had to rid himself of the trauma so that he could get on with life.

Lani was glad when Debbie and Frank arrived. Bryan had been in the back room of the house all afternoon, and judging from the clacking of the typewriter she assumed he had been working on his journal. But because of the occasional outburst of expletives she'd overheard, she was reluctant to ask. The few times Bryan had come out of his room, he hadn't looked as if he would welcome a conversation about it. An hour before their guests were due, Lani had called out a reminder to him, but hadn't waited for a reply. When he finally emerged, he tried to appear as though nothing were wrong, but Lani could tell it hadn't been a good day for him.

Debbie handed Lani a bag of tortilla chips and a bowl of her homemade avocado dip. "I couldn't show up empty-handed," she explained.

"I would never turn down your guacamole," Lani assured her. "I think I've become addicted to it. Come into the kitchen, and we'll pour the chips into a bowl. Frank, you'll find Bryan out by the barbecue pit. We bought an off brand of charcoal, and it doesn't want to light. Bryan is having to reinvent fire."

"I'll give him a hand. I never saw a charcoal I couldn't set fire to one way or another."

"Uh oh," Debbie said with a laugh. "The last time Frank said that he singed his eyebrows, and the steaks tasted like gasoline."

"It wasn't gasoline, it was kerosene. But I learned from the experience," Frank assured her with mock dignity. "Now I only use charcoal lighter."

Lani laughed. "Don't you two get into trouble out there. I don't want the grill blown up."

When Frank was gone, Debbie asked, "How is it going?"

"Fine. I've already made the hamburger patties and sliced the tomatoes and cheese. We're just waiting on the charcoal."

"I don't mean supper, and you know it. How is Bryan adjusting?"

Lani stopped pulling leaves off the head of lettuce and looked at her friend. "I don't know. Debbie, I'm scared. This afternoon... well, he all but asked me if I wanted to continue our marriage."

"He did! What did you say?"

"What could I say? I said we should give it more time."

"Then what did he say?"

"Nothing! He didn't say anything at all!"

Debbie frowned. "Maybe he didn't mean it the way it sounded."

"Now what else could he possibly mean? I don't think I could stand losing him again!"

"People are tough, Lani. You could handle it."

"Don't give me that. You know what I mean. Sure, Bryan's changed. He's changed a lot! But I still love him."

"Does he love you?"

"He says he does, but if he means it, why would he ever suggest that our marriage might not last? I don't know what to do." She went back to shredding the lettuce, her fingers working frantically. "I think a lot of the problem is that the job market is so tight around here."

"That could do it. Men seem to worry more about who supports whom than women do." Debbie rescued the lettuce from Lani. "Did he try the Lazy A ranch?"

"Yes, he's tried everywhere. Debbie, I can't conjure up a job for him out of thin air!"

"Of course not."

"I heard him typing. I think he's turning his journal into a book."

"I hope so. I'd like to read it."

"But would anyone else? Maybe it's a waste of time, and I shouldn't have encouraged him."

"Nonsense. Writing is good therapy. I've heard Frank say it over and over."

"Bryan won't go to see Frank at the office," Lani said as she set the table. "I'm not sure why, but he says he won't."

"Too bad. I really think Frank could help him work through it."

"He doesn't want help. Not from anybody, even me." Lani turned to face her friend, her eyes filled with confusion. "Before he went away, Bryan always asked my opinion. Now he just goes ahead and does things, and then tells me about it."

"Such as?"

"Take the back room, for instance. We've always used it as a sort of den, and while he was gone I painted it pale green. The day before yesterday he bought paint, and now it's a very strange shade of blue."

"Maybe he doesn't like green."

"That's not the point. Wouldn't most couples discuss something such as that first? When he was through, he said he didn't mention it to me beforehand because I was working and he didn't want to disturb me. But how many people do you know who decide to paint and then do it immediately? I always think about it a day or two. Don't you?"

"Yes, but I hate to paint. I try to put it off until Frank volunteers to do it for me." Debbie shrugged. "Maybe Bryan feels he has wasted five years and he doesn't want to lose any more."

"That's exactly what he said!"

"That's not too hard to accept, is it?"

"No, but to tell you the truth—" she glanced at the doorway to be sure they were still alone "—it's a shade I would never have picked. It's much too dark."

Debbie laughed as she put ice in the tea glasses. "You have to admit, Lani, your light colors do make a house more feminine."

"Is it? I never noticed." Lani looked at the frilly Cape Cod curtains at the window as if she were surprised to see how dainty they were. When she had hung them next to the daisy-patterned wallpaper and lemony woodwork, her only thought was that they merely looked clean and fresh.

Debbie shook her head teasingly as she laughed again.

Outside Frank and Bryan had finally coaxed a flame out of the charcoal. "I'll never cut corners on charcoal again," Bryan said with a shake of his head.

"It's going now. You just needed to use more charcoal lighter." Frank capped the can and wiped his hands on his pocket handkerchief. "Have you squared things away with your license yet?"

"You mean my recertification? The medical exam went okay. All I have left is my biannual flight review, but I haven't bothered. It won't do me much good since there are no jobs for pilots around here, and I can't afford a plane." He glanced around at their house, the small barn and the orchard beyond it. "I guess I could mortgage the farm, but that's out of the question. I know now how chancy life is. If anything happened to me, Lani could lose everything."

"How are you keeping busy? That's important, you know." Both men stared down at the struggling flames since the subject seemed too personal for eye contact.

"There's plenty to do around here. The barn was in bad need of repair, and I've found a number of smaller jobs that needed my attention such as caulking and that type of thing. Lani managed very well while I was gone, but she never got up on the roof and cleaned out the gutters or crawled up under the porch to jack up that sagging corner." Bryan grinned. "I painted the back room a couple of days ago. It was a sort of faded color. Now it's blue. Sure does make it easy to work in there with some color on the walls."

"I like vivid colors, too. What are you working on in there?"

"Oh, this and that," Bryan evaded self-consciously. "I wrote a sort of journal while I was gone. There wasn't much else to do. I decided to type it up in case I ever wanted to show it to anybody."

"Hey, that's a great idea! Maybe you could sell it to the movies."

"It would sure be dull." Bryan laughed. "The set would be cheap though—just one small cell."

"Could I see it sometime? If it's not an imposition, that is."

"Sure, why not? Lani even said something about me trying to sell it as a book."

"That sounds like a good idea to me."

"Come on, Frank. I'm nobody special. Hell, I don't know if I can even write at all. At least not something a stranger would pay to read."

"Well, whether you sell it or not, it's good for you to get it down on paper. I have a feeling you're bottling a lot up inside."

"Yeah, maybe so." Bryan made an offhanded gesture to signify he could handle it.

Twenty minutes later, the charcoal was covered with a uniform white ash and Bryan declared the fire was ready for cooking. He went in to get the hamburger patties, and when he returned, he said, "Lani and Debbie are talking a blue streak in there."

"They always do. I don't know how they find so much to talk about as often as they see each other."

"I don't either," Bryan agreed as he put the meat on the grill.

Frank studied his new friend a moment before he said with careful casualness, "How is Lani adjusting to having you back home?"

Bryan's gaze seemed locked on the glowing coals. "Okay."

"It's none of my business. Forget I asked."

Bryan sighed heavily. "Sorry. I guess I'm touchy about that. The truth is, I can't tell how she's doing. I know it's been a big change for her. After all I was 'dead' for five years. That's almost twice as long as we were together!" He thought about Jay Harmond and the proposition he had overheard. "It must be hard on her, but she doesn't admit it."

"I'm not sure 'hard' is the way I'd describe it. Maybe 'different.'"

"She had a life of her own. Now I'm back in it. She could hardly tell me to hit the road." Bryan tried to laugh, but his uncertainty showed through.

"Knowing Lani, she would say it if she felt it. Debbie and I have gotten to know her quite well since we moved here. She talked about you a lot."

"She did?" Bryan's eyes searched Frank's face.

"I thought you were some paragon of perfection, to hear her," Frank said with a grin. "It was a relief to find out you're as human as the rest of us."

"Somehow I assumed she had managed to pretty much forget about me." Bryan eased the spatula under a patty and flipped it.

"Well, she's a survivor. She had put her life back together."

"How much 'back together' was it?" Bryan asked with a disconcertingly direct look.

"If you're asking if she was involved with anyone around here, the answer is no. She would have told Debbie, and I would have heard by suppertime. She wasn't seeing anyone."

Bryan nodded. "Thanks." Frank had said she wasn't seeing anyone locally, but Jay Harmond was from Houston. If Lani had been having an affair, she might not have been all that open about it. Despite her gregarious nature, Lani had a secret core most people never knew existed.

When the meat was done, Frank and Bryan carried it into the air-conditioned kitchen. Lani's colorful plates were set on the antique oak table she had salvaged from an auction. Above the table hung a stained-glass lamp that cast rainbow hues onto the ceiling. Bryan set the meat between the baked beans and the potato salad, and everyone sat down to eat.

The conversation rose and fell as Lani, Debbie and Frank discussed the current gossip of Laredo. Bryan tried to keep up with who they were talking about, but he felt like a stranger at his own table. Only now and then did a familiar name float by, and whenever it did, he grabbed at it eagerly. Then the talk shifted to the national news, and Bryan was even more lost. Any event over a few weeks old was a mystery to him, and he felt awkward asking for too many explanations. He finally decided he would spend the next week or so at the library boning up on the news of the last five years.

As Lani was serving the peach cobbler, Frank grinned at Debbie and said to her, "I guess you've already told Lani, haven't you?"

"No, I said I wouldn't. I can keep a secret, Frank." Debbie tried to look stern, but her smile broke through.

"What secret?" Lani asked. Then she paused and said, "You aren't moving are you? You had better not say that!"

"No, no." Debbie laughed. "Tell her, Frank."

"No, you do it."

"Well, somebody tell me," Lani said with a laugh, then her eyes grew round. "You aren't!"

Debbie nodded, her eyes sparkling.

"What?" Bryan asked. "She isn't what?"

"Pregnant!" Lani exclaimed as Debbie nodded again.

Bryan grinned as he shook Frank's hand. "Way to go!"

"It's not due until spring," Debbie said almost shyly. "We only found out this morning."

"And you didn't tell me? Debbie!" Lani pretended to scold.

"I'm having trouble convincing myself. So far I don't really feel very different."

Frank nodded sagely to Bryan. "She's *always* had a fetish for saltine crackers and ice cream."

They laughed as Debbie blushed even redder.

"You'll have to come over and help me plan the baby's room," Debbie said to Lani. "The baby's room. My goodness, doesn't that sound odd?"

"It sounds wonderful!"

"We're going to put her in the room Debbie's mother uses when she comes to visit," Frank said smugly. "Maybe my mother-in-law will get the hint and stay with Debbie's sister in El Paso."

Debbie punched his arm, and Frank pretended to flinch.

"'Her?'" Bryan asked.

"Think pink," Frank advised. "I've always wanted a daughter."

Although Lani couldn't have been happier for her friends, she felt a twinge of sadness for herself. Would she ever have a baby of her own? She was already twenty-eight. Time was flying by for her. Debbie was nearly two years younger.

When Lani lifted her eyes, she found Bryan watching her. Quickly she glanced away. What was he thinking? Did he think it was already too late for them? That he no longer wanted the responsibility or the bond of raising children? Lani couldn't tell, and she was afraid to speculate. "We went by the park today," she said in a rush. "I love to see the children playing there."

"Before long ours will be one of them," Debbie said in wonder.

"Have you seen a sale on tricycles?" Frank asked with mock seriousness.

Debbie shook her head in happy exasperation. "He's been like this all day. By noon he had chosen a college!"

"There's no reason to leave everything until the last minute," Frank protested. "I was going to leave the selection of graduate school up to her."

Bryan laughed and winked at Lani. "We had better sign up now if we want to get to baby-sit her."

The breath caught in Lani's throat, but she nodded. Was Bryan merely going along with the teasing, or did he mean it? "I had better get to baby-sit her," Lani said, "or her parents are in big trouble. I can still take back this cobbler, you know."

"No, no," Frank protested, clutching his bowl. "Not that! I've had your cobbler before. You can be chief baby-sitter."

"She can call you Aunt Lani," Debbie added. "Can I keep the cobbler?"

"It's a deal. Does anyone want ice cream on top? Crackers as garnish, Debbie?"

"All right now. I can see I'll never live that down. I'll take ice cream, though."

"Enjoy it while you can," Frank advised. "Tomorrow the diet starts."

Debbie groaned and rolled her eyes.

As Lani put a bowl in front of Bryan, she said, "These peaches came from our orchard."

"Do you mean those trees finally started to produce?" he asked. "Amazing. I was about to cut them down before..." He hesitated, not wanting to bring up their years apart. "From our orchard. That's great."

Lani nodded. "The apple trees don't do well, but we get plenty of pears and peaches."

"Got any crackers?" Debbie asked in a stage whisper.

Bryan got the cracker tin and watched in amazement as she ate the concoction with obvious relish. He had no brothers or sisters so he had rarely had close contact with pregnant women. He found himself wondering what Lani would be like if she were carrying their baby. Would she glow like Debbie? Lani was definitely the glowing type. He pictured her blossoming and imagined himself holding a baby—he didn't care if it was a boy or a girl, but he hoped it would have Lani's coppery hair.

At once he forced himself to look at life realistically. Lani might not even want a baby anymore. He had heard it was harder on a woman to have a first child as she got older; in two years Lani would be thirty. Even if she still wanted a child, she might not want his. She didn't seem certain that she even wanted to continue the marriage.

He watched as Lani leaned forward, her face bright with happiness as she discussed nurseries and baby clothes with Debbie. He loved her so much he ached inside. Would he be able to give her up if that's what she wanted? If it would make her happy, he knew he would do it, but he also knew his heart would break.

"Dads-to-be are the forgotten people," Frank said philosophically. "From here on out the women have all the say."

Bryan nodded, but he thought that if Lani were pregnant, he would want very much to be a part of the planning and excitement. Bryan had always loved children and very much wanted at least one of his own—his and Lani's.

The big farmhouse seemed hollow to him when he thought of the empty bedrooms they had planned for their tribe of children to grow up in.

"The cobbler is good," he said to mask his real thoughts.

Chapter Six

When the camera flash went off, Lani jumped. "Good heavens, Bryan! I didn't hear you come in."

Bryan grinned and rolled the film to another frame. "I wanted to catch you in a natural pose."

She went back to smoothing a thick collar onto the neck of the clay statue. Testily, she said, "If I promise to be natural, will you not sneak up on me with a flashbulb?" As soon as she'd spoken, she was sorry she had been so abrupt, but he had startled her. She had no intention of discouraging his renewed interest in photography, because it seemed to be helping relieve him of some of his boredom.

"Who have we here?" he asked as he peered over her shoulder, obviously unaffected by her sharp remark.

"I decided to make a goddess to watch over women in childbirth. Since the Mayans believed that a woman who died giving birth was the equivalent of a warrior dying in battle, I figure there must have been some goddess or other to preside over the event. My little lady here is meant to insure a safe delivery and healthy baby. I'll use it as a prototype for others; this one I'm giving to Debbie. She likes my little people," she added with a pointed glance at Bryan.

"I'm getting used to them, though I have to admit I was glad when the hearth goddess moved off the stove, and I feel sorry for the little fellow buried in the woodpile. I sort of like this one."

"Woodpile! I forgot all about him."

"He's moldering nicely."

"I'll bring it in after a while. I don't want to stop now. I'm on a roll."

"Can you roll and talk at the same time?"

"Sure. What do you want to talk about?"

"Nothing in particular." Bryan was trying to find an excuse not to work on his journal. After the first day he'd worked on it, he had had terrible nightmares. The dog-eared and stained pages had the power to put him right back where he had been, and it hadn't been a pleasant experience. "Have you talked to Debbie today?"

"No, not since they were here the other evening."

"I wondered if morning sickness is bothering her."

Lani glanced curiously at him, then resumed rounding the belly of the clay figure. "She didn't mention it. Not every pregnant woman has nausea."

As he watched her deft movements, he wondered how to bring up the matter that was really on his mind: namely, did Lani want to continue their marriage and have children? "I looked in the guest room a few minutes ago."

"Oh?"

"It seems a shame not to use it."

"I suppose so. Do you want to invite out-of-town friends for a visit? To tell you the truth, I've lost touch with most of them."

"No, I didn't have company in mind."

"Well? What are you talking about?"

"Never mind." He bent and snapped a shot of her fashioning the goddess's facial features. He had been foolish to try to broach the subject of children in such a clumsy way. He moved around to the other side to put the statue in the foreground. "Smile," he said.

"I won't look natural if I smile while I'm working."

"I was talking to the goddess."

Lani looked amused, but she kept working. Bryan straightened. "I don't guess you want to go for a walk."

"Now? Bryan, I have a dozen things I need to do."

"Would you like for me to do some of them?"

"No, thanks."

"Okay." His face was unreadable as he set his camera on a shelf and went out back.

Lani paused. She hadn't meant to sound so abrupt, but she didn't really like to talk when she was concentrating on her work. She watched him through the window as he crossed the yard. He looked as if he felt rejected. With a sigh, Lani wrapped the clay figure in a wet cloth and washed her hands.

Bryan was out of sight by the time she went outside to talk with him, but she felt sure she knew where he had gone. One of Bryan's favorite places had always been the stream lined with willows that meandered across the back of their small farm.

She saw him before he heard her approaching, and as she had expected, he was sitting on a rounded rock that jutted into the stream's path. The stream wasn't much more than a narrow band this time of year because of the lack of rainfall, but because it was spring fed the water never dried up entirely.

Bryan sat with his elbow resting on one bent knee. He looked more despondent than she had ever seen him, and she had a quick stab of fear that he might be contemplating leaving her. As she watched, he lifted his head and gazed up as if he were watching something. She followed his line of sight but saw only a bit of sky framed by willow leaves and a sparrow that was hopping from twig to twig. Then she understood: these were common sights that had been denied him for so long.

Bryan pulled a leaf from a nearby branch and studied the pattern of its veins and shape, then lifted it to his nose to smell its fresh leafy scent.

Lani's heart was full of tenderness as she watched him. Bryan had always loved to be outside with nature; being in jail must have been hell for him. She wondered if he had had an exercise yard or if he had had to stay in the cell all the time. He had never said, and she had felt awkward about asking.

As if he sensed her presence Bryan looked around, and Lani stepped forward.

"I thought you were busy," he said.

"I wasn't that busy as it turns out." She went to him and sat beside him on the cool rock. "Do you want to talk about it?"

He shook his head. "There's nothing to say."

She felt the wall of reserve between them and put her hand on his thigh to bridge the gap. "We used to be able to talk about anything."

He nodded. "Yep."

"I appreciate your offering to help me. I really do. It's just that the things I need to do are things I have to do myself or things I could do in less time than it would take to explain to someone else what needs to be done. For instance, I need to call Jay and tell him when the next batch of figures will be finished."

"I could have managed the phone call to Harmond."

"I know how you feel about him, and I was trying to spare you the unpleasantness."

"I don't need to be protected."

"Jay might," she said with a smile. When Bryan gave her a sharp look, she said, "I was joking."

He looked away and seemed intent on studying the reflection in the water of the leafy boughs overhead.

"Honey, won't you go talk to Frank? You like him and—"

"Don't nag me, Lani!"

She drew back. "I wasn't nagging. I was trying to help you." Her voice was cold in her attempt to hide her hurt.

"I don't need help. I don't need anything."

"I don't think you even need me."

He frowned at her. "What do you mean by that?"

"You can figure it out. You've already said you don't need my help."

Bryan sighed. "I'm not trying to fight with you."

"No? You could have fooled me."

He ran his long fingers through his dark hair. "I'm sorry. I guess I'm hard to live with these days."

"I've noticed that. Why is it?"

As he shook his head, he said, "I guess it's that damned journal. Working on it brings back all the bad times to me."

"Then put it aside. Don't look at it again. We'll burn it if you want."

"That wouldn't solve anything. Everything written in it is stuck in here." He tapped his forehead angrily. "Ignoring it won't make it go away. I have to write it to get it out of my head."

"But why? It seems to me that if you give it time, the pain will go away on its own."

"Don't you see, Lani? It's not just the bad memories. I've given it a lot of thought. Whoever set me up to fly out that cargo of drugs, or whatever it was, hired me because he thought the risk that he would be caught was high. That was no spur-of-the-moment operation. When the men were loading my plane, they seemed nervous, but they knew exactly what they were doing. They had obviously done it many times before."

"So? I still don't see why you have to torment yourself with the journal."

"Whoever set me up has been walking around free, while I had five years of my life taken from me. I have to find out who it is and see that he's punished."

"But Bryan! How can you—"

"I have to try. I can't just sit back and pretend it was all a quirk of fate that I lost five years of my life. No! Someone is responsible, and I have to find out who."

"The man who hired you—would you recognize him again?"

"Probably not. He was a tall Mexican with a mustache. He said his name was Juan Garcia, which is almost like saying John Smith here in the States. It probably wasn't even his real name."

"And you have no idea what was being smuggled? None of your jailers ever gave you a hint?"

"We didn't exactly have long conversations. Besides, you know how little Spanish I spoke at the time. They could have told me everything, and I wouldn't have understood."

"You once mentioned that you thought it was drugs."

"That seems the most likely possibility. I can't think what else anyone would be smuggling that would fit into boxes of that size unless it was jewels, and I never heard of any mines in that area. Besides, jewels could be carried over the border in a lot of things smaller than a cargo plane. It almost had to be drugs."

"You know how I feel about drugs. I agree that we have to do all we can to stop it from continuing, but how will your journal do that?"

"It may supply me with a clue to someone who knows more about it than I do. I just have to get enough public notice to get the attention of someone who can put the puzzle together."

"It seems like a long shot to me."

"It is, but it's the only shot I have."

"Could I type it for you?"

"No, I have to do it. Some of it is almost illegible, even to me, and other parts trigger memories that I'm adding as I go. No, I have to do it myself."

"Be careful, Bryan," she said.

"Nothing else can happen to me. I'm safe here in the States and the Mexican government doesn't even have a record of my imprisonment."

"I know, but you hear such awful things about people being mixed up in the drug traffic. You know, like the mob and all."

"You've been watching too many old movies. I'll be okay. We don't even know for sure it *was* drugs."

"No, but it does sound like it. What else could it be? Especially since the IOTA Company doesn't exist. And they sure weren't shipping piñatas and flower pots!" She shook her head and added, "I still don't see how this will stop whatever was being done—assuming it's still going on at all. That was five years ago."

"Whether it is or not, somebody set me up. I can't just let it go."

She nodded. He was so intense it almost frightened her. Whoever would have thought she could ever be frightened by calm, gentle Bryan?

Lani slid off the rock and walked down to the water's edge. The stream had washed the sand to powdery softness, and the trees cooled it invitingly. Lani stepped out of her sandals and stood with her toes in the clear water. "It's been hot this summer. I hope we have an early fall."

Bryan looked at her in amazement that she could discuss such a mundane subject when his thoughts were strung as tight as violin strings.

"I'll bet you don't remember what we did here right after we bought this place?" she asked.

The corners of his mouth turned up in the hint of a smile as he recalled a much happier day. "I'll bet I do."

"That seems like a lifetime ago." She lifted her head so that the sun and breeze mingled through her hair. "Have I changed much?"

"We both have."

"I'm eight years older now." She looked up at him, her long lashes veiling the green of her eyes.

"You're more beautiful now than you were then. And when I first met you, you were about the prettiest girl I'd ever seen."

"I wasn't fishing for a compliment."

"Weren't you?" This time he did smile. "We all need compliments, Lani. Everybody needs affection."

"At times you don't seem to need anyone but yourself," she observed.

"That's not true," he said as he avoided her eyes by looking down at the slow-flowing water. "I wonder where this stream comes from and where it goes."

"I was wondering the same thing about time. We can't stop it or back it up or even stay abreast of it. There is only past and future, really. The present is here and gone faster than it takes to comment upon it."

"You've become philosophical."

"I've had a lot of opportunity to observe the passage of time. I wish we could go back and relive selected parts. Say, the part where you decided to fly to Mexico City and back that day. If I could do that day over again, I would keep you from going, even if I had to shoot you in the foot."

"That would have done it."

"But constantly regretting that it happened the way it did doesn't solve anything. You're back, and as far as I'm concerned that's nothing short of a miracle."

"I can go along with that."

Realizing what she was about to do was risky, but wanting desperately to regain the close bond they had once had, she said, "I think we should start over." With only the briefest hesitation, she started unbuttoning her blouse.

Bryan watched her with curious interest. "What are you doing?"

"We're starting over." She quickly undressed and tossed her clothes onto the rock. The sunlight spangled her body with green and gold and brought to life the pale freckles on her nose and shoulders. She stood slim and strong, her head thrown back and her arms raised, her feet braced in the pale gold water. "I claim this land in the name of us," she announced.

"*Us?*" he asked with a laugh. "I don't recall that part."

"Things have changed. I'm making this up as I go." She lifted her face to the shimmering green leaves of the willow trees. "From where the sun now stands, we will fight no more!"

"Is this the part where we give Indian quotes? I'm afraid I don't know many. And I didn't know we were fighting all that often."

In a serious tone, she said, "A couple can fight without ever saying a word." Her eyes pleaded with him for understanding. "I don't want to fight with you." She had dropped her defensive mask, and as she stood naked before him she had never felt more vulnerable.

Bryan rose slowly, towering over her. He searched her face for what seemed an eternity to Lani, then to her great relief he removed his own clothes. With a stern expression, he lifted his arms overhead as Lani had done. In stentorian tones he said, "We camp here!" Grinning down at her, he added, "It's the only quote that I could think of."

Her laughter burst forth with the release of her tension. Beaming her smile back at him, she said, "You delivered it beautifully."

Taking her hand, he lithely led her down from the rock, across a wedge of fine sand and into the water. "I sure hope we don't have surprise company right now."

"No one could come out here to look for us," she said as the water pooled around her knees. "I wish it were deep enough to swim."

"Maybe we can put in a pool someday."

"I'd like that." Her eyes followed the lean lines of his body. Although his torso was still pale from his imprisonment, his preference for staying out-of-doors was beginning to darken his face and arms and legs. And by contrast with her alabaster skin, which rarely saw the sun, he looked almost tan.

They waded downstream to a point where the creek narrowed between banks of billowing grass. Beneath their feet the sandy bottom was cool and, with each step, their feet were clouded with golden whorls of the fine sand.

"It's beautiful here," she said.

"I was just thinking the same thing," he replied, as he reached out to stroke her sun-kissed waist and hip. "Beautiful."

She looked over her shoulder at him and smiled. The filtered sunlight bathed her creamy skin with a green-gold translucence, and her eyes took on the hue of the leaves above. Her hair blew around her face like radiant flames, and when she smiled, her lips were moist and rosy.

"You remind me of a water sprite," he said softly as he turned her to face him. "I think you should always dress like this." He ran his fingers lightly over her gold-freckled shoulders and down her chest to where her breasts lifted proudly. The breeze had beaded her coral nipples, and the sun's reflection in the water spangled her luscious body.

He swept his hand lower over the familiar and enticing plane of her stomach, over the dip of her navel and lower to touch the light auburn curls at the junction of her thighs. "I'm glad you have this curious tendency to take your clothes off every time we come to this spot."

"It's not the spot that inspires me, it's you. I haven't taken off even my shoes here in a long time."

He looked at her as if he wanted to believe her, but wasn't sure he should.

"Well, I haven't," she affirmed.

"Lani, you're young and desirable and passionate. I know you had a life of your own while I was gone and I don't blame you."

Anger flared in her eyes. His lost years always came between them! As she tried to get past him, her breasts grazed his firm chest. Bryan caught her arms and pulled her against him. Their bodies molded together like two pieces of a whole, and she felt the hot insistence of his manhood against her hip.

"I wasn't trying to make you mad," he said.

"Then don't imply I've had a steady stream of lovers!"

"*From where the sun now stands*—remember?" He reached up and smoothed his thumb over the angry furrow on her forehead. "Quit frowning before your face freezes like that."

Lani laughed in spite of herself. She didn't want to be angry, either. "It must be a hundred degrees out here. Nothing is likely to freeze."

"You never know. I wouldn't chance it." He bent to kiss the smooth skin where the frown had been. "Besides, fighting with you is the last thing I had in mind."

"Oh?" she asked innocently. "What did you have in mind?"

His hand cupped her breast, then his fingers brushed sensuously over the nipple. Taking the taut bud between his thumb and forefinger, he rolled it gently. "A bit of this," he said lazily. His other hand closed over her nape, and his thumb lifted her face to his. His lips gently met hers in a lingering kiss, as if he were savoring the taste of her. "A bit of that."

Lani opened her eyes halfway to gaze up at him. His fingers were sending flames through her breast, and her lips felt swollen and hungry for his kisses. "You always could kiss better than anybody in the county," she murmured.

"Have you been holding contests?" he asked with a soft laugh.

"Pure hearsay."

Again his mouth claimed hers, and she opened her lips, inviting him to explore her mouth. She met his tongue with hers and licked across his inner lips and over the serrated edges of his straight teeth. Bryan pulled her closer and kissed her with a passion that left her breathless.

When he pulled back, she laid her cheek against his chest and listened to the quickened beat of his heart. "Yes, if there were an Olympic category for kissing, you'd walk off with all the medals."

He laughed as he put his arm around her and led her back to the tiny beach. "You're damned good yourself."

Retrieving his shirt, he spread it out on the dry sand and pulled her down to sit on it. Putting his arm around her, he laid her back in his arms. "We don't want a grain of sand to spoil our day," he explained as he felt to make sure the cloth was between her hips and the ground.

With a smile she drew his lips down to hers and wrapped her slender arms around him. The sun kissed their bodies, and the breeze cooled them as a butterfly skipped above them in the air. Scentless wildflowers nodded in the tangle of grasses near their wedge of sand and shielded them in a bower of love.

Bryan lowered his head, leaving a string of kisses over her jaw and neck, pausing to lick the pulse that fluttered in the hollow of her throat, then eased lower until he had captured the coral-and-ivory treasure of her breast. He ran his tongue over the warm swell as his hand mounded it to tempt his lips.

Lani sighed with pure delight as his lips and tongue teased her to hot desire. She loved him with all her heart! Couldn't he see? Couldn't he tell?

When his hand circled her thigh, she eagerly opened herself to him. She felt his fingers, larger than her own and slightly rougher, as he fondled the center of her passions. He stroked and tempted until she was wet from wanting him. Lani moved restlessly and murmured his name, but

Bryan took his time, pleasing and loving her in a way that wouldn't be rushed.

At last he joined with her, moving slowly, strumming her nerve endings to throbbing ecstasy.

A wild and demanding passion seized Lani as every movement he made seemed perfectly targeted to heighten her enjoyment. Quite by surprise, a primeval need caught her and set her whirling and spinning to her culmination. As hot waves pounded through her, she held onto Bryan tightly and buried her face against the hard strength of his neck and shoulders.

As the ecstasy began to mellow, he softly spoke words of love and desire that stirred her again. Sensing her response, he once more began moving in the ancient and ever-new dance of love. More quickly this time Lani felt the fevered need for him spread through her. Something as elemental as life itself swept her up and carried her on the magic spell Bryan was casting. He was her man, and she wanted him in the fullest sense of the word.

Her hands urged him on, and her words mingled with his. Civilization was forgotten as they loved with a passion that tolerated no temperance. She sensed an increased urgency in him, and she held her breath as his movements became more demanding. When he reached his peak, the sensation triggered her own release. Clinging tightly to her lover, Lani let all her love and passion explode into ecstasy.

Afterward she lay in his arms, enjoying the feel of his warm, naked body against hers. "With a little practice," she whispered, "we could become decadent."

"What do you mean *become*?" He rolled on his side so that they were nose to nose. "Damn! Lady, you'd kill an older man. I'm out of practice."

"I can fix that."

He laughed and kissed the tip of her nose, then her eyelids. "You're one hell of a woman."

"And you're one hell of a man."

"Want to get a divorce so we can become lovers?" he suggested as he stroked her bright hair.

"Maybe," she quipped, then it occurred to her that he might be serious. A veil slid behind Lani's eyes, and she looked away.

"Hey," he said gently. "Where did you go?"

She smiled in a bittersweet way. "Who, me? I'm right here."

"No, you're not." He sighed and looked up at the emerald leaves. Cold dread seeped through him. He knew he shouldn't have joked about a divorce. He should never have mentioned the subject. Was she thinking of leaving him, even at a time like this? "I love you, Lani," he said almost defensively.

"I love you, too."

She sounded as though she meant it. He turned his head to gaze at her. Not only was she loving and fun and desirable, but she was so beautiful, it made his heart ache. And she was a talented artist, too. Those waterfalls and clay gods were really great, even if he didn't care for Mayan sculpture. How could he hope to hold her when so much had changed? He looked away.

"Now who's leaving whom?" she asked in the silence that ensued.

"I'm not going anywhere."

Tentatively she reached out and touched the chiseled planes of his face. Not going anywhere? She could feel him going farther away with every second that passed. She wondered if he had meant he also wouldn't leave her life again. There was so much restlessness in him, so much intenseness. At times he reminded her of a puma preparing to leap and run. Run away? "Don't go," she whispered as her fingers traced the hard line of his jaw.

"What?" He turned to face her.

"We'd better go," she amended.

He got to his feet with a fluid movement and pulled her up. For a moment their bodies kissed along their full length, then Lani stepped away.

As Bryan watched her shake the sand out of her hair and get dressed, he shelved the despondency that threatened to overtake him. This was no time to worry; he and Lani had just made love. He pulled on his clothes, except his shirt, which he casually tossed over one shoulder and held with only his crooked index finger. He watched her run her fingers through her hair to remove the remaining tangles. Only minutes before she had been a seductress. Now she was a pixy who might dash off without any warning. "You're a dozen women all rolled into one," he commented. "I never know who I'll see next."

"At least I'm never lonely," she teased.

With a smile he put his arm companionably around her shoulder, and she slipped hers around his bare waist.

"Remember what happened the first time we made love here?" she asked.

Bryan laughed at the recollection. "We got so sunburned that neither of us could wear clothes for days. You were as pink as a lobster."

"I think it's happened again."

He solicitously lifted his arm from her shoulders. "You're kidding!"

"I burn easily. Fortunately I keep lots of lotion on hand."

"But first, vinegar."

"Yuk!"

"Vinegar is the very best thing for a sunburn," he said firmly.

"I'll smell like a pickle vat!"

"You'll be the sexiest pickle vat around," he reassured her. "And I can't wait to rub lotion all over you."

With a grin Lani said, "If I'm not sunburned, we'll pretend I am."

"It's a deal."

Hand in hand they walked back to the house, each hoping the bond between them would strengthen before the tension separated them forever.

Chapter Seven

Lani brought in the day's mail and routinely sorted through the bills, advertisements addressed to Occupant and sales fliers from the local supermarkets. The last envelope was made of heavy white paper and was addressed to Bryan. The return address caused her eyes to widen.

"Bryan?" she called out. "Bryan!"

"In here," he answered from down the hallway.

She took the letter with her to the bathroom door. Bryan was lying on his back on the tile floor, his head and shoulders under the sink. An array of tools were scattered all around. "I think you should come out and read this."

"I can't turn this loose. What's wrong?"

"You got an answer from *The McPherson Show*."

Bryan swung around and looked up at her. "Are you kidding?"

"Nope. It's right here."

"Wait a minute."

She heard the clank of wrench on pipe and saw Bryan's muscles bunch as he tightened the joint.

He eased himself out from under the sink and sat up. "What does it say?"

"I don't open your mail." She handed it to him; for some reason she felt apprehensive.

Quickly he tore open the envelope and scanned the page, then reread it more slowly. "They want me to come to Chicago and be on the show."

"Chicago?"

"That's where they do the show. It says they are gathering a panel of guests who have been wrongfully imprisoned, and they want to interview me." He looked up at her. "This is exactly what I've been hoping for."

She felt cold, and she clasped her hands together so they wouldn't shake. "Are you sure you should do this? I've seen that show and sometimes McPherson makes his guests look like fools."

"I'm not worried."

"Bryan, what if you're opening a can of worms with this publicity? Maybe someone will want to extradite you or something. Maybe the Mafia is involved in this smuggling, and you'll get in serious trouble."

He smiled up at her and scanned the letter again. "I'm to call them right away and confirm that I'll be in Chicago for the show next Wednesday."

"So soon? I thought these things took weeks. Months maybe."

"It seems the show has been planned for some time, but one of the guests they had scheduled can't make it. I'm to take his place."

"I feel nervous about this."

Bryan stood and turned on the faucet. "There's nothing to worry about. This might help me get some clue about who set me up. At the least we'll have a trip to Chicago."

"We?"

"You don't think I would leave you behind, do you? The letter says they are paying for my airfare and hotel, but we can scrape up money for a ticket for you, and we'll just pay the difference in the room rate for a double."

"I can't drop everything and go dashing off to Chicago!"

"Sure you can. When was the last time you had a vacation?"

"That's beside the point."

"What do you have going that can't be postponed a few days?"

"I have to fire the birth goddess."

"When we get back I'll help you."

"I have to deliver some bowls and pitchers to Monica."

"We'll take them before we leave. What else?"

"Bryan, this is crazy! People like us don't go on *The McPherson Show*!"

"Here's the invitation," he said. "Read it for yourself."

Lani read it; Bryan was right. She had hoped he had somehow read it incorrectly. "This doesn't mention bringing a wife along."

"I'm telling you it's no problem. We'll pay the extra expense, and it'll be just fine."

Lani nodded slowly. She knew there was no way to talk Bryan out of this; maybe she was wrong to try. It was only that she was afraid of changing anything now that she had him home. She no longer took things for granted.

After changing planes in Houston, Bryan and Lani had a nonstop flight to Chicago. For all those years that he was gone she had assumed Bryan had died in a plane crash, and her anxiety over flying had become increasingly worse. Knowing that he had not met that fate had done little to relieve her concern, though having him next to her helped. Secretly she was glad Bryan had not resumed his flying career again, and hoped he wouldn't, though she would never ask him to give it up.

Although the flight was uneventful, when they landed at O'Hare airport under clear skies, Lani was relieved to be on the ground again. However, much of her nervousness remained, and she stayed close to Bryan. She felt unaccountably shy in the Chicago crowd and very far away from home.

They were met by a car from the hotel, and when they were deposited on the walk in front of the impressive building, Lani again felt a cold apprehension. What was she doing here? There was a sense of unreality about it all.

At the desk the clerk looked at Lani with cool disapproval. "I'm afraid you are booked for a single, Mr. Cameron."

"I sent word that I was bringing my wife."

"No one noted the change. It says here that you're booked for a single."

Lani glanced around the luxurious marble-floored lobby with its gold velvet appointments and Aubusson carpet. She definitely felt out of place.

"Whatever that card may say," Bryan was saying firmly, "you can see that she is here. We'll take a double."

"I see your room is being paid for by a third party. It's not customary—"

"I'll pay the difference." Bryan's dark eyes commanded the man to get on with it.

Heaving a sigh that spoke volumes, the desk clerk made an issue of striking out the single booking and changing it to a double. When he told Bryan what the difference in price would be, Lani's eyes widened. The difference was more than they usually spent on an entire room.

After Bryan signed the register and they were given a key, Lani whispered, "How much are these rooms anyway?"

"Don't ask," he said with a wink.

Lani decided that was good advice.

The elegantly appointed room was decorated in the same shade of gold as the lobby. The curtains, chairs and bedspread were oyster white; the thick carpet was a rich shade of golden tan. "There must have been a sale on gold fabric," Lani murmured as the bellhop unloaded their suitcases from the dolly.

Bryan tipped him and closed the door. "Here we are! How does it feel?"

"Scary as hell."

"That's the spirit," he said with a laugh. "I knew you'd enjoy it."

She hadn't seen Bryan this enthused since his return. "Bryan, I shouldn't have come. The hotel didn't expect me."

"So what? This isn't a private home where we're barging into unannounced. It's their business to accommodate us."

"If the hotel didn't know I was coming, maybe the TV people didn't know it, either. Didn't you mail that letter telling them?"

"Sure I did. Everything is going to be fine."

"I don't think the desk clerk believed we're married. He probably thinks I'm some floozy you picked up on the plane."

Bryan laughed and put his arm around her. "He's probably wondering how I got so lucky."

"I wonder how long it will take for the vice squad to get here."

"Just relax and enjoy yourself."

Lani went to the window and opened the curtains to a dizzying view of the streets below. "We seem to be still cruising on the plane."

"It's pretty far down there, isn't it?" Bryan said with enjoyment. "Isn't this great?"

"Yes," she said with a smile. "It is." Bryan had always loved seeing new places as much as she enjoyed things that were familiar. She had forgotten that about him. In her mourning-embellished memories she had convinced herself they were much more alike than they really were.

"Let's go out to eat. I'll call the desk and ask what they recommend for a Texan and his floozy." His broad wink drew a hearty laugh from her.

Early the next morning they were picked up by a limousine that had been sent from the television station. As the driver got out to open the door for Bryan, he looked suspiciously at Lani. "They said I was to pick up a Mr. Cameron."

"That's right," Bryan explained patiently. "I'm Mr. Cameron. This is Mrs. Cameron."

"They didn't say anything about no Mrs."

"It was an oversight." Bryan stood aside and propelled Lani into the car.

"Maybe I should stay here."

"Nonsense. If I get nervous, I'll need you there to hold my hand."

"You've never been nervous in your life."

"They don't know that."

The driver got in and threw Lani a frosty look through the rearview mirror. She returned it, then looked away. She was getting tired of feeling like unnecessary baggage.

The television studio they were taken to was quite different from what Lani expected. The front lobby, where they were greeted by a young woman who identified herself as their escort, was small but tastefully decorated. They were led through the doors marked Employees Only and down a long, winding hall that appeared to have been in need of repainting for quite some time. The offices off the hallway were similarly austere, with desks piled high with books, papers, computer printouts and ledgers.

As they neared the end of the hall, their escort again cast an intimidating glance at Lani. "I still think you should wait in the lobby, Mrs. Cameron. You can see it all on closed-circuit television."

"She stays with me," Bryan said.

The woman pushed her hip against a door marked No Admittance, and Lani found herself looking at the familiar set of *The McPherson Show*. Seeing the studio firsthand left her with a disjointed sense of reality. Her first impression was that it was much smaller than she had expected, the second was that it wasn't nearly as plush as the camera's eye had led her to believe.

A chubby man with a shiny balding head rushed up to them. "Mr. Cameron? You're just in time. I'm Preston. Nick Preston. Rob McPherson never meets his guests before the show goes on. Doesn't want to leave the show in the Green Room. Ha, ha." He saw Lani. "Who's this? How did you get in here? The studio audience isn't being seated yet."

Lani opened her mouth to explain, but Bryan beat her to it. "She's with me. This is my wife, Lani Cameron."

"Was she in jail, too?"

"I'm just along for the ride," Lani said.

"Oh." Preston looked at her as if he wasn't at all sure what to do with her.

"I won't be any trouble," Lani reassured him.

"Trouble? What do you mean trouble? You can't go on!"

"No, no. I don't want to. I mean I'll stay put. Maybe I could sit in the audience?"

Preston scowled as if having to deal with anything out of the ordinary was a great imposition. "All right. Sit there on the left." To Bryan he said, "Come along, come along. The others are already in the Green Room."

Lani went to the group of seats the chubby man had indicated and gingerly sat down. She had rarely felt so out of place. She examined her nails, then checked her makeup in the mirror from her purse.

About fifteen minutes later, the camera crew entered the studio and began checking their equipment. Then the doors behind Lani opened and the ushers brought in a crowd of people. Lani moved over so they wouldn't have to step over her.

"How did you get in here so early?" the woman next to Lani asked. "We've been in line since six-thirty."

"Just lucky, I guess." She smiled, but the woman didn't return it. Lani turned back to the set.

Soon the brilliant stage lights went on, and she heard the familiar theme music of *The McPherson Show*. When the show's logo appeared on the studio monitors, Lani knew the show was about to begin.

A man stepped out from one of the doors nearest the set and strode toward the stage. As if by magic his foot hit the lighted area just as the music faded, and a wide, boyish grin leaped to his face. Rob McPherson, the Heartbeat of America, sauntered out onto the set. Lani was close enough to tell he was several years younger than she had supposed, and he wore stage makeup that was a startling shade approaching orange. His curly brown hair was groomed to perfection and his teeth were as white and perfect as modern dentistry could make them.

As the guests were announced, each came out onto the stage and sat in one of the red fabric chairs. Bryan was the last to be introduced, and Lani smiled proudly as she joined in the applause. He was a head taller than McPherson and more handsome.

With all the charm that made his show a national favorite, McPherson said a few words to each of his guests before returning to the first one to begin the interview. Lani couldn't help but wonder if the other members of the audience shared her feeling that McPherson's familiar voice with its distinctive Scots burr seemed to be coming from the wrong body—he had looked quite different on television.

All the guests had heartrending stories. One had been arrested because he had the misfortune to have the same name and a physical resemblance to a wanted felon. A woman had been arrested because circumstantial evidence made her appear guilty. The next was more militant in his denial of his guilt, and it occurred to Lani that perhaps he protested a bit too much. Then it was Bryan's turn.

His quiet Texas drawl contrasted sharply with the northern and eastern accents. At one point McPherson's questions brought a smile to Bryan's face and Lani noticed, as if for the first time, how sexy he was.

When the show broke for a commercial, McPherson's professional grin vanished, and he called out to one of the cameramen to get a close-up of chair number two. To Lani's amazement the endearing Scots burr had vanished along with the disarming grin.

The woman next to Lani nudged her. "That tall one on the end is better looking than Rob McPherson."

Lani nodded, her eyes shining with love for Bryan. "I think so, too."

"Watch and see if Rob don't cut his interview short."

"What do you mean?"

"He's got what they call charisma. Rob don't like it when someone better looking is on camera."

"Are you serious? What difference does it make to him? It's his show."

"It is today, but who knows about tomorrow. You ought to come to more of these shows and you'd know these things."

In the final segment of the show, Bryan mentioned the fact that he had kept a journal during his confinement. At once the audience clamored to know if it had been published and where they could buy a copy. Bryan admitted it wasn't sold to a publisher, but that he had considered it. His dark eyes met each questioner as if she were the only person in the room. On camera this translated to a degree of sensuousness that Lani found unsettling. Bryan had always had the quality of making another person feel important, but she had never given it much thought until now. His intense gaze and slow drawl had every woman in the studio audience sitting on the edge of her chair and feeling special.

When the final music sounded and McPherson leaned forward to speak earnestly but inaudibly to the man on the opposite end from Bryan, the woman beside Lani whispered. "I sure wouldn't mind going home with that Cameron. Would you?"

Lani smiled. "I won't mind at all." When the woman looked surprised, Lani said, "I'm his wife."

The woman actually looked offended. "You might have told me!"

Lani watched her join the crowd surging toward the stage. The stage crew held the audience back, directing them toward the exit, but she saw that they were all trying to speak privately to Bryan as if he were a celebrity. She lingered, waiting for the crowd to clear.

"Okay, lady, time to go," a stagehand said brusquely. "The exit's over there."

"I'm with him," Lani said as she nodded toward Bryan.

"Sure you are." He pointed again at the door.

Lani lifted her chin defiantly as Bryan strode off the low stage and came to her. McPherson had already disappeared, presumably back to his dressing room. When Bryan reached her, Lani turned to the stagehand. "See?" The man shrugged and walked away.

"How was it?" Bryan asked.

"You were terrific. I've always thought you were sexy—but I never realized how widespread your appeal was."

"Is something wrong?"

"Of course not." She smiled and put her hand in his. How foolish of her to be jealous of a studio audience! She felt churlish for begrudging him his moment of fame. "Are we supposed to leave now?"

"I guess so. McPherson took off as soon as the cameras quit rolling."

"Were you nervous?"

"I was for a minute or two, but as soon as I started talking I was fine. Did I sound as if I came from the sticks?"

"You sounded great. The woman next to me all but said she craved your bod, and that seemed to be the general consensus."

"But did my story make sense? Do you think it did any good to go public?"

"How can I tell? You made perfect sense. You didn't sound like a nut—like the man sitting beside you. We'll have to wait and see if anything comes from it."

They left the studio and made their way back to the lobby. Their driver was waiting beside the limousine, cleaning his nails, but when he saw Bryan he hastily put away his pocket knife and opened the car door. This time he didn't give Lani as much as a glance.

"I'm glad it's over," Bryan said as the car pulled into traffic. "I did what I felt I had to do, but I'm glad it's over."

"So am I." She put her hand in his and smiled up at him. "It's been quite an experience, but I'm ready to go home."

He squeezed her hand companionably. "So am I."

When they walked into their hotel room, the telephone was ringing. "I wonder who that can be," Bryan said as he went to answer it.

"Probably the Floozy Control Board," she teased.

"Hello...? Yes, this is Bryan Cameron.... Who...? You're with what show?" His eyes widened, and he covered the mouthpiece with his palm. "It's somebody calling from the *Oprah Winfrey* show!" He turned back to the telephone.

A wave of apprehension washed over Lani. So the woman in the studio was right. She put her purse on the dresser and sat in the wing chair to gaze out the window.

When Bryan hung up, he sat still for a minute as if he were stunned. "They want me to be on a show in the fall. I told her I would have to get back to her."

Lani couldn't think of a reply. The phone rang again.

"It's a radio show," he said to her after he answered.

She watched him as he agreed to stay over another two days to tape a show for that station and three of its affiliates. She wanted to be happy for him, but she only felt numb. "You're going to stay?" she asked when he hung up.

"This is my chance to get it all out in the open. They agreed to pay for our room."

"I can't stay another two days. You know I have to finish that order for Jay."

"Look, honey. I'm not doing this for the thrill of it. It's hard to pour out my feelings over the air to all those strangers. But if I don't, that smuggling ring may never be stopped and those years will have been wasted."

"You don't know that the smugglers are still operating, and nothing will bring those years back." She tried to stay calm, but her voice rose. "Bryan, nothing you do will ever bring those lost years back!"

She saw the closed look on his face, and her temper flared. "Don't look at me like that!"

Bryan turned away and thrust his hands into his pockets. "This is something I have to do, Lani."

"Why! Why do you have to? Why can't you come back to Laredo and help me put our lives back together?"

"Because I can't! There may be something I saw or heard that will make it easier for the authorities to arrest those crooks. You know how I feel about drugs!"

"You don't even know that it *was* drugs!"

"What else could it have been? Maybe you can just write off those years, but damn it, I can't! You didn't spend them cooped up in a cell smaller than this hotel room. You didn't have to wonder if you would live or lie there until you rotted! You had a life of your own, and from all the evidence, you were doing just fine for yourself!"

"What's that supposed to mean!"

"You know what I'm talking about!"

"Jay Harmond?" she gasped. "Bryan!"

"Who else would I mean? Or were there others? Five years is a long time for a woman like you!"

She drew back as if he had slapped her. "A woman like me?" she asked in icy tones. "Exactly what does that mean?"

"You aren't cut out for the celibate life."

"Jay is a business acquaintance. Nothing else!"

"Sure. He probably propositions all his business associates. Give me some credit, Lani."

She walked stiffly across the room and got her suitcase. All her muscles were aching and shaking as if she had the flu. Anger had always made her feel sick. With jerky movements she threw her belongings into the bag and zipped it with a yank. Going to the phone, she dialed the desk and asked for a bellhop and a cab to the airport.

"Just like that?" Bryan demanded. "You're leaving?"

"Surely you don't expect me to hang around here and be insulted."

"You're flying back to Texas? Alone?"

"Brilliant," she said frigidly. "Where else would I be going with my suitcase?"

"Don't go, Lani." He didn't move to stop her, but his hypnotic gaze commanded her to stay.

"Come with me," she countered. "Let's forget all of this and be Bryan and Lani Cameron again, just average people. If the smugglers are still operating, somebody else will catch them."

"You mean good always triumphs in the end? Sometimes you have to give it a hand."

"Then you won't come with me?"

"I can't."

She stared at him stonily. She had never felt so alone in all her life.

"Try to see it from my point of view. At home I'm your husband—no job, no prospects for one. If I go on these shows, I may be able to accomplish something with my life."

"Or you may do no good at all."

"Thanks for your words of support," he said dryly.

"All I know is that Chicago and its listening audience are a long way from Laredo and even farther from southern Mexico. You could do more in Laredo than here."

A knock sounded at the door, and Lani picked up her suitcase and purse. "Goodbye, Bryan."

"I'll be home in a few days."

Her eyes met his, and she had to steel herself not to rush into his arms. She turned and walked to the door.

All the way to the airport she hoped Bryan would come after her. As she checked in her suitcase and traded her ticket for a boarding pass, she listened keenly to every announcement and paging. When they called for her flight to board she hoped to see him racing to join her, but he didn't come.

She sat in a window seat and stared back into the terminal until the plane pulled away.

Even as the plane revved its engines and began to taxi with taunting slowness to its takeoff position, she had a fantasy that Bryan would somehow stop the plane and get on board to be with her. The flight attendants walked down the aisles, checking seat belts, putting seats in the upright position and answering last-minute questions. Lani looked out at the flat expanse of runway. She had thought she was used to being alone, but she felt as if part of her had torn away and was staying in Chicago.

The plane turned, paused and started its takeoff roll. Faster and faster the scenery flew by. Farther and farther she went from Bryan.

What was she doing here? her brain screamed. No deadline was reason enough to leave Bryan like this!

She felt the nose of the plane tilt up and the thrust of the takeoff pressed her back against her seat. A familiar churn of apprehension about flying twisted in her stomach, and with considerable effort she stilled it with the force of her will. Unlike Bryan she didn't consider the sky to be her second home.

Bryan. They were apart again, and this time it had been her own doing. Tears welled in her eyes and blurred the sight of lake and city below. Would he come home? She wasn't at all sure. They had never parted in anger before, nor had their marriage ever been so shaky. If he didn't, could she fly back to Chicago and find him? A tear rolled down her cheek, and Lani glanced over to see an elderly woman watching her.

"Is it your first flight?" the woman asked compassionately.

"No. No, I'm just going to miss my husband."

"That's sweet," the woman cooed. "I remember when I was your age and my Arthur used to travel. Why..." The woman's voice droned on in comforting tones, but Lani's thoughts were on Bryan.

By the time the plane reached Houston, Lani knew more about the woman's marriage than her hairdresser did. She was glad to disembark and board the plane to Laredo. Fortunately her seat on this flight was beside a portly businessman who wanted only to read the paper and drink scotch. Lani closed her eyes and lay back, feigning sleep. Bryan seemed so far away!

When the plane landed in Laredo, dusk had fallen. Only the faintest red smudge in the west hinted there had been a sunset, and it quickly faded to black. Lani claimed her luggage and carried it to the parking lot shuttle bus. After a jolting ride that was more hair-raising than the flight, Lani got off at her car. She glanced around to be sure she was alone, then unlocked the car and tossed the bag into the back seat. Airport parking areas at night weren't her favorite places.

She paid the parking fee and drove home. Although she had often gone out alone at night, she was uneasy. Tonight she had expected to return with Bryan. Lani was more than a little surprised to see how much she had again come to rely on Bryan for protection.

Instead of pulling into her dark garage, Lani parked in the driveway and hurried toward the back door. Crickets sang in the black bushes, and the sliver of moon cast almost no light. When an armadillo rustled in the hedge beside the porch, Lani jumped nervously. She had often gone out at night, but she had never liked it—especially when she had to return to a dark house.

She opened the door and switched on the porch light and the kitchen light. At once she felt better. Locking the door behind her, she carried the suitcase to the bedroom. Slowly she unpacked as she listened to the silence of the house. How quickly she had grown accustomed to the small sounds of another person in the house. In the familiar surroundings she was no longer afraid, but she was so lonesome she ached.

After her things were put away, Lani sat on the bed. Never had she lost her temper to such an extent before. Why had she ever considered leaving? Had she expected Bryan to refuse to let her go? Lani had never considered herself to be manipulative, but she had also never thought she was crazy enough to fly away and leave Bryan in Chicago, either.

After a while she stood up and went back into the kitchen to make herself a supper of cheese and crackers; cooking for one was too lonely to even consider.

She hoped her loneliness would only last two days. She hoped Bryan would come back to her.

Chapter Eight

Although she had cut short her trip—and possibly her marriage, she thought morosely—to work on her clay gods, she found herself unable to concentrate. She spent a good deal of the morning straightening shelves and sweeping and doing other busywork. The rest of the morning she stared at the lump of clay that was only beginning to take the shape of a figure. She had no inspiration as to how she could portray this figure differently, and she was too much of an artist to take the easy way out and copy one of her earlier works.

Resolutely she waded in. There were some things that were always the same: the figure had to have two arms, two legs, one head. She hoped the details would come to her as she worked. Her strong fingers pressed and pulled and molded the clay as she tried to get her mind on the right track. She had to think like a Mayan, to see the god as a

Mayan would have. All she could see, however, were visions of Bryan.

As her movements dwindled and stopped, Lani wondered what he was doing. Taping radio interviews would hardly take an entire day, even if he did all three back-to-back. That left him a great deal of free time. Would he miss her? After the way she had acted, he might be glad she had gone. With all her heart she wished she could go back and live that day over. She promised herself that when—if—he returned, she would be easier to live with.

But what about his behavior? a stubborn little voice in the back of her mind demanded. He hadn't been all that amiable, either. There was no compelling reason for him to stay in Chicago. Radio interviews could be taped over a telephone just as easily as in person. He had been perverse in his insistence that they stay. Even before the trip, he'd been so moody that she never knew what he was thinking or what to say to him. Why, he was even thinking of ending their marriage!

All the more reason to have stayed in Chicago, another part of her insidiously prompted.

Lani doubled her fist and bashed in the head of the statue. Both thoughts were valid, and she didn't know what to do. She rolled the clay into a lump, moistened it and started over. She would make a fertility goddess. Jay had said those were perennial favorites. Her hands worked with little guidance from her brain, sculpting heavy breasts and a rounded belly.

When the phone rang, she almost dropped the statue. Bryan was calling! She ran to answer it, perfunctorily wiping her hands on her jeans. "Hello?"

"Hello, Lani. How are you?"

"Jay." She tried to keep the disappointment from her voice. "I'm fine. And you?"

"Great. Say, I'm in town for the afternoon. Why don't you meet me for lunch at Mi Casa? That is, if your husband will let you out of his sight. I don't want any more trouble from him."

"No, no. He's... Sure, I can meet you for lunch." For some reason she was reluctant to tell Jay that Bryan was still in Chicago. "I was working, and I have to change. Would twelve-thirty be all right?"

"Perfect. I'll have a table waiting when you get there."

Lani hung up and wiped the receiver clean with her shirttail. Bryan hadn't called. She went back to the studio and wrapped the clay in a wet cloth and replaced it in the old refrigerator. Since Bryan was gone she could work on it all night if need be and make up her lost time.

After a quick shower, Lani dressed and drove to town. Mi Casa was a restaurant that served the best Mexican food for miles around, and it was as crowded as always. She found Jay in one of the booths that resembled adobe huts and slid onto the seat opposite him.

"Did you have any trouble getting away?" Jay asked.

"Bryan is my husband, not my keeper," she answered testily.

"I didn't want to cause more trouble between you."

"What do you mean, trouble?" Lani hadn't told him of her marital problems.

"I thought he was going to punch me the last time I saw him."

"Oh, that." She relaxed and looked down at the menu. "You should have known better than to proposition me. I've told you before not to do that."

"Well, if you ever decide to take me up on it, the offer still stands."

She shot him a warning glance as the waiter approached. "I'll have *tacos al carbón*," she told the young man.

"The enchilada dinner for me," Jay said as he gave the man his menu. When they were alone he said, "I saw your husband on *The McPherson Show*. That was quite a story he was telling."

"I'm just glad it's all over, and he's safe."

"There were a lot of things he didn't mention. Does he know why it happened, for instance."

"No, that's the strange part. There was no reason at all for Bryan to have been held. He wasn't involved in smuggling."

"Are you sure? I hear it's awfully lucrative."

She frowned at him. "Of course I'm sure. Bryan would never do anything illegal. Especially not smuggling! You've never heard him on the subject of drugs."

"Drugs?"

"What else could it have been?" She sipped the tea the waiter had brought.

Jay smiled. "Does he have any idea how he got in such a mess?"

"None. That's one reason he wanted to be on *The McPherson Show*. He hopes his story will help shed some light on the smugglers if someone is about to catch them."

"He's playing a dangerous game," Jay said.

"I know. I told him it's probably the Mafia or something, and that he should leave well enough alone."

"Yes. Organized crime is nothing to fool around with."

"He wouldn't listen, though. He's changed." She added sugar to her tea and stirred it idly.

"Changed?"

"Before this happened Bryan was so easygoing and gentle. Now he's more like Dirty Harry." She smiled reminiscently as she recalled their nights of fevered loving. "Not that I object." She caught what she was saying and blushed as she said, "He's just different."

"People change," Jay said philosophically.

"Usually their wives are with them to see the change, though, and it's not as obvious. I'm still trying to get used to it." She tasted the tea again. "I'm making a fertility goddess."

"Good. Those are very popular."

"I prefer the rain goddess personally."

"To each his own."

"When do you want to pick up the next order? I'll be firing the birth goddess this afternoon. That's the last of this lot."

"How about next week? Maybe you should bring them here."

"Jay, that's silly. Bryan wouldn't have been upset if you hadn't said what you did to me."

"But you're so beautiful, I can't help myself," he said with a winning smile.

"Don't start that or I'm leaving."

"Okay, okay. I only wanted to remind you where I stand." Jay paused as their waiter served their food, then casually asked, "Did Bryan mention who hired him for the flight?"

"It was someone named Juan Garcia. Bryan didn't know him."

"Did he say what the man looked like?"

Lani thought a minute. "I believe he mentioned a mustache. Why?"

"I just wondered; curious I suppose. I fly to Mexico City often on business."

She smiled indulgently. "If you're worried about running into the man, I wouldn't. Mexico City is huge, and this happened five years ago."

"No, it's not that. I was just thinking that this Juan Garcia won't likely ever be caught. As you say, it's been a long time."

"On the other hand, Bryan is awfully determined, and stranger things have happened."

Jay didn't answer, and Lani turned her attention to her food.

After the plates were cleared, Jay signaled for the check. Lani tried to pay her portion of the bill, but he waved her money away. "This one is on me."

She shrugged. This was, after all, a business lunch. "Now about these clay gods. It seems to me we would do better if you got an order for some particular type, and I made it, rather than the other way around. What if I made a batch of hearth gods and everyone wants fertility goddesses?"

"Let me worry about that," Jay said with a smile. "So far I've placed everything you've made."

"I wish you would look at my waterfalls. I have a new design that resembles a pueblo ruin. I think it would interest anyone who likes Mayan sculpture."

"As I've told you before, Lani, I'm only interested in the clay gods. Your waterfalls are nice, but they don't fit my decorating style."

"But it seems to me—"

"If it works, don't change it," Jay said. "That's my motto. The clay gods are a great item. Let's not rock the boat."

"Whatever you say."

"Come over to the hotel with me," Jay suggested as he paid the waiter and got a receipt. "There's something I want to show you."

"I'll bet there is."

"No, really. It's an article on a new Mayan find. I thought it might give you inspiration."

"You know I make up my own designs."

"I know, but it's an interesting article."

Lani considered it for a minute. She had been running dry of new ideas lately. "Okay. But I'm not going up to your room. You can bring the article down to the lobby."

"The lobby is so public. All right, I'll meet you halfway and make it the bar."

"Okay."

As the hotel was only two blocks from the restaurant, Jay had walked, but Lani drove him back in her car and parked out front. "Let's make it quick, Jay. It takes hours to fire a statue, and I don't like to do it after dark. It's too hard to paint the patina on and get it just right when I can't see what I'm doing."

"This won't take long."

Lani left him at the elevators and went into the bar. At this hour there were few patrons. She ordered a soft drink and waited.

When Jay returned he ordered a bourbon and pushed the article toward her.

"Can I take this home and read it?" she asked.

"Sure. I have another copy. I want you to pay particular attention to this part." He pointed to a paragraph near the bottom. "There were more of the women statues, similar to those that were found at El Zapotal in Veracruz. They are supposed to be Cihualeotls, the goddess who watched over the souls of women who died in childbirth."

"I can't imagine there would be much of a market for such a sad figure," Lani protested. "It seems to me my birth goddess would be better. No one wants to think of death in relation to childbirth."

"I think I have a client who would be interested. See? There's a detailed description of the patina, and here's a photograph."

"I won't copy. You know that."

"Of course, of course. I only thought it would inspire you. And look here. There were more of the penitential statues of women with thick ropes around their necks."

"No way. Those look more like a punishment than a personal choice for penance. See? It looked as if this one is fitted with a kind of chastity belt. No, I'll stick to my little gods and goddesses."

Jay looked displeased, but then he smiled. "Far be it for me to tell an artist what to sculpt. If you do want to try one, however, I know I can sell it. In fact, I would be willing to pay considerably more for a penitent or a Cihualeotl."

"Why?"

"Because they're hot items right now. This new archeological find has rocked the art world. It's being compared in significance not only to El Zapotal, but to the life-size army figures found a while back in a tomb in Sian, China."

"Sorry. That's too close to forgery. If I made one, I would have to change the design so much to make it an original that it wouldn't be a true penitential or a Cihualeotl. You wouldn't be pleased with the result, and neither would I."

"You can be stubborn at times."

"No, I'm stubborn all the time. You just don't often cross me." She tempered the harshness of her words with a smile.

"Lani, Lani," he sighed. "Let's go up to my room and discuss it."

"That does it," she said lightly, but with definite determination. "I'm leaving. Thanks for the lunch, Jay." She folded the article and slipped it into her purse. "I'll have the gods ready for you next Wednesday."

"I'll be out at two o'clock." He walked her to the door of the hotel and dropped a brotherly kiss on her forehead. "Forget I got out of line. Okay?"

"Sure, Jay," she said with a laugh. "Why should today be any different?"

He grinned and stepped back inside. Lani shook her head, still chuckling. Jay was incorrigible, but he could be charming when he wished. As she turned to go she almost ran into Monica Denton.

"Good heavens, Lani," Monica exclaimed. "What are you doing here?"

"I had a business lunch with Jay Harmond. Didn't you see him?"

"I thought that was Jay." Monica's eyes narrowed speculatively. "Is Bryan with you?"

"No."

"I saw the television interview, and he was gorgeous!"

"I'll tell him you said so."

"Could you give me a lift? I see your car is here."

"Sure. Where are you going?"

"Back to the downtown store. I should have driven, but I didn't realize it would be so hot out."

"No trouble at all." Lani and Monica got into the car and Lani pulled out into the traffic.

"Did you enjoy yourself in Chicago?" Monica asked as the air conditioner cooled the car.

"I was only there one night."

"You didn't stay longer? I would kill for a few days in a city."

"I had some statues to finish for Jay."

"I see. That does sound like more fun than shopping and sight-seeing and staying in a marvelous hotel."

Lani laughed. "The hotel was marvelous, all right. I felt as if I should have been wearing diamonds, so I wouldn't look out of place in the lobby."

"Not to mention having Bryan with you." Monica gave her an appraising glance. "Where did you say Bryan is?"

"I didn't."

"Do I detect a certain evasiveness?"

"Of course not," Lani said quickly. "I just have a lot on my mind today. I have quite a bit of work left to do in order to finish the statues to meet my deadline with Jay."

"I suppose. Personally, I'd have told Jay to cool his heels and stayed in Chicago with Bryan for a few extra days."

"I wish I had."

"I'm surprised Bryan didn't insist that the two of you stay. After being apart for so long, I would have thought you both would have wanted a second honeymoon."

Lani shot her a reproving glance. "Not really. The fact that we have each other is what's important."

"Yes, I said something similar myself—just before my divorce, in fact."

"We aren't considering a divorce," Lani protested with a nervous laugh. "My goodness, Monica, I never said a thing like that." She wished she hadn't offered a ride to Monica, and tried to think of a polite way to tell her to mind her own business.

Monica smiled, seemingly pleased at Lani's response. "Of course you aren't. All marriages take some work to keep them smooth. Everything will work out."

"I'm telling you, there is no problem."

"That's nice. Here we are. Just let me out anywhere." When she got out of the car, Monica said, "Thanks for the lift. Give Bryan my best."

"Right." Lani watched Monica cross the sidewalk and enter her store. She wished it had been anyone but Monica who had seen her leaving Jay Harmond's hotel.

She was reluctant to hurry back to her farmhouse with its silence and loneliness, so she drove to her parents' home. Both cars were in the driveway, so she parked and went around to the back door.

Edna and Charles were sitting in the deep shade under the trellis of rambling roses and bougainvillea. When Lani approached, Edna put aside her magazine and said, "Hello. I'm glad you dropped by."

Her father grinned at her and went on sketching his plans for an underground lawn sprinkling system. Lani peered over his shoulder. "How's it going?"

"Fine, fine." Charles said. "I'm going to start digging the trenches for the pipe next week."

"Charles, I've told you over and over, wait for fall." Edna shook her head and said to Lani, "All my flowers are blooming now. See if you can talk sense into him."

"She's right, Dad. Why disturb the beds now? Besides, it'll be cooler in the fall."

"We're not getting any younger," Charles said cheerfully. "I keep telling your mother that, but she won't listen. Never put things off or they might not get done. That's what I say."

"You're not exactly on your last leg," Lani said with a laugh. "You've only been retired a few months."

"Yes, and he's driving me crazy," Edna pretended to complain. "Get another job, Charles. Drive somebody else crazy for a change."

Charles grinned and winked at his wife. "You couldn't do without me around here, and you know it."

Lani sighed. "Unfortunately jobs aren't all that easy to get. Bryan still hasn't found anything."

"He looked very handsome on TV," Edna said. "Like a movie star."

"I saw a glimpse of you in the audience," Charles added. "You looked as pretty as ever."

"Thanks." Lani smiled at her parents. "I don't know what I'd do without you two."

"He's changed quite a bit, hasn't he?" Edna had always been the more empathetic of the two.

"Who?" Charles asked as he went back to sketching.

"Yes, he has. And I don't know what to do about it. He's not happy."

"Who isn't?" Charles repeated.

"Give it time," Edna said.

"Who are you talking about?" Charles asked again.

Edna shook her head in exasperation. "Bryan, of course. Keep up with the conversation." To Lani she said, "I can't do a thing with him since he retired. I guess it's all the time he has on his hands."

"Time!" Charles demanded as he looked at his wife. "I have less time now than I ever had. It's fix this, fix that, do such and such. I'm going to have to go back to work to get some rest."

Edna laughed. "He's just running on," she confided to her daughter. "He loves it."

Lani smiled. "When I was growing up I always wanted to have a marriage like you two have. You're friends and I like that."

"I thought you and Bryan had that," Edna said.

"We did. We don't now. Mom, he's changed so much!"

"So have you," Edna reminded her. "Nothing stands still."

"I know, but he's so...intense. It's as if there's a spring wound tight inside him. He almost never laughs anymore. You know how Bryan was always joking before. Bob isn't his friend any longer, though with Helen running the show I'm not surprised. Bryan doesn't see much of Albert, either. He says Albert reminds him of when he was a pilot and had his own cargo service."

"You see the Goldmans, don't you?" Charles asked.

"Yes, and that helps. By the way, did I tell you they are expecting?"

"No!" Edna said as if pregnancy were the rarest of miracles.

Lani nodded. She didn't want to admit, even to her parents, how much she wished she were carrying Bryan's baby. She knew she shouldn't consider having a child until she knew the marriage would survive. Logic had nothing to do with it, however, and she longed for a baby with Bryan's dark eyes.

Edna gave her a scrutinizing look as if she saw straight into her thoughts, but she made no comment.

"Maybe Bryan ought to think about going back to college," Charles said. "I always thought he should have finished. Sure, money gets tight for newlyweds, but he could have stayed in if you had taken a job."

"I know, but he didn't want me to work. He still doesn't."

"Well, it seems to me if he would finish his years out it would be a fair trade. He only had two to go."

"I know, Dad. I'll suggest it to him."

"My offer still stands to loan you the money," Charles continued. "If Bryan won't borrow it from me, there are student loans. I think I'll suggest it myself. Can't hurt."

"I'd appreciate that."

Edna stood and put her magazine on the table. "Come walk with me and see the vegetable garden."

"Watch out for the squash," Charles warned. "It's a man-eater."

The women walked down the shady path and through the wooden gate that hid the less-lovely vegetables from the yard. "Dad's right. The squash is taking over, isn't it," Lani observed.

"I didn't bring you back here to talk about squash. What's really the matter?"

With a sigh, Lani looked away. "I don't know if we're going to make it, Mom. At times I'm sure Bryan is considering whether we should split up."

"It's as serious as that?"

"He hasn't come right out and said the words, but yes. It's as serious as that."

"Can't you go to a counselor? Frank Goldman is marvelous, I've heard."

Lani shook her head. "I'm too close to Frank. Besides, I don't want my friends to know about the trouble we're having. Even if I went to another psychotherapist, Frank would know. Bryan wouldn't go anyway. He won't go to Frank for his own problems, much less marriage counseling."

"You could at least ask him."

For a minute Lani studied her clasped hands, then looked away as she said, "Bryan didn't come home with me from Chicago."

"What?" Edna leaned forward as if she couldn't make sense of the words. "He didn't come home? Why not? Where is he?"

"He's still in Chicago. He stayed to do radio interviews."

Edna relaxed. "Good heavens, Lani, I thought—"

"Mom, he could have done them by phone!"

"Maybe the radio station didn't want to do it that way. Why didn't you stay with him?"

"I couldn't. I have all that pottery to do and those statues to finish, and—"

"None of which are as important as your marriage."

Lani was silent.

"Go back up there. Be with him."

"I can't. Not only is there the expense, but I don't know if he's even in the same hotel."

"You could find him if you tried."

"He'll be home in a couple of days."

"Are you sure Bryan is the only one who wants out of the marriage?"

Lani looked up sharply. "Mom! What a thing to say!"

"It's a good question. You've changed, too. I can see it, and I haven't been away from you for five years. The differences must be quite unsettling to Bryan."

"What do you mean? I haven't changed all that much!"

"Haven't you? When he left, you were so sensitive to all his wishes that you didn't get a job even though it meant Bryan had to drop out of college. Now you're supporting both of you and you have a chance to really break into the art world with your waterfall sculptures."

"You make it sound as if I were a clinging vine before! We discussed whether I should get a job, and Bryan said he preferred to quit college."

"How does he feel about you working now?"

Lani turned away. "He will have to get used to it. I'm good at what I do and I enjoy it too much to give it up."

"You don't even look the same," her mother continued. "Your hair is short and you almost always wear jeans."

"I like the way I look," Lani said defensively.

"So do I. But the point is, you're different."

Lani looked back at her mother. "So is he."

"Bryan has been through a lot. I'd be amazed if he wasn't."

"Not all of the changes are easy to live with. I think he would live outside, if he had a choice. When he's in the house he's as restless as a caged animal. And he doesn't take anything for granted anymore."

"That doesn't sound like an abrasive trait."

"It can be. I can't turn on a light without him glancing at it. For days after he came home, I would see him standing at the kitchen sink, turning a faucet on and off as if he were fascinated. Whenever I can't find him anywhere else, I know he's in the shower. I never knew anybody could bathe so often. And the microwave! You'd think it was magic the way he treats it!"

"Why do these things irritate you?"

Lani shook her head. "I guess it's because they aren't things I've always associated with Bryan. And too, they remind me of all he went through, and I hate to think about that."

Edna went to Lani and comfortingly stroked her hair as she had done when Lani was a child. "It must be even harder on Bryan, don't you think?"

Reluctantly Lani nodded. "I wish we could just forget those years ever happened."

"So do I, baby, but you can't. Neither can Bryan. Good or bad, they're part of your lives and have contributed to who you are. You have to accept them, not forget them. In time they will fade."

"I guess. I just wonder if our marriage will fade, too."

"You two are right for each other. You can work it out if you try. All his changes aren't bad ones, are they?"

"No." Lani thought of the way Bryan now made love with her. She had to admit that was an improvement, though she had believed it had already been as good as it could get. To her mother she said, "Bryan never puts things off these days. You know he used to be a procrastinator. Now he does things as soon as he sees they need to be done."

"So does your father."

Lani smiled. "That's true, isn't it!" She thought a minute. "Bryan doesn't like for me to work, and it really galls him that I'm supporting us, but he hasn't insisted that I quit when he finds a job."

"That's a big advantage. I couldn't see why you didn't want to work to start with. It's very chic these days."

"It's very necessary," Lani corrected with a smile. "One salary doesn't usually get the bills paid."

"You two have more going for you than you seem to realize. Now you put this idea of divorce out of your head and get on with your marriage."

"Yes, Mother," Lani said teasingly.

"I know it's not all that simple," Edna said. "You probably never knew it, but your father and I had some rough spots in our marriage, too."

"You did! I had no idea."

"Back then we didn't believe in 'letting it all hang out' as they say. We patched it up and went on. Now we're as married as they get."

Lani hugged her mother. "Thanks, Mom. You've been a big help."

"That's what I'm here for. Now," Edna said briskly, "we had better get back to Charles before he digs up my impatiens. The man is a maniac when he has a shovel in his hands."

With a laugh of genuine relief, Lani followed her mother back to the shady patio. Somehow she and Bryan would make it. She hoped.

Chapter Nine

Lani was outside when the phone started ringing, and by the time she reached it, she was out of breath. "Hello!" she gasped, praying it would be Bryan.

"Hello, Ms. Cameron?"

Lani forced herself to relax. "Yes, this is Mrs. Cameron."

"I'm Ella Marset with the Houston Museum of Cultures."

Lani's muscles tensed again. "Yes?"

"I'm calling to ask if you could do a one-woman exhibition for us in October." She paused for Lani's response, but Lani was speechless. "Hello?"

"Yes! Yes, I'm here. My own exhibition. Just me?"

"We saw your water sculptures in Abilene recently. They are unique, unlike anything we've seen here, and I think they would be perfect for our museum. We have an opening in October. Would you be interested?"

"Yes," Lani said as she fought to control the eagerness in her voice. "Yes, I'm available in October. Where is your museum located?"

"We're quite new. Are you at all familiar with Houston?"

"A bit, yes."

"We are located west of Rice University near Braes Bayou."

"I know the area."

"Splendid. We would like to have your showing from October tenth through the twenty-second."

"That will be fine." Lani's heart was racing. A museum show!

"That will put you between the African mask exhibit and the impressionist we're bringing from San Francisco."

"I'm looking forward to meeting you." She had been discovered!

"Actually that brings up another point. I'm not the president, and he is, well, somewhat eccentric. Our museum is rather small and quite new, as I've said. Our president, Mr. Robert Garrison, likes to meet the artists prior to the show since they are, naturally, on hand for the exhibit. You understand, I'm sure."

"Yes, I do." Lani knew this must not only be a small and new museum, but an exclusive one—otherwise they wouldn't be so careful to weed out the extremists and aging hippies. Lani had met a number of artists, some of whom were eccentric to the point of being weird.

"Good. I knew you would. If you could fly up this afternoon, Mr. Garrison could discuss all the arrangements."

"This afternoon! You mean now? Today?"

"I know this is quite short notice, and I hate to suggest it, but Mr. Garrison is going to France tomorrow and isn't expected back for at least a month. Naturally we will reimburse you for your expenses."

"I see." That meant he wouldn't have time to interview another artist if Lani didn't meet his approval, unless he did so immediately.

Ella Marset dropped her voice a bit and added, "Frankly, Ms. Cameron, I think Mr. Garrison's insistence on a personal interview on such short notice is a bit much, but this showing would be important to your career. I know you're a newcomer to the art scene, and we really are an exclusive museum. However, if you can't make it, we'll understand and will keep you in mind for a showing at a future date."

But not a named one, Lani noticed. This was too good an opportunity to pass up. She was almost caught up on her work, and if she went now she wouldn't be taking time away from Bryan. "I understand, Mrs. Marset, and I can manage to fly up this afternoon."

"*Ms.* Marset," the woman corrected. "Delightful. I'm looking forward to meeting you."

"Thank you." Lani took down the address and phone number, but she was so nervous she could hardly write.

After she hung up, Lani felt stunned. It had all happened so fast. Why should she fly to Houston so she could be inspected by a man she had never heard of who was the president of a museum that was unknown to her? She knew why. It was a *museum* and not a mall or even a gallery. And if she was in Houston, she wouldn't feel so lonely. She went back out to finish painting the aged patina on her clay goddess and thought about what she should wear.

* * *

The Camerons' farmhouse was quiet. Lani had carefully locked the doors, leaving on a couple of lights so anyone passing would assume she was home. Only the dry tick of the antique mantel clock disturbed the silence. The house seemed suspended in time, awaiting the return of its owners.

Suddenly the phone rang. Its metallic voice called out several times, then the telephone answering machine clicked on. Lani's voice sounded in the empty house, explaining that she was working and couldn't answer the phone. She always used the same message, feeling it made her less vulnerable to a burglar who had the foresight to call first. After the loud beep, a man's voice spoke to the tape.

"This is Jay. I just wanted to be sure you understood what I meant yesterday morning at the hotel. Give me a call when you can."

The call ended, and the recorder cut off. Once more the house was silent and waiting.

Bryan was tired when he got off the plane. He had had trouble sleeping alone, and he was suffering from jet lag on top of everything else. He wasn't at all sure how Lani would receive him when he got home. If anyone had told him that he and Lani could have an argument in Chicago that was so bad she would go home without him, he would have said it was impossible.

For hours after she'd left, he had fumed angrily, expecting her to return at any moment. Sure, she had said she was going home, but he didn't believe her. No, she would ride around until she cooled off, then come back to the hotel.

When she wasn't back in two hours, Bryan became worried. He called the airport and learned a flight had just departed for Houston, but they refused to say whether Lani had been on board. Bryan tried to argue with the airline, but he knew it was against their regulations to reveal the name of a passenger while the plane was in flight. Bryan had hung up and paced.

After she had had time to reach home, he called, but when she answered he hung up. Lani had actually done it! She had gone back to Texas, and he was furious.

For the next few days Bryan had struggled with what to do. He was afraid to call her for fear she would tell him not to come home at all. If she was ending their marriage, Bryan didn't want to hear about it long-distance.

Bryan's pride had prevented him from leaving before the interviews were over, but as soon as he finished the last one, he had gone straight to the airport. The flight had been rough, and he'd had a two-hour layover in Houston, but he was finally in Laredo.

Naturally Lani had taken the car home, and he considered calling her but again he stopped. She might say she didn't want him, and if that were the case, Bryan had to hear it face-to-face.

Bryan's cabdriver left with as much haste as he had driven the several miles out of town. He obviously was anxious to return to the airport for the more lucrative short-haul fares. Bryan slowly walked up the front steps. The house was quiet, and he assumed their car was inside the garage. When he unlocked the door and went in, however, the house felt and sounded empty. "Lani?" he called.

There was no answer. Maybe she was in the studio. Bryan shut the door and called out more loudly, "Lani, I'm home."

Only silence greeted him. Bryan went to their bedroom and dropped his suitcase on the bed. If she was in the studio, she was ignoring him. That was a bad sign.

He went into the kitchen and looked up at the light. Odd. Lani didn't have a reason to turn on the light when the room was so sunny. A prickle of apprehension touched him. "Lani?"

He flipped off the light and went to the studio. There, too, the lights were on, but Lani was nowhere to be seen. Bryan went through the room, his eyes searching for signs that she had been there. But there was no evidence of clay on her workbench, and the pots of glaze she normally used were all on the storage shelf.

Although the back door of the studio was locked from the inside, Bryan opened it anyway and stepped into the yard. "Lani! Are you out there?" Nothing.

With a worried frown he went back inside. Where could she be? Visions of all sorts of catastrophes assailed him, and he hastily searched the house. When he found neither her body nor signs of violence, Bryan went into the bedroom and tried to calm down. Had she left him? No, he reasoned, she hadn't been *that* mad. Debbie. That was it; she was visiting Debbie.

Feeling rather foolish for his fears, Bryan went to the phone and dialed the Goldman's number. "Debbie? Bryan. Is Lani over there? How long has it been since you've seen her? No, I've been out of town, and she isn't here. Her parents? I'll try them. 'Bye."

When Edna assured him that she had no idea where Lani might be, Bryan felt the panic rising again. Logic told him she could be at another friend's house or at the grocery store, but he was still uneasy. Lani rarely went anywhere during the day because she preferred to work when the light was best.

Again Bryan searched the house, this time looking for a note. He found nothing. A glance in the garage told him the car was gone, so he didn't waste time searching the farm. He could do nothing but wait until she returned.

This time when he entered their bedroom, Bryan noticed the message light was lit on the telephone recorder. He fiddled with the unfamiliar machine until he figured out how to rewind it, then played back the message.

"This is Jay," the voice said. "I just wanted to be sure you understood what I meant yesterday morning at the hotel. Give me a call when you can."

Bryan's face grew stony, and a muscle bunched in his jaw. What in the hell was Lani doing with Jay Harmond at a hotel! What exactly did Harmond say that Lani had misunderstood?

The droning hum of the machine indicated there were no other messages. Had she called him back, or had she gone down to see him?

Bryan yanked the telephone book out of the drawer and riffled through it until he found the hotel's number. "Is Jay Harmond there?" He waited impatiently as the desk clerk checked. "He left? Checked out this morning? Thanks." He shoved the receiver back down onto its cradle.

He went to the closet where they kept their suitcases. Lani's was gone. A red haze formed behind Bryan's eyes. So she had needed to return in order to work? To see Harmond was more like it!

Bryan's hands were shaking, and he felt sick to his stomach. The woman he loved more than life itself was off with that...that paunchy interior decorator. At that moment Bryan was capable of tearing the man in half. An audible groan of sheer anguish rose from Bryan's throat, and it wasn't without great effort that he managed to refrain from punching the wall. A broken hand wouldn't help him; he wanted to save it so he could punch Harmond instead.

Who would know where they had gone? Bryan forced himself to think. There was only one other person he knew who might know—Monica Denton.

He strode through the house and out to the barn. The ancient Jeep was there under the shed. He hadn't used it since his return, but he knew Lani drove it occasionally. After several false starts Bryan coaxed it to life and drove toward town.

He found Monica at The Outpost and said with no preamble, "Where's Lani?"

Monica looked surprised and replied, "Lani? Bryan, you look upset. Is something wrong?"

"No. Of course not."

She put her head to one side thoughtfully. "Come in the back room. You look as if you need to talk."

Bryan had no need or inclination to discuss anything with Monica, but this was his last lead. Monica sent the salesclerk to watch over the store, and she went to the pot of coffee. "Can I get you a cup?"

"No thanks. Look, Monica, I really don't have time to talk right now, and since you don't know where Lani is, I'd better go."

As if he hadn't spoken, Monica said, "I saw Jay Harmond a couple of days ago."

Bryan stopped in the act of leaving and looked back at her suspiciously. "So?"

"He was staying at the hotel downtown."

Bryan waited.

"Lani was with him. Well," Monica added hastily as if she had made a slip, "she wasn't *with* him. I only saw them talking at the door." She widened her eyes innocently. "Maybe Jay knows where she is."

"Two days ago? Tuesday?"

"That's right. I remember being surprised to see her there at that time of the morning."

"In the morning?" Bryan's voice dropped to a menacing rumble.

"I think it was morning. It might have been afternoon. I'm sure it was business. Jay is a good-looking man and he has money, but Lani has *you*." The invitation to change that situation was clear in her eyes. "Or does she?"

"I was in Chicago on business. I don't know what she told you, but that's all there was to it."

"I see." Since Lani had told Monica nothing at all, this was news to her. So there was a rift in their marriage. "Interesting."

"I have to go."

"If you're looking for Jay, he's gone. I called his hotel less than an hour ago to invite him to have lunch with me, but he has already left. He lives in Houston, you know."

Bryan felt sick. Everything pointed to the fact that Lani must have left with Jay.

"Since I hate to eat alone, maybe you will join me." Monica sidled closer, a hungry glint in her blue eyes.

"Do you know whether Harmond went home?"

"No, but I'm sure Lani must know. They've had a...business relationship for quite a while. Oh, but then, you said you're looking for Lani, didn't you. Well, she will show up." Monica stepped closer and put her hands on Bryan's chest. "In the meantime, have lunch with me. We can go to my house, and I'll whip up something for you. I promise you'll like it." She undulated toward him suggestively.

Bryan pried her away and tried to keep his disgust from his face. "I would rather find my wife."

"Have you thought of trying Houston?" Monica asked sharply. "Jay lives at 423 Court Drive."

"She isn't there," he said angrily. "I don't know where she is, but I don't believe she's with him." He wished he meant those words. He turned on his heels and left by way of the back door.

"'Bye, Bryan," he heard Monica say from the doorway. "See you again soon." He didn't bother to look back.

Two women stood on the sidewalk at the end of the parking lot, passing the time of day. He recognized one as Bob's wife, Helen, and he nodded brusquely to her as he passed. He saw her shocked expression and how she leaned her head toward her friend as he went by, but Bryan ignored it. He was bent on finding Lani.

He arrived home in record time and slammed into the house. Running his fingers through his hair, he tried to determine his next move. He now knew Harmond's address, but he would look like a fool if he flew all the way to Houston and she wasn't there. He would feel like a bigger fool if she *was*. As much as he wanted to find her, he was reluctant to confront her and her lover in a situation that could mean only one thing. Bryan loved Lani, and if she had any excuse at all, he wanted to believe it—otherwise he would lose her. In his anger it never occurred to him that it was odd that Monica had Harmond's address on the tip of her tongue.

He heard a car drive up and stop. The last thing he wanted was company. He heard footsteps coming up the walk, then a key being fitted into the lock. The door opened, and there stood Lani.

She jumped, and her eyes widened. "Bryan! You scared the life out of me! I didn't expect you to be home so soon!"

At the same time he demanded, "Where have you been?"

She saw that absence hadn't improved his temper. "Houston."

"What!"

Holding her head up, Lani repeated, "I was in Houston."

"Why!"

"Since you ask so politely, I'll tell you. I was being screened for a showing of my waterfalls at the Houston Museum of Cultures."

He glared at her. "I never heard of such a place."

Ice gripped Lani's middle. He was so angry! "It's new and it's small. There's no reason for you to have heard of it."

"I'll bet it is!"

"There's no reason for you to take that tone with me. It may not be the Fine Arts Museum, but it *is* a museum and it's a big step for my career."

"Do you expect me to believe you flew all the way to Houston just to talk to someone about an art show?"

"They paid my way."

"That's not the point! What happened to using the telephone?"

"The president of the museum wanted to make certain I would be right for the museum's image. For all he could tell over the phone I might smell bad or have purple hair."

"Lani, that's the most farfetched story I've ever heard!"

"No, you staying in Chicago to be on a radio show is! Why did you do that, Bryan!"

"You should be glad that I did! *The McPherson Show* was seen by an agent who says he thinks he may be able to sell my journal!"

She looked up at him in surprise. "Are you serious?"

"You needn't sound quite so amazed. *Someone* writes books. Why not me?"

"I didn't mean that. I just didn't expect this."

"Neither did I."

They glared at each other, both wishing they could back down, but neither wanting to be the one to give in. Finally Bryan said, "Do you want to make up, or would you rather keep fighting?"

"I'd rather make up," she answered warily. "Would you?"

"If I didn't, I wouldn't have suggested it." They watched each other, both too afraid of rejection to take the next step.

Finally Bryan reached out and drew Lani to him. She went gladly and put her arms around him. He breathed in her sweet fragrance, and held her as if he would never let her go. "Let's start this over," he said. "Hi, honey. I'm home."

"How was your trip?" she responded.

"I missed you." He tilted her head back and gazed into her eyes. "I really did."

"I missed you, too. I forgot how lonely this place can be when you're not around."

Had she been lonely? He wondered if she had turned to Jay because of it, and had made up the museum story to cover her true reason for going to Houston. "Did you really go to a museum in Houston?"

"Of course I did. Why else would I go there?"

He could think of at least one reason, but he tried to shove it aside. "I'm glad you're home."

"So am I." She stepped back and lifted her suitcase. "I'll go put these things away."

Bryan nodded and watched her go down the short hall to the bedroom. Against his will, his eyes went to the telephone. There was one way of finding out if the museum existed. He went to the phone and dialed the number for directory assistance.

All at once he realized what he was doing, and pressed the button to disconnect the call. He had never even considered checking up on Lani before! He would not do so now. As he walked toward the bedroom the nagging voice in his head said that it wouldn't prove anything anyway. If Lani were going to lie, she would surely be smart enough to name a museum that really existed. Bryan wouldn't consider actually calling the museum to see if Lani had been there.

He leaned against the door and watched as she unpacked first her things, then his. She didn't act as if she had recently come from a tryst with a lover. Instead she was chatting about the flight and the Houston traffic and how she almost didn't reach the museum in time. Was she being a bit too talkative? Lani frequently tumbled one word over another when she was nervous.

She stepped out of her heels and unfastened her skirt. Bryan watched as she folded it in a pile with her blazer and a silk dress that needed to go to the cleaners. "Something ought to be done about the air pollution in big cities," she said as she began to unbutton her soft blouse. "You really notice it when you come from a place like this."

Bryan made no comment. Surely if she had been with Harmond she couldn't undress so casually as he watched. But she did seem unusually nervous about something.

She removed her panty hose, then her blouse. Wearing only her sheer bra and lacy panties, she put the blouse in the stack of clothes to be washed, then reached in a drawer and pulled out a cotton T-shirt. "Boy, it's hot out there," she commented. "At least it's dry here. You know how humid Houston is."

In a smooth stride Bryan was beside her and caught the T-shirt before she could pull it on. "There's no need to be in a rush." Surely she would pull away if she had anything to hide.

"I have to get these things in the wash and—"

"I'll wash them for you."

"I have to glaze the pottery for Monica."

That reminded him of Monica's inference that Lani and Harmond were lovers. Bryan took the shirt from her and tossed it aside. With a practiced motion he removed her bra.

"Bryan," she began to protest.

He covered her breasts with his palms, and drew her closer so that her bare back rested against his chest. "Yes?" His hands moved in sensuous circles over her tender skin, teasing her nipples.

"I've missed you," she sighed, letting her head rest against his chin. "I've missed you so much."

"Lani, don't ever leave me again," he said in a low voice.

"Me, leave you? I never would do that."

But she had. She had done so twice, if he counted her trip to Houston. The idea of anyone, especially Jay Harmond, touching her like this sent a shaft of pain through him. Almost roughly he turned her to face him. "Love me, Lani," he commanded as his eyes searched hers. "Love me as you used to."

"I can't," she answered truthfully. "We've changed. Both of us. I can't go back, and neither can you."

He hadn't wanted to hear this. Was she saying there was no hope for them? A need to convince her otherwise drove him, and he lifted her and laid her on the bed. As he yanked off his clothes he gazed down at her. She was so damned beautiful! No other woman in the world aroused him the way she did. He desired her above all others.

Her hair was like a coronet of flame against the pale coral bedspread. Sunlight from the window poured over her, turning her skin to glowing ivory, accentuating the supple curves of her body. Her nipples were a rosy apricot and were pouting under his scrutiny.

Bryan lay naked beside her, his length pressed next to hers. Overhead the ceiling fan turned with a rhythmic hum, cooling their bodies. Bryan cupped his hand over the lush velvet of her breast and kissed her. Lani's lips parted under his, and she returned his kiss with all the eagerness he could have wished for, yet the nagging in his head persisted. Had she made love with Harmond like this? Had he stroked her breasts and drawn from her a murmur of soft love words? Jealousy flared in Bryan, and he kissed her more passionately. If she had any thoughts of Harmond, Bryan would drive them from her head. Lovemaking had always been good between them. Surely it would overshadow any desire she had for someone else.

Bryan lowered his head and took Lani's nipple into his mouth. It beaded against his tongue, and he drew on it gently. She curved her body toward him as if she wanted to give him all of herself. Bryan was willing to take all she gave.

Enjoying the velvet of her skin, he ran his hand over her sides and hips and caught her buttocks, pulling her closer. He pressed her body to his; it fit as perfectly as if they had been made to measure.

With a sure movement he removed her panties and with his hand he caressed the firm flesh of her inner thigh. He felt the heat of her womanhood before he touched it. She wanted him. When his fingers found the fount of her desires, he realized she was already moist and ready.

He wanted to take her and love her so passionately that she would be his forever, but he knew the secret to Lani's heart was by way of a more subtle path. With knowing touches he stroked and probed until she pleaded for him to take her.

With controlled eagerness, Bryan entered her and held her close as he fought to retain his control. Slowly he moved, drawing out her pleasure more and more until she cried out, and he felt the rhythmic pulsing that meant she had achieved her summit. He enjoyed the sensation until she began to relax, then he again moved deep within her.

Lani was responsive as he had known she would be. Their bodies were perfectly tuned and each was sensitive to the other's desires. Once more he coaxed her to ecstasy, marveling at the way she could be pleased time and again. She was his; he was sure of it now. She would never be so willing in his arms if she had been with someone else. Lani had too much honesty and fidelity to switch from lover to lover with no compunction. And he was her lover as much as he was her husband. They had always been primarily lovers.

Once more her wants became needs, and her needs fulfillment. This time the pulsing deep within her drew him inescapably to his own completion, and Bryan groaned with a mixture of intense enjoyment and disappointment; he had wanted to give her more pleasure.

Love and pure ecstasy twirled through him, and he held Lani tightly as their souls touched for a shining moment. Gradually his pulse slowed, and his heartbeat grew more steady. Bryan rolled to one side, still holding Lani in a lover's embrace. "I love you," he whispered, trying to somehow make her see that they belonged together. "Don't ever leave me."

"I won't leave you. I love you." She kissed the hot pulse in his throat, her warm breath stirring against his skin. "I'll never leave you."

Through his still-heightened senses he heard the tight note in her voice. Even now when she should be relaxed in the warmth of his embrace after making love, she sounded worried, and he didn't know why. Bryan had always been able to sense the subtleness of her moods. He gathered her close and laid her head on his shoulder.

As he gently stroked her silky hair, he wondered how he could put their world back together. He wasn't going to give her up; that was for sure. A love like theirs was too rare to give up just because of a rough spot.

Rough spot? Hell, she could be thinking of divorcing him! Bryan closed his eyes and pressed her body to his. He would do whatever was necessary to keep her. They belonged together, and he wasn't going to give up.

"I love you, Lani," he repeated almost fiercely.

"I love you, too." She put her arm further around him, and clung to him as if she were drowning and he was her only hope.

"I won't give you up," he whispered, but he said it so quietly, he wasn't sure that she heard him. When she made no reply, he rubbed his face in the tumble of her hair. No, he wouldn't give her up.

Chapter Ten

As she pushed the grocery cart along the supermarket aisles, Lani thought about Bryan. He seemed happier these past few days. The intenseness was still there, but she was growing accustomed to that. He no longer seemed as if he had a coiled spring inside him. Also, he was more attentive to her. At times she would find him watching her for no reason.

Lani glanced at the list and put some cans of green beans and corn in the basket. She didn't know what made Bryan suddenly become so aware of her, but she liked it.

As she went up the next aisle, she saw Helen Edwards approaching, also with a loaded cart. Lani considered faking an interest in her list until the woman passed by, but her honesty prevented her. She might not like Helen and she might secretly wonder if Helen had been instrumental in breaking up Bob and Harriet's marriage, but that was beside the point. Laredo was relatively small, and Lani didn't want hard feelings between herself and a woman she would see off and on for possibly the rest of her life.

Helen had already seen Lani, and her eyes had a gleam in them. Lani hoped Helen wasn't going to try to sell her bazaar tickets or something of the sort. They rarely talked unless Helen's church or one of her clubs was trying to raise money.

Lani tried giving the woman a friendly nod and passing on by, but Helen said, "Hello, Lani. I haven't seen you in a long time."

"It has been, hasn't it?" Lani responded in the too-friendly tone people reserve for casual acquaintances.

"You must be very busy these days."

"As a matter of fact, I am." Lani wished Helen would make her sales pitch so she could get on with her shopping. "I have a show coming up at a museum in Houston."

"My goodness, that must be exciting." Helen smoothed the shirttail of her maternity blouse and pointedly stared at Lani's flat stomach. "I just came from a doctor's appointment, and he says the baby and I are doing fine."

"That's nice." Lately Lani had felt vaguely jealous of pregnant women. She wanted to start her own family.

"I saw Debbie Goldman in the waiting room, and she said you had been in Chicago."

"Yes, Bryan was on *The McPherson Show*, and I flew up with him."

"That's what she said."

Lani moved restlessly. There was never any way of speeding Helen up when she was making a plea for a donation.

"Did Bryan mention that I saw him in town the other day?"

"No, I don't think he did."

"I believe it was about the middle of last week. I saw him coming out of The Outpost."

"You did?" Lani wondered why Bryan would go to Monica's store. He never went there except to help Lani with a pottery delivery.

"I thought at the time it was odd not to see you with him."

"My mother's birthday is coming up. Bryan was probably buying her a gift."

"That's strange, because he was coming out the back door."

Lani frowned. That *was* strange. "I have no idea why he was there. I guess he had to drop by and check on some of my pottery."

"That must be it. What else could it be?" Helen's eyes glinted as she added, "I heard Monica say she would see him again soon. She must have meant when the two of you bring her more pottery."

"I'm sure that was it. Helen, I hate to rush, but I do have a lot to do today."

"Don't let me keep you. I know how it is to be busy. Everyone tells me I won't have a minute to myself once my baby is here."

Lani wasn't listening. She was trying to figure out why Bryan would go to see Monica and not tell her.

As quickly as she could, Lani finished shopping and checked out. Why would Monica say she would see him later? That had an ominous ring to it. Could that be why Bryan was being so nice to her lately? Maybe he was watching her closely to see if she was suspicious.

No! Lani wrote out the check and gave it to the checker. No, Bryan would never see another woman behind her back; he wasn't like that. At least the old Bryan wasn't.

Lani had the sacker put all but the refrigerated goods into her trunk; the sack with milk and eggs she put up front on the car seat. Before her conversation with Helen, she had intended to go straight home, but instead she went to Debbie Goldman's.

When Debbie opened the door, Lani, with her sack of cold groceries, stood on the porch. "I need to talk," Lani said. "Can I put this food in your refrigerator so it doesn't spoil?"

"Sure. Come on in." Debbie led Lani into the kitchen and made a space in her refrigerator for the sack. "What's up?"

"I don't know. Nothing."

"That sounds serious. Come sit down. Can I get you a Coke or a glass of iced tea?"

Lani nodded. "The tea would be great. It's still so hot outside."

"I almost dread fall. Usually I love to teach, but this year is going to be difficult with my pregnancy and all."

"Maybe it won't be so bad. I've heard of some women who work right up until the baby comes."

"The doctor says if I stay well and want to, I can do that. I guess only time will tell." Debbie and Lani had gone into the den, and Debbie sat opposite Lani in an overstuffed chair. "But you didn't come here to talk about my teaching or my pregnancy."

Lani was silent a minute as she studied the amber liquid in her cold glass. "I saw Helen Edwards in the grocery store."

"Isn't she something else? I was trapped in the obstetrics waiting room with her. You'd think no one else ever had a baby. No one has ever been sicker or felt her baby kick as early or has such an understanding husband. She makes me ill."

"She isn't the highlight of my life, either."

"She isn't selling more raffle tickets, is she? Frank thinks I'm crazy, but I can never tell her no. That's easy for a psychotherapist to say, but Helen is always saving some starving tribe in Africa or earthquake survivors in Guam. I can't turn down causes like that."

"Neither can I. No, she isn't saving anyone right now." Lani thought for a minute, but could think of no tactful way to say what was on her mind. "Helen said she saw Bryan and Monica together."

"Monica Denton?"

"Is there another one?"

Debbie's smile faded to a frown. "Where were they?"

"At The Outpost."

Debbie's smile returned. "That's not too difficult to explain. Maybe he was buying something. Monica's stores have the cutest gifts in town."

"He was coming out the back door."

The frown threatened to return, but Debbie was determined to remain optimistic. "He must have been there to check on your pottery."

"That's just it. I do all that by phone. Bryan has made a big deal out of telling me he doesn't want to be anywhere near Monica. So why would he go there alone?"

"I don't know. Have you asked him?"

"I haven't had time. I just came from the store. Remember the groceries?"

"If it were me, I'd forget the whole thing. You've said things are getting better between you and Bryan. This could needlessly rock the boat. Bryan wouldn't do anything wrong."

"But Helen saw him there."

"Helen is nothing but a troublemaker, and you know it. She probably still has her nose out of joint over Bryan not knowing Bob had divorced Harriet. The Outpost is a public place."

"The back room isn't."

"I think you're worrying needlessly."

"Helen heard Monica say she would see Bryan again soon."

Debbie's frown returned. "There are a dozen explanations for that."

"I can only think of one. What if he has been so nice to me lately because he's feeling guilty?"

"Ask him why he went to The Outpost. You won't be happy until you do."

"What could he possibly do but deny it? If he's seeing her, he certainly won't admit it!"

"Look, Lani, I'm the one who is supposed to have weird notions and cravings. You're the one who is supposed to be rational."

Lani slid lower in the chair and took another sip of her cold drink before resting it on her thigh. "I don't feel rational. I feel suspicious and angry and jealous. Debbie, I've never felt like this before in my life. On top of everything else, I think I'm coming down with something."

"Oh?"

"I feel sort of odd. Nothing I can really put my finger on, just different."

Debbie leaned forward with interest. "How long has this been going on?"

"Just yesterday and today." Lani moved restlessly. "I guess it's the heat."

"Maybe so." Debbie smiled slightly. "If it keeps up, you may want to see a doctor."

"I don't feel that bad," Lani said offhandedly. "My main worry is over Bryan."

"Take my advice and either forget about it or ask Bryan. I have a feeling there is nothing to worry about."

"Would you say that if it were Frank?"

"Of course not," Debbie answered with a laugh, "but it isn't, and I can be more objective."

"Thanks. It's helped to talk about it."

"I wish I could do more. Do you want me to talk to Monica?"

"Lord, no! If there isn't anything going on, I wouldn't give her the satisfaction of knowing I thought so."

"Then forget all about it. Just concentrate on that museum show."

"I have to go to Houston tomorrow to see that the waterfalls arrive safely. You can tell these people are new to the business, wanting the sculptures so far in advance. I suspect it's so that the artist won't exhibit in the area ahead of time, stealing the museum's thunder. This Mr. Garrison, the museum's president, isn't the most trusting man I've ever met."

"I guess everyone in the field of art is allowed to have quirks."

"Thanks, pal."

"You know what I mean. Is Bryan going with you?"

"No, there's no reason for him to do that. I'm flying there and back the same day. He suggested joining me, but the museum is only paying my fare." Lani looked thoughtful. "Maybe I should ask him to come along anyway—all things considered."

"Lani, I'm surprised at you."

"So am I. If I can't trust him to be alone in town with Monica, we don't have anything worth saving."

"Bryan loves you. I can see it every time he looks at you. When a man is in love with a woman—really in love—he won't look at anyone else."

"I know. I guess I sometimes worry about whether he's truly in love with me."

"Lani, what am I going to do with you? Of course he loves you."

"I guess so. But he's changed so much. You never knew him before, but at times he isn't the same at all."

"Do you love him?"

"You know I do."

"Then treat him as if you do, and it will all work out. Nothing is more contagious than love."

"I just hope whatever I seem to be catching isn't contagious. I shouldn't have come here if it is. I wasn't thinking." Lani got up.

Debbie's smile was broad as she, too, stood. "I have a feeling you aren't contagious at all."

"I hope not. I'd never forgive myself if I gave you something in your condition. Condition," she said with a laugh. "That makes pregnancy sound like a malfunction."

"Come see the nursery while you're here. I couldn't wait a whole nine months to decorate. I even have the curtains up."

Lani followed Debbie down the hall to the bedroom they had set aside for the baby. Lani and Debbie had scoured the area's flea markets and garage sales to find inexpensive baby furniture, and they had spent an entire day painting it all a pale yellow.

The curtains were white with a parade of toys along the bottom and balloons at the top. Lani admired them enthusiastically. "How adorable! No baby could resist them."

"Look at this." Debbie opened a drawer and took out a tiny sleeper. "Isn't it darling? My mother sent it yesterday. She did the embroidery work herself."

"It's so tiny!"

"She says it will swallow the baby at first. I can't imagine a human so small. You know, I've never held a newborn? All my sisters had their babies in other states and the babies were several months old before I first saw them." Debbie held up the small garment. "I've seen dolls larger than this."

Lani touched the soft cloth. "I have to admit I'm a little envious, Debbie. I wish Bryan and I were starting a family."

Debbie smiled slightly as if she suspected something Lani didn't. "Maybe you will before long. When you do, you can borrow this little outfit."

"I wish I thought I would have a reason to, but I'm not even sure the marriage will work out—much less that I'll ever have a baby. Time is getting away from me."

"You aren't over the hill yet. As for the marriage, I know a terrific counselor."

"So do I. I only wish Bryan would talk to Frank."

"You know, maybe he will. Not in the office, but unofficially."

"What do you mean?"

"Frank could ask him to go fishing. I hear that's as good as a beauty shop for talking things out."

"I couldn't ask him to do that. Counseling is his job."

"But we're friends. Okay, I'll make you a deal. Trade me one of your clay gods for the counseling. Bryan will never know, and it will all work out."

"I've already made you one. I was going to give it to you for your anniversary."

"Great! I've always liked those little rascals."

They went back to the kitchen, and Lani took her sack out of the refrigerator. "Thanks, Debbie. I appreciate your listening to me."

Debbie smiled. "That's what friends are for."

When Lani left, she felt considerably better than when she had arrived. Even the odd sickliness was almost gone.

The flight to Houston wasn't pleasant. Not that the air was rough, but because of the argument she had had with Bryan before leaving. It had been the worst kind—the kind where no heated words had been exchanged.

"Why will it take you all day to deliver these sculptures?" he had asked.

"I have to show Ms. Marset how to put them together. They don't have interchangeable parts, you know."

Then he had fallen silent. Lani had no idea what was wrong with him. He and Frank planned to go fishing that morning so it wasn't that he would be lonely. True, she had had to get up early in order to get herself and the crates of sculptures to the airport in a rented van, but that was no big deal. Lani had hauled herself out of bed to send Bryan off with a predawn breakfast on many occasions. It was almost as if Bryan didn't believe she was going to Houston on business.

Lani shifted in the seat as the plane approached Houston. She was feeling odd again, and the changing cabin pressure and constant roar of the engines were only aggravating her near-nauseous sensation. Not the flu, she whispered almost prayerfully. Please, not the flu today of all days.

With the airport in sight, the plane banked, lining up with the runway for landing. Lower and lower they flew, then the ground seemed to rush up at them. For Lani, the landing was by far the worst part of flying. She heard a scraping sound as the wheels touched down, then felt a jolt as the aircraft solidly contacted the ground. As the pitch of the engines changed to a protesting growl, she released her grip on the seat's armrests.

Ms. Marset and a burly driver were waiting for Lani in the terminal. Ms. Marset was an impressively chic woman with perfect nails and hair that the wind never tousled. Next to her Lani felt gauche and coltish.

The crates of ceramics were unloaded from the plane's baggage compartment and put in the museum's van by the driver, who never said a word of greeting. Lani thanked him, but he looked at her as if he understood no English.

Ms. Marset chatted all the way into town, and Lani tried to make all the proper responses, but the unaccustomed rush of Houston traffic and the driver's apparent attitude that they all led charmed lives kept her from being able to concentrate on the woman's conversation. The man zipped from lane to lane, braking and accelerating into openings Lani would never have dared try. She was glad when they finally passed downtown and exited the freeway.

The Museum of Cultures, housed in a large round building that resembled a Styrofoam igloo, was located near Rice University off Shepherd Drive. Massive iron sculptures were displayed on the lawn, and the entrance was colorfully decorated with the six different flags that had flown over Texas.

They circled around to a loading dock at the back where Lani supervised the removal of the crates. The air was oppressively heavy with the typical Gulf Coast humidity, and in moments Lani's silk blouse was plastered to her back. Ms. Marset, who was obviously acclimatized, looked on as collectedly as if she had her own personal air conditioner.

Lani was relieved to enter the cool interior of the building, and quickly surmised from the relaxed demeanor of the museum's employees that Mr. Garrison, the stern taskmaster, must still be out of the country.

"We'll set them up in here for now," Ms. Marset said as she ushered Lani into an empty back room. "As soon as the current show has been packed away, I'll supervise the relocation of your pieces to the showroom."

"I'll come back and help if you want me to."

"There's really no need. Mr. Garrison will be back by then, and he decides on the placement of the exhibits. Once I've seen them assembled, I can recreate it."

"I just assumed you'd want me here."

"It's up to you, of course, but we will work Sunday and most of the night preparing for your show on Monday. There's no need to wear yourself out. Of course, Mr. Garrison will want you here when we open the doors for the show."

"I understand."

"After the opening, we won't need you back until it's time to remove the exhibit. Then we will reverse the procedure and replace your sculptures in the crates."

"I appreciate your inviting me to the exhibit here." Lani had liked the museum from the first moment she had seen it on her previous trip. It was accessible and perfectly lit to show off its treasures. Aside from the stuffiness that seemed to be inherent in all art museums, it was a pleasant place to visit.

The driver opened the crates, and Lani showed Ms. Marset how to arrange the ceramic bowls in each sculpture so that the water splashed or flowed or bubbled just as Lani had planned.

Eventually the room was full of her sculptures and all the pumps and bowls and reservoirs were in place. Although the driver had done all the lifting and carrying,

Lani was exhausted. Telling someone else how to put the pieces together was almost as difficult as doing it herself.

She stood back and critically examined them. The adobe "ruins" had its trays slanted so the water would slide off in droplets that would resemble a shower of rain on each level. The set of staggered lily pads were angled in such a way that a musical stream of water gurgled down into the lotus "pond" below. The curving lines of a series of spiraling water slides in opalescent white was arranged to permit a smooth and almost silent flow of water through its intricate maze. One by one Lani examined them and explained to Ms. Marset the precise effect she wanted to achieve. Although the woman was diligent in her note taking, Lani decided she would be there herself when they were to be moved. Water was tricky, and if it didn't flow properly, the entire artistic effect of the sculpture would be wrong.

When she was finished, Lani glanced at the clock on the wall. As she had hoped, she had some extra time before she had to leave for the airport.

"You can stay here if you like," Ms. Marset offered. "We have the African exhibit in the showroom."

"Thank you, but I need to see someone while I'm in town. Could I call a taxi?"

Before long Lani was being driven with hair-raising recklessness through the streets of Houston. After several minutes the taxi stopped at the address she had given him. Lani leaned forward and looked at the building. "There must be some mistake. This is a restaurant. It's supposed to be Harmond Interiors."

"I can't help that, lady. This is the address you gave me."

"Wait here. Maybe someone inside can tell me where I need to be."

"Don't take all day," the cabbie growled.

Lani slid out and hurried toward the door. Inside she found the manager and said, "I'm trying to find Harmond Interiors. Can you tell me where they've moved?"

"I never heard of them. Wait a minute." He turned to one of the waitresses. "Ever hear of Harmond Interiors?"

She shook her head and went on with her work.

"Sorry, ma'am. We can't help you."

"Surely someone knows. They must have been the previous tenants of this building."

He looked at her as if she were crazy. "This restaurant has been here for a dozen years at least. Maybe longer."

"That's impossible!"

"Look, I'd like to stand here and discuss it with you, but I'm trying to get ready for the dinner crowd."

"Can I use your phone?"

"Is it a local call?"

"Yes." She was trying hard to be civil, but she was losing the battle. When the man put a phone on the counter, she noticed he hovered near enough to be sure she dialed only seven digits.

Lani waited impatiently while the phone rang. This was the number she always used to contact Jay's business. It was printed clearly on the card he had given her years ago, but so was this address. After several rings an answering machine clicked on, and she heard Jay's recorded voice explaining that he was out of the office.

She hung up without leaving a message. To the manager she said, "You're sure this restaurant has been here that long?"

"I've worked here since it opened."

"May I ask who owns it?"

"It's owned by the Atoi Company."

"A foreign firm?"

"Beats me. I just draw a salary."

Lani thanked him and hurried back out to the impatient cabdriver. She ignored his surly comments and gave him a new address. She would go to Jay's house and ask him where his business was.

Disappointment clouded Lani's face as she discovered that 423 Court Drive was not quite as prestigious as she had expected, but at least it existed. It was in the middle of a short row of tall, narrow town houses that she estimated to be fifteen to twenty years old. The facade of each town house was different. Jay's was of a Tudor design, nestled between a colonial and a Georgian.

Lani didn't dare ask the cabbie to wait again, so she paid him and went up the short walk. The town houses had been set close to the street, and it appeared that the developer had piled a mound of dirt in front of each of the end units in an attempt to create the illusion of hills to break the monotony of Houston's flat terrain. That had been years before, however, and the grass that had covered the yard had become a tangled mat of St. Augustine and multiple varieties of weeds. The shrubbery in front of the units was in desperate need of trimming.

Again Lani compared the number on the house and the name on the nearby street sign to the address Jay had written on the reverse of his business card. This was 423 Court Drive; there was no mistake. Lani felt uneasy as she went to the door and pressed the doorbell. She could hear it jingling far off inside the house. As she waited, she looked at an oblong tan water stain that marred the curtain at the window. Why would a successful interior decorator allow his own house to become shabby? Was he so busy tending to his clients that he shelved his own needs?

She recalled the ancient adage that it was the cobbler's children who had no shoes.

She rang the bell again. Why would Jay live in a neighborhood that was clearly going to seed? She looked at the nearby intersection as the traffic light changed and a river of cars and trucks roared by. Just beyond was a convenience store and beside it a dry cleaner's and a service station. None of them were new. A closer inspection of the front of Jay's town house revealed that the stucco was peeling and the black Tudor beams were splitting from Houston's capricious weather. Lani frowned. Her own house needed painting, too, but she wasn't a well-known and highly paid decorator.

After the third ring she had to admit defeat. Jay wasn't home, and she had to get to the airport. Lani dodged traffic across the intersection and called another taxi from the convenience store.

During her ride back to the airport, she puzzled over the mysteries she had discovered. It was possible that Jay no longer lived in the town house; he might have moved from there years before. But the restaurant was baffling. All the correspondence she'd ever had with him went to the address where the restaurant was located, and she had always received a reply. The manager could have been lying for some inexplicable reason, but the restaurant *looked* as if it had been there for years. It was almost as timeworn as the town house.

Lani boarded the plane, wishing she could tell Bryan about this. He was good at unraveling mysteries, but naturally she couldn't discuss Jay Harmond's business and *home* addresses with him. Knowing how strenuously he had objected to Jay coming to her studio to pick up his shipments, Bryan would really be upset if he knew she had gone to Jay's house for any reason.

As the plane taxied and roared off into the sky, Lani concentrated on this perplexing question to keep her mind off the flight. Jay had to be all he said he was; his checks had always been good, and Lani had never had a reason to doubt him—at least not until now. She tried to recall the name of the company that owned the restaurant, but she couldn't remember. If she called them to ask again, however, they would probably think she was as loony as the restaurant manager obviously had thought her. She decided to get Jay to explain it all the next time she saw him.

When she got home, she found Bryan hard at work in the back room. "You're home? I thought you and Frank might still be fishing."

Bryan pushed away from his typewriter and came to her. "Guess what!" he said with excitement as he put a hand on each of her shoulders.

"You caught our supper?"

"Better! I got a call today!"

Struggling to sound excited for him, Lani asked, "You found a flying job?"

"No, it was from that agent I met in Chicago. He's read the part of my journal that I sent him, and he thinks he can sell it!"

"What?" she asked in delight as she caught his mood.

"He asked me to finish the rest of it, and mail it to him as soon as possible! He said he really liked my writing style and wants to see anything else I try after I finish the journal."

"I'm so glad!"

"Don't you see what this may mean? If I can write, it could mean a whole new career for me! I could work right here."

Lani looked up at him. Did that mean he planned to be here, with her, permanently? "That would be wonderful. But what about your flying?"

"I hadn't mentioned it to you, but I've been hoping to find a way to support us without taking to the air again. I know it always made you uneasy." Not seeing the relief in Lani's face, Bryan changed the subject back to his writing. "I've always heard the first book is the hardest. I have some other ideas floating around in my head. Can you imagine me as a writer? I never even finished college!"

"Maybe now you'll have the time and money to finish your degree."

Bryan ran his hand over his dark hair. "I might at that! God, Lani! You don't know how I've dreamed of doing that!"

"You have? You never said so." She stared at him. "Why didn't you ever tell me that before?"

"There didn't seem to be any way around it."

"Bryan, you need to know this. Even if you make a million dollars, I'm going to continue my sculpting."

"That's fine!"

"It is?"

"There's a big difference in you working because you want to, and you having to work to support us."

She shook her head and smiled. It all sounded the same to her, but if Bryan was happy, she was, too.

"This has been a terrific day," he was telling her. "We caught all the fish Frank and I were willing to clean, then when I got home, there was a message from the agent. *My* agent! Doesn't that sound great?"

She nodded happily.

"You know, I really enjoyed being with Frank. I never knew anyone so easy to talk to before."

Lani smiled and put her arms around him. Maybe it was all going to work out after all.

Chapter Eleven

"Hello, Bryan? This is Richard Sinclair. Did I call at a bad time?"

"No, this is fine." Bryan covered the mouthpiece to say to Lani, "It's my agent."

"I've talked to several editors about your book and the feedback is very good. How is the manuscript coming along?"

"Pretty well. But I haven't finished it yet." Bryan didn't want to admit that it was coming along very slowly.

"Keep working on it. I think we need to sell it while interest is high. A lot of people saw you on *The McPherson Show*."

"Oh?"

"What is he saying?" Lani whispered.

"How soon can you send me the rest of the manuscript?"

"I don't know. I've never written a book before. I have no idea how long it will take."

"Well, as I said, time is of the essence. Just keep after it, and get it to me as soon as you can."

"Has anyone made an offer?"

Lani came nearer. "Is someone interested in your book?"

"Not yet," Sinclair said matter-of-factly. "Since this is your first effort, an editor will want to see the complete manuscript before making an offer."

"What if it isn't good enough? I've never written a book before."

"Just keep doing what you've done already. The chapters I've seen are a bit rough, but as I told you before, you have talent. I'll look over the completed manuscript when it comes in, and between the two of us, we'll get it shaped up so I can formally submit it."

"How long do you think it will take you to sell it after we get it all together?"

"Not long, I hope. But sometimes these things can take months."

"All right." Bryan met Lani's eyes. "I'll get it to you as soon as I can."

After he replaced the receiver in the cradle, Bryan stared at it silently.

"Well?" Lani demanded. "What did he say?"

"He said I should send him the manuscript as soon as possible. There is some interest in it, but he says he can't even try to sell it until I finish and he feels it's ready to show to an editor."

"That's wonderful!" She looked at him more closely. "Why don't you look as if you think it's wonderful?"

"Lani, I've never written a book before. It could take me months just to finish the first draft. Sinclair said the first few chapters I sent him were pretty rough."

"I have confidence in you," Lani said with a bright smile, hoping to cheer him up.

"Thanks. I'd better get back to it."

"Sure. I understand. I'll be in my studio if you want to talk."

For an hour, Bryan stared at the handwritten pages of his journal and the blank sheet of paper in his typewriter. At this rate, he would never finish the book. This wasn't earning a penny, and there was no guarantee that it would sell at all. Bryan slammed his open palm on his desk top and headed out back to take out his frustrations by working on his old Jeep. They didn't need the Jeep, and Bryan was thinking he ought to sell it to help pay for the Chicago trip that had severely dented Lani's budget.

"Hey, man, you still looking for a job?"

Bryan raised his head from beneath the hood of his aging Jeep and laid his wrench to one side. "Hi, Albert. I didn't hear you drive up."

"I was out this way and thought I'd drop by." Albert leaned against the Jeep's fender, gazing with interest at the old engine. "I heard this morning that Swayco is hiring."

Bryan folded his arms and looked down at the dusty ground. "Swayco? The trucking line?"

"Hell, man, there's jobs other than flying. My brother works for them, and he says it's a good company."

"I didn't know Floyd was working there."

"Been there for a couple of years now."

Bryan looked thoughtful. "Did Floyd say what they are paying?"

"No, but it must be pretty good. He just bought his wife a new Cadillac. But then he's on the road more than any of Swayco's drivers. He says he enjoys the scenery."

"I'd hate to be gone very much, but nothing else has come up."

Albert reached down and tugged on the fan belt. "Looks like you could use a new one. I don't know how this one is holding together."

"I wish a fan belt were the only thing wrong with this old heap. I'm amazed that it runs at all." He looked back at his friend. "I guess trucking cargo isn't all that different from flying cargo."

Albert grinned. "You just fly lower, that's all."

"I think I'll give Swayco a call."

"There you go, my man. Hey, it's not forever. Just until you find a pilot's job."

"Yeah. That's right." Bryan slammed the hood shut and wiped his hands on a greasy rag. His pride wouldn't let him admit to a fellow pilot that he no longer wanted to take the risks associated with so much time in the air. "I'll go call them now."

"Well, I got to be going. I told Marlee I'd pick her up early."

"Marlee? I thought you were still dating Carol."

"No, we quit seeing each other. Dating Carol was about like dating Khaddafi."

Bryan laughed as he gathered his tools back into the box. He was pleased that during one of his recent visits to the library he'd learned who Khaddafi was. "I've always thought Marlee was sweet on you."

Albert grinned. "She's quite a woman. The better I get to know her, the better I like her."

"Sounds like this one may be getting serious."

"Could be. You know it's about time I thought about settling down."

"With the right woman you couldn't do any better."

Albert studied Bryan. "You and Lani doing all right?"

"Sure. It's been an adjustment for her, but we're okay. Why do you ask?"

"No reason." Albert paused. "I saw Bob Edwards the other day." He paused as if this might mean something to Bryan.

"So? How is he?"

"Okay, I guess. Well, I've got to go or Marlee will think I got lost."

"Good seeing you. I'll go call Swayco."

Bryan watched Albert walk away. For a minute he had thought that Albert was going to say something important about Bob. Bryan shrugged. Whatever Albert had had on his mind, he must have decided not to mention it.

He went inside and looked up Swayco's number, then dialed it before he could back out. This could be a sure thing. The book might never make him a dime. "Hello, this is Bryan Cameron. I hear you're looking for a truck driver?" He listened to the job description, making affirmative sounds as the man on the other end talked.

Lani heard Bryan's voice and came into the living room. She could tell from the strained look on his face that something was bothering him.

"How much does it pay? Okay. Yeah, that sounds good all right." His eyes met Lani's, and his expression didn't match his words. "Okay, I'll be down about four o'clock."

When he hung up the receiver, he said, "I got a job."

"What? A job? With whom?"

"Swayco."

Lani sat on the arm of the chair. "That's a trucking company."

"I know."

"You aren't a trucker."

"No, but I need a job, and they are willing to hire me without my having had any experience." He was unwilling to meet her eyes. "Of course it means I'll be on the road some."

"So I assumed." She stood up and paced over to the window. If they were having this much trouble now, what would happen under the added strain of Bryan being gone for days or weeks on end. "I didn't know you were considering going to work for Swayco."

"Albert came by and said they were hiring. I know the man who is doing the interviews, and he hired me over the phone."

"I wish you had discussed it with me." She crossed her arms as if she were hugging herself and continued to stare sightlessly out the window.

"You aren't my mother," Bryan said defensively. "I don't need your permission."

"I am your wife. Before, we would have discussed it at length before you did something that would alter our lives."

"I had a job before. Things were different then."

"We aren't penniless," she snapped. "We aren't rich, either, but I make a good living!"

"That's just it! *You* make a living."

"You sound as if you're still living in the dark ages! What difference does it make who earns the living?" Her voice rose angrily, and even her hair seemed to crackle with emotion.

"I have my pride! I don't—"

"How are you going to write your book and drive a truck at the same time?"

"Obviously I won't. I'll work on that damned thing when I'm home," he said in an exasperated voice.

"I don't understand why you don't just forget the job with Swayco and stay home and work on the book. All I've heard lately is how badly you want to write this book. I know it's important to you. What happened to your dreams of making a career of writing?"

"The book hasn't sold. Richard only said there is interest in it. I don't even know what that means."

"It must mean that someone thinks it'll be worth publishing and may be willing to give you money for it. That's a job, Bryan!"

"There's a big jump between 'may be willing to give you money' and 'the check is in the mail.' Richard made no guarantees. At Swayco I know I'll be making a salary."

Lani stared at him. "I can't believe what I'm hearing. Are you saying you are going to give up writing the book to drive a truck for Swayco?"

He scowled at her. "I don't know what I'm saying!"

"Let's talk about it. Let's make the decision together." Her eyes pleaded for him to hear her.

"I have to decide this on my own."

"Why! This impacts my life, too!"

"You aren't the one driving the truck or writing the book. You have your own career. Remember? The one we never discussed?"

Lani drew back. "You needn't snap my head off!"

Bryan ran his fingers through his hair. She was right, of course, but he couldn't bring himself to admit it. She seemed to have no concept of how it felt to come back after so long an imprisonment and find everything changed and to feel you were no longer needed. "It's my decision, and I'll make it alone." He felt broken and stiff inside, and he wanted to put his arms around her, but she looked so angry that he didn't attempt it.

"I see. I forgot for a minute that you had turned into Mr. Macho."

He glared at her. He didn't feel macho—only worried and confused.

Lani went to the door of their bedroom and got her purse. "Since you don't need me for anything at all, I'm going over to see Debbie. I'll be home in time to put on a ruffled apron and cook you a perfect meal. Later I can sit on a cushion and do some tatting. Or maybe I'll just improve my mind by reading about new ways to take stains out of clothing—something feminine and nonthreatening."

Bryan was too angry to answer. Couldn't she be empathetic enough to see he was confused about what to do and know that he didn't want to fight? Evidently she couldn't, because she charged out of the house with such force the noise reverberated through the entire house. Feeling as weary as if he had been doing hard physical labor, Bryan sank into a chair. He had to figure out what to do, and he felt he had no margin for error. If he made a mistake, his marriage could be over. He wished Lani were as easy to talk to as she had been before.

As Lani drove to Debbie's house, tears clouded her vision and trickled down her cheeks. By the time she parked in Debbie's driveway, her nose was red and her face felt puffy. She blew her nose as she went up the walk and rang the bell.

"Good heavens!" Debbie exclaimed when she answered the door. "What happened!" She stepped aside to let Lani come in.

"We had another argument. Do you have any diet drinks? I'm hungry for junk food."

"Of course." Debbie's face mirrored her concern. "Go in the den and sit down while I get it."

When Debbie came in with two cold drinks and a bag of tortilla chips, Lani was sitting on the floor, leaning back against a chair. Debbie sat on the floor beside her. "Do you want to talk about it?" she asked, as she opened the bag of chips and offered it to Lani.

"No." Lani fished out a handful of chips and said, "Why are husbands so damned hard to understand?"

"Beats me."

"Do you know what Bryan has done? He took a job as a truck driver with Swayco!"

"That doesn't sound so terrible to me." Debbie began to munch on a chip.

"But he never even said he was considering it! Wouldn't Frank tell you if he was going to become a truck driver?"

"I would assume so."

"So did I. Debbie, he will never be home anymore. His cargo business had more travel than I was happy with, but he enjoyed flying so much I never said anything. Now he will be gone more often than he's home!"

"Many people have jobs that require them to travel these days," Debbie said reasonably. "Even Frank has seminars he has to attend in other cities and things like that. More chips?"

Lani took out another handful. "That's different. Frank is seldom away from home. Bryan will be gone more than he was as a pilot. And he didn't discuss it with me!"

"That's what really bothers you?"

"I don't know which bothers me more." She took a sip of her drink and added, "I don't want to talk about it."

"Okay."

"If we're having all these problems with him here, what will happen to our marriage if he's gone?"

"Maybe having some distance between you will help?"

"No, it won't. It will finish breaking us apart. And do you want to hear the corker? The agent called and encouraged him to finish the book as soon as possible, and now Bryan can't decide whether to do that or drive for Swayco!"

"Can't he do both?"

"Not and write as fast as he should. He can't type and drive at the same time."

Debbie sipped her drink. "What does he plan to do?"

"How should I know? He never tells me anything these days."

"Are you sure you aren't blowing this out of proportion? How are you feeling these days?"

"I'm fine. I still feel dizzy once in a while, but I'm getting used to it." She got more chips as she drank her drink. "I guess it's not the flu, or I'd be sick by now."

"Have you been nauseous?"

"No, I never get sick like that. Debbie, what am I going to do? Bryan acts as if he is the only one to make any decision or to earn any money. He wasn't this obstinate before."

"I guess Frank had better take him fishing again."

"Poor Frank. I don't think he's done this much fishing since I've known you."

"He doesn't mind, and as long as he cleans the fish, I don't object to cooking them."

"You're feeling all right then?"

"Better and better. Maybe I'll be one of those women who blooms when she's pregnant."

"I'll probably never get a chance to see what I would do in that condition," Lani said gloomily.

Debbie suppressed her smile.

"Take these chips away from me. I've eaten almost half the bag."

"Don't worry about that. I have more in the pantry."

Lani shook her head. "I can't seem to get enough tortilla chips these days. I'm becoming a junk-food junkie."

"I wouldn't worry about it."

"At least Helen Edwards hasn't called to say she saw Bryan with Monica again. At least that's something."

Debbie looked away.

Lani looked at her suspiciously. "What aren't you saying?"

"Bob told Frank that it's around town that Monica has her eye on Bryan. I'm sorry, Lani, but I thought you should know."

"Oh, great! That's all I need. Rumors that Bryan is seeing Monica really make my day."

"You know it isn't true."

"I know it and you know it, but everybody else in Laredo doesn't know it."

"Helen is a troublemaker, and Bob has gotten almost as bad. You talk about somebody changing, look how Bob is now that Harriet is gone."

Lani was frowning. "You don't think I'm being naive, do you? About Monica and Bryan, I mean?"

"Lani, when would he have time? He is always right there with you."

"You're right. I'm being silly."

Together they finished off the bag of chips and their soft drinks. Lani got up and wadded the bag into a ball. "I had better go home. By now Bryan may have decided to sell our home and become a ricksha jockey in China."

Debbie laughed. "Keep your sense of humor and try to get him to talk. If you can communicate, you can work it out."

"Okay. And you get ready to fry some more fish. Tell Frank I really appreciate all he's doing for us."

"That's what friends are for."

Lani drove home and parked her car under the shade of the cottonwood tree. For a minute she sat there, feeling the heat from outside seep into the car's cool interior. Whether or not Bryan wanted to hear it she had to voice her opinion. She firmly believed a marriage had to be give-and-take, and that both partners should be equals. She wasn't willing to settle for less.

As she caught her lower lip between her teeth, Lani asked herself what she really wanted Bryan to do. The trucking job involved travel, but it was also security. As an artist she lived with the risk that she might fall out of favor or that she might lose the whisper of the Muse that gave her inspiration. An artist's income was always a chancy thing, and Lani was too levelheaded to believe it offered real security.

Also, there was the matter of Bryan's pride. It had always been a major facet of his personality, but now it seemed to be his motivating force. Perhaps, she thought reluctantly, that was because he had had to live with no pride at all for years. She hated to think of that. The idea of Bryan in misery and poor living conditions made her feel physically ill.

On the other hand, what could bolster Bryan's wounded pride more than the sale of his own autobiography? Not to mention the fact that as a writer he wouldn't always be traveling all over the United States, and they would be more likely to work out their differences.

She got out of the car and walked across the lawn to the kitchen door. Bryan was leaning against the countertop as if he had been watching and waiting for her to come in.

For an awkward moment they stared at each other. "Are you still mad at me?" she asked at last.

"No. Are you mad at me?"

"Not anymore." She put her purse on the table and vaulted up to sit on the countertop so she was eye to eye with Bryan.

He leaned forward and put a hand on the counter on either side of her thighs. "You have a bad habit of storming off when you get mad. Next time stay put until we can work it out."

She looked at him warily. "Have you been thinking about what to do?"

"Yes, and I've come to the conclusion that you're right. We need to discuss it."

"I agree."

"Logically I know what to do. I should take the job as truck driver because it's a sure thing. There are no guarantees that this book will sell, and Richard Sinclair has told me a single book rarely brings in enough money to live on for long. I have no guarantee that I have another book in me or that it would sell if I did have. Oh, sure, I have lots of ideas, but I don't know if they are any good when it comes to writing."

"It sounds to me as if you've already made up your mind." She started to slide down from the countertop.

"Stay put. You aren't going to run away until I'm finished. I was going to say that on the other hand, I would rather write books than drive a truck. It's risky, but so is life. If I can manage to be a writer, we would probably make more money than I would as a trucker. And I still think the publicity could help nail the smugglers if they haven't already been caught."

"That's true, isn't it? They could have been caught and sent to prison—even years ago—and we would never have known."

"Or they might still be hiring gullible private pilots to haul their smuggled goods across the border."

"That's also true."

"So what do you think? Do we go for the sure thing or take a chance?"

"As you said, life itself is risky. I think we should go for broke. Write the book."

He nodded. "That's exactly what I had decided."

Lani finally smiled. "You had?"

"I've done a lot of thinking while you were gone. I enjoyed my cargo business, mainly because I would enjoy anything that gave me a reason to fly, but I was away from you more than I wanted to be. And I knew it would never be any different. I also knew that I would never make really big money. Oh, sure, I could have expanded, but the cost of insurance and other overhead expenses would also have gone up. I might never have made enough to retire comfortably. That's one of the problems with working for yourself."

"You'd be working for yourself as a writer, too."

"But I might be able to put enough aside to have a retirement account. Maintenance on my typewriter isn't nearly as expensive as it was on my plane. Right now we only deduct expenses related to your workshop on our income tax. I figure that we can add the back room and even our plane fares." He smiled. "Best of all, I'll be with you."

Lani's eyes softened. "Would you like that? I thought you were getting cabin fever from being here all day."

"I'll be the first to admit that I like to be busy. I have to have something to do or I feel like a caged lion. But finishing that book will keep me busy."

"Good point."

"So I'm going to try it." He went to the phone and dialed the number of the Swayco Company.

Lani listened as Bryan explained to the manager that he had decided not to take the job after all. She hoped he was making the right decision. It was what she had wanted him to do, but she had no special insight as to whether or not this book or any other would sell. She liked the way Bryan wrote, but she was far from impartial. Could he handle the uncertainty of not having a regular paycheck?

Bryan turned back to her. "It's done. I'm officially a writer. Again."

"I'm very proud of you," she replied.

"Go make some more of your little clay gods. We may need a lot of them to feed us until Richard can sell the book. You're the supporter in this family."

"I love you," she said.

"Jay, I'm not popping these things out of molds and spray painting them. It takes time!" She cradled the phone between her cheek and her shoulder and wiped off the clay mud on her hands.

"I'm not asking for that many more," Jay protested in a cajoling voice.

"I'm turning them out as fast as I can as it is. These aren't the only things I make, you know. I have pottery to send to shops, and there are my waterfalls."

"If you can't increase your production, I have another suggestion."

"What is it?"

"Make authentic reproductions of artifacts."

Lani was silent.

"Did you hear me?"

"Yes, I heard you. Jay, you know how I feel about that."

"I'm not suggesting anything illegal. I'm surprised that you think I might!"

"Come off it, Jay. What else would you call copies of actual artifacts that are even fired the way the Mayans did it? That's forgery no matter how you want to look at it."

"I can sell them for a lot of money," he said in a tempting voice. "A lot of money, indeed. Not that I would ever market them as originals. We could both get in trouble for that!"

"What else would they be good for that my original gods wouldn't serve?"

"Ever since the scandal about the Brigido Lara statues, people have been particular about buying Mayan art. It will be years before Lara can sort out with the museums which are fakes that he made and which are really authentic artifacts."

"I know. So why would that make me eager to jump in there with him?"

"His statues were sold as artifacts. I will sell yours as incredibly good copies."

"No way."

"At least think about it. With another mouth to feed I know you must need the money."

"Not badly enough to break the law."

"We wouldn't be breaking it. You trust me, don't you?"

Lani paused. "Of course I do." She had been surprised to find her instinctive answer hadn't been "no." "Jay, I've been meaning to ask you something. When did you move your studio?"

"What?"

"Your studio. Harmond Interiors. I went to the address you gave me, but I didn't find your studio. That is the address for a restaurant."

There was a pause on the phone line, then Jay laughed. "I have a new place a block over. Didn't I tell you?"

"No, you didn't. And the manager said he's been working in that restaurant for years."

Again there was a brief silence. "He has," Jay said with quick joviality. "I had rooms above the restaurant. The owner is a friend of mine, and he sends over my mail when anyone addresses it to the old place. Yes, I have a bright new office not far from there."

Lani frowned. Something about this wasn't ringing true. "When I couldn't find you at work, I went to your town house."

"Oh?"

"You weren't home." She wondered how she could say she had been surprised at the lack of elegance in his home. There was no tactful way to put something like that.

"I'm sorry I missed you. I'm in the process of redecorating the place, and I must have been out." This time his voice didn't sound quite so jovial.

"That's my fault for dropping by."

"Next time call first, and I'll be waiting for you with champagne in one hand and roses in the other."

"That won't be necessary." She felt suddenly awkward as if there were something going on just beneath the surface. "I shouldn't have come by."

"Nonsense. Nonsense, you're always welcome. Of course you'd have had to step over drop cloths and fabric samples, but I'd love to have shown you my place."

Lani's uneasiness grew. The town house had not had the look of a place with painters and other workmen about. And now Jay was actually pressuring her to copy authentic artifacts. Something was definitely wrong here! "Listen, Jay, I have to go. I'll have the order of gods ready for you in two weeks."

"And the other things I mentioned?"

"I won't copy any authentic artifacts. Not ever."

His voice was noticeably cooler as he said, "You're making a big mistake, Lani. A costly mistake, indeed."

"I have to go, Jay. Goodbye."

She hung up quickly and stood staring at the phone. She was actually trembling! Nervously, she backed away. There had been a misunderstanding—that was all. Naturally Jay was upset with her for not doing what he wanted her to do, but that was all there was to it. That last thing he had said about her having made a mistake—he had meant she had made a financial blunder. Only her overactive imagination had shaped it into a threat. That was all.

Lani closed her eyes and drew in a steadying breath. Her nerves were on edge because of Bryan's decision to write. Nothing else. There was no reason to be suspicious of Jay Harmond, and certainly there was no reason to fear him. The very worst that could happen would be for Jay to cancel his orders for the clay gods.

Actually, she thought to herself, that could be rather bad indeed. Those little clay gods would be the main source of their income until Bryan could sell his book.

Lani went back to her workbench. Income or no income, she wasn't going to break—or even bend—the law.

Chapter Twelve

Once Bryan resumed work on his book with a more positive attitude, he was amazed at his progress. Of course, allowing Lani and Debbie to do the bulk of his typing literally saved him weeks. Much sooner than he ever would have guessed, Bryan had his manuscript ready to send to Richard Sinclair. Richard read it and offered some suggestions to tighten the writing. Bryan revised the manuscript, put it back in the mail, and began pacing nervously.

"Bryan, you can't walk the floor until you get a reply. Didn't Richard tell you it could be as long as six weeks or maybe more before you hear anything?"

"Surely he was exaggerating. How could it take someone six weeks to read a book?"

"Beats me. I know, why don't you start another one? It will give you something to do besides wearing a hole in the floor."

He shook his head. "I'm too nervous to write. Maybe I made a mistake in not going with Swayco."

"You didn't make a mistake," Lani said comfortingly.

"Maybe if I had gone over the manuscript another time or two, I..."

"It was perfect. Quit worrying."

Bryan paced the length of the room again.

"I know what your next book can be about. It can be the story of a man who drove himself and his wife crazy while he waited for his manuscript to be sold."

"Very funny. How can it take six weeks for anybody to read a manuscript?"

Lani shook her head and sighed.

Three weeks later Richard Sinclair called Bryan. "Bad news, I'm afraid. They turned it down."

"What? But why?"

"The editor said she likes your writing style, but they recently bought an autobiography with a similar story—one about an Iranian hostage."

"My book isn't about Iran or a hostage."

"I know. She also said the ending wasn't satisfying."

"Satisfying?" Bryan was trying hard not to grit his teeth.

"She said it has a weak resolution—the bad guys get away scot-free."

"I know! That's one reason I wanted to write the book—so someone can catch the 'bad guys.' I'm not writing fiction. I told the story the way it happened. Is this editor playing with a full deck?"

Richard laughed. "That was just one editor's opinion. Not to worry. I haven't heard anything from the other two publishing houses I submitted it to."

"I can't believe anyone could turn it down. I poured my soul into that book!"

"All good writers do. I think the story is compelling and commercial. I was very pleased with the manuscript myself, and I am confident that it will sell. What else are you working on?"

"Nothing, really. I was too nervous about this one."

"The worst thing you can do is to sit around and worry about whether the book will sell. Get busy on something else for me."

"Should there be another one? Maybe I should forget it all."

"Nonsense. You have talent. Nobody ever said writing is easy. Get to work."

Bryan laughed. "You sound like my wife."

"Then she must be a very sensible lady. Take her advice."

"Okay. I'll do my best."

"Great. I'll let you know as soon as I hear anything about the book."

Bryan hung up. "Lani? That was Richard. I just got my first rejection."

A worried expression crossed her face, but then she brightened. "Big deal. I read somewhere that everyone gets rejections eventually."

"Where did you read that?"

"You aren't the only one in this family who goes to the library." She went to him and smoothed her hand over his soft beard. "You know, now that I've gotten used to this beard, I can't imagine you without it. Yet I never pictured you with one before."

"I'll shave it off, if you want me to."

"No, this is a reminder of who you are now as opposed to who you were then. It helps me remember that you won't necessarily think or act the way I expect."

"Am I that different?" he asked seriously.

"In some ways you aren't the same at all. In others I see the familiar Bryan I used to know. In fact you've become a bit more gentle than you were when you first came home, even a bit more vulnerable."

Bryan stiffened. "I hope I never get vulnerable again. It's a dangerous way to be."

Lani withdrew her hand. "I would never do anything to hurt you. There's no reason for you to keep your guard up constantly."

Bryan caught her hand and kissed her curving fingers. "If you were my only worry, I might be more trusting. But you aren't. Until I know what happened to me and why, I can't let down my shield. Maybe the Mexican government has no record of me, but someone knows that I was in jail and that I'm not now. They could come after me."

Lani's eyes grew large. "What? Why would they?"

"They may think I know more than I really do. They may even be right. There may be some scrap of information in my brain that means nothing to me, but that would incriminate whoever was behind it. I saw faces, I know the location of the pickup point. That alone could be enough to place us in some jeopardy."

"Why didn't you tell me this earlier?" Lani demanded. "Call Sheriff Armbruster and tell him."

"I already have. When I go to the library, I frequently stop by and talk to Armbruster."

Lani stepped closer and put her arms around him. "When will it all be over?"

Bryan shook his head. "I'll take care of you, Lani. You can depend on that."

"I do, Bryan." She closed her eyes and leaned against his strong body. She had no doubt that Bryan would defend her to the death, if need be, but who would defend Bryan? "Maybe Sheriff Armbruster was right, and you should have left well enough alone. Your book could stir up a hornet's nest."

"Yes. I know."

Lani had the feeling that Bryan was smiling. She held him tighter.

Lately Lani's odd, disjointed feeling had been replaced by a queasiness that always seemed to hit her around supper time. She didn't mention it to Bryan because she felt he had enough to worry about over the book. While she didn't feel ill enough to actually be sick, it was unlike Lani to feel bad for any length of time. She hoped it wouldn't be necessary to go to the doctor. With the pottery sales down, as they typically were after the big tourist season was over, she didn't want to spend the money just to have the doctor tell her she was suffering from stress.

Bryan loaded another box of pottery for Monica's store into their car's trunk as Lani fished her keys from her purse. "Are you sure you don't want to ride into town, Bryan?"

"No, I should stay here in case Richard calls."

"You can't hatch that phone like an egg. Remember about the 'watched pot' and all that? Our telephone recorder will take the call, if it comes in."

"I've had an idea lately I want to get on paper. You go ahead."

"Is it because I'm going to Monica's?"

"You got it." Bryan gave her a disarming smile.

"Why didn't you say so in the first place?" She tiptoed up and kissed him lovingly on his nose. "I'll be home in an hour or so. After I exchange this pottery for the ones that haven't sold, I'm going by Debbie's to give her the birth goddess I made for her."

"Take your time. I'll be right here keeping an eye on the phone."

Lani laughed as she got in the car and drove away. There had been less strain between Bryan and herself these past few days. Maybe he was becoming more accustomed to ordinary life. Or maybe it was only that the blistering heat of summer had finally moderated into early autumn, and his temper had followed suit. Soon she would have to return to Houston for her museum exhibit. She hoped Bryan would go with her; she was reluctant to go there alone.

Monica answered Lani's knock on The Outpost's back door and let her in with a casual greeting. She had just finished boxing the older bowls and platters. Lani opened the top of the box of the replacements and took out one of the new bowls. "I hope these sell well. See? I used a new glaze. What do you think?"

Monica took the bowl and examined it critically. "Very pretty. These will give a new look to the pottery section, and maybe that will stimulate sales. You know how it is, though. After tourists and before Christmas, it's always slow here."

"I know." Again she hoped that whatever was making her stomach churn and her skin feel clammy would go away before she had to consult a doctor.

Monica put the bowl on a worktable and wrote out a price tag as Lani continued unpacking. Offhandedly, Monica said, "How are things going with you?"

"Just fine."

"I've heard... never mind."

"Don't do that to me," Lani snapped, feeling quite dizzy and out of sorts.

Monica's eyes darted to Lani, then back to the bowls she was pricing. "I have heard you and Bryan are having, well, serious problems."

"What?" Lani's head snapped up. "Where would you hear a thing like that?"

"I forget exactly. You know how gossip is. You hear a bit here and a bit there. Before long everyone has heard."

"Are you saying it's all over town that Bryan and I are having marital problems?" Now Lani felt sick indeed.

"I wouldn't say it's all over town, but I have heard people mention it. Naturally I told them that it's news to me."

"It is to me, too. Bryan and I are doing just fine."

Monica didn't answer.

"Well, we are!"

"I believe you, Lani. My goodness, I have no reason to doubt your word."

Lani recalled what Helen Edwards had said about seeing Bryan and Monica together. The queasiness increased, and claustrophobia began to close in around her. "I have to go. Can you unpack the rest of these?"

"Of course." Monica's eyes narrowed as her red lips smiled. "Is something wrong?"

"No. No, of course not. I just have a lot of errands to run today."

Lani picked up the other box and didn't see Monica's calculating smile. "Goodbye, Monica. I'll check back with you in a couple of weeks."

"You do that," Monica purred.

Lani carried the box outside and balanced it on her knee as she fumbled with the trunk lock. The cooler air outside helped to clear her head, but as she struggled to get the box in the trunk, her hands slipped, and she heard the sickening crunch of dishes breaking. Lani lifted one side of the box and felt loose pieces slide to the other end. "Damn!"

she muttered. She had assumed Monica had used packing material between the pottery pieces.

She drove to Debbie's house and found her friend waiting for her on the breezeway. "Look!" Debbie said, standing to model her new blouse. "My first maternity top. I know I don't really need it yet, but somehow wearing one makes it feel more official."

"It's very pretty." Lani put the box she carried on the glass-topped table. "I brought you something."

"You did?" Excitedly Debbie unfastened the box and marveled as she removed the clay statue. "How lovely!"

"She's a birth goddess."

Debbie touched the figure's delicately molded features and her intricate headdress. "To look at it, you'd think she was a thousand years old!"

"Actually she has only been around a few weeks. I should have brought her over earlier but I've been snowed under with work."

"Business is booming?"

"No, only my work load. Jay seems to think I can mass-produce these things. Now he's pressuring me to make copies of real Mayan pieces."

"I hope you told him no! You could get in trouble doing that."

"You're telling me. Of course I refused, but he was really upset. He said I was making a big mistake." She frowned as she recalled the tone in his voice when he had said that. "He sounded almost threatening."

"Threatening?" Debbie stared at her friend in concern. "He threatened you?"

"No, no. Not in so many words. I guess it was just the way I took it. Debbie, I've been so out of sorts here lately."

"You still aren't feeling well, are you?"

"No, I'm not, and it's starting to worry me. I've never handled stress well, and I've been under an unbelievable amount these past few weeks."

"I see. Do you have any interesting symptoms?"

"Just what I told you before. Dizziness, queasy and just, well, odd."

"Lani, don't you see what it must be?" Debbie asked gently.

Lani looked blank, then her eyes widened. "You think I'm *pregnant*?"

"It could be."

Lani eased herself down in the nearest chair. "Pregnant! No, I can't be." Her eyes darted around the room as she tried to remember the last time she had looked at her calendar. A slow smile lifted her lips, and her green eyes became dreamy. "I guess I *could* be." Then she shook her head, and the light went out of her eyes. "I don't know what Bryan would say about it."

"He would probably be tickled pink like any other father-to-be."

"The old Bryan would have been, but this one is full of surprises. And if his book doesn't sell, we frankly can't afford to have a baby."

"It may be a little late to consider that."

"What are we doing?" Lani said with a laugh as she jumped up. "We don't know that I'm expecting a baby, and here I am trying to figure out how to pay the doctor bills! Pretty silly, huh?" She looked at Debbie as if for support.

"We may be jumping to the wrong conclusion, but if the symptoms are still there a couple of weeks from now, I think you should go to the doctor."

"A baby!" Lani said softly. "Bryan's baby."

Bryan was busy sorting through papers on his desk. Somewhere he had written down some notes about an Indian tribe that had lived on the land he now owned. A history of the tribe would be interesting, and there were plenty of legends to add spice. His father had once told him that their own bloodline could be traced to the chief of the tribe. Bryan wondered if this book would have enough general interest for Richard to sell it.

The jangle of the telephone startled Bryan. He looked for the phone, but didn't see it. It rang a second time. Where had he put it? he wondered. Not for the first time he wished he'd replaced this new phone—with its bird-tweeter ring—with one of the older types that had the familiar bell. On the third ring, he discovered it beneath a stack of booklets and papers on his desk. Grabbing it, he said brusquely, "Hello?"

There was a pause. "May I speak to Lani?" a male voice asked.

"She isn't here right now. Who's calling?" He balanced the phone on his shoulder as he continued to search for his elusive notes.

"This is Jay Harmond."

Bryan became rigid. "She isn't here," he repeated. "Can I take a message?"

Again there was a pause. "I just wanted to ask her when she will be in Houston for the Museum of Cultures show. I thought it might be a good time for us to get together and talk about the business deal I proposed to her."

What deal? Bryan wondered. "*We* will be down for the show on the evening of October eighth. That will give Lani a full day to set up her waterfalls. We could possibly meet with you later that day to talk business."

"I see."

The constraint Bryan detected in Jay's voice caused his anger to flare. "I'm sure Lani would prefer for me to come along since you'll be discussing business. I'm more or less her manager now." This much was true. Lani disliked handling bank accounts and keeping records, so Bryan had started doing this for her.

"I see," Jay repeated. He didn't sound pleased. "Tell Lani I'll have to check my appointment calendar and get back to her."

"Sure thing." Bryan smiled grimly. He was damned if he was going to make an appointment for his wife to have a tête-à-tête with the man who was trying to get her into the sack. Bryan hung up more forcefully than was necessary.

Again Bryan ruffled through the papers. He found a receipt that he would need for his income tax return, a phone number in his handwriting but without a name, a pamphlet on raising chickens and a news clipping on Christmas tree farms, but not a shred of information on Indian tribes.

He thrust his hands into the hip pockets of his jeans and frowned at his disheveled office. One day soon he was going to have to take the time to organize it. He still found it remarkable that he had accumulated so much disorder in so little time.

The doorbell rang, and Bryan went to answer it. He wasn't expecting company, but it wasn't unusual for Albert to drop by if he was driving out this way. With his mind still on the missing article, Bryan opened the door.

"Hello," Monica sighed seductively.

Bryan stared at her. "Monica? What are you doing here? Lani has gone in to see you."

"Yes, I know. May I come in?"

Although he wanted to refuse, he knew he couldn't. "Sure. Come on in."

"Lani was in a hurry when she came by and she forgot to get her receipt." Monica's talonlike nails dipped into her alligator bag and produced a slip of paper.

Bryan took it gingerly. "I'll see that she gets it."

"Let me go over it with you so there is no misunderstanding." Monica glided past Bryan in such a way that her breast grazed his forearm. He was sure it hadn't been an accident.

She went to the waist-high entry table and put her purse and car keys to one side. When she bent over the table to point at the itemized sheet, her silk blouse gaped open revealing the shallow cleavage of her breasts. "See?" she asked innocently. "Lani left five bowls; one large, two medium and two small. I also have three small platters; one medium and two large ones. The large ones may not sell, I'm afraid. The size is rather difficult to store in a kitchen cabinet. But, we'll see." She shifted, and her lace-enclosed breasts were in plain view.

Bryan scowled and forced himself to nod. The woman was as blatant as a hooker. "This all seems quite clear to me."

"Yes, but look here." Monica reached over his hand to point at a notation on the far side of the paper. "I forgot to include the small carafe from the last batch she brought me. It's too large for a milk pitcher and too small for wine. I don't think I can sell it."

"Did you bring it with you?"

"No, foolish me. I forgot it. Could you come by and pick it up?" Monica's eyes slanted as she tilted her head coyly. "I have it in my back room."

"*Lani* can pick it up the next time she's in town." He wasn't about to agree to go himself.

"Whatever." Her red lips pouted.

Bryan straightened. "Is that all? I'll show the receipt to Lani as soon as she comes home."

"I hate to bother you, but could I ask your advice about something?"

"I suppose so."

Monica moved farther into the living room, her blue eyes appraising the decorating touches Lani had added to her home. "As you know, I haven't lived here for long."

"Yes?"

She looked back at him over her shoulder. "It's rather embarrassing for me to mention it, but I haven't met very many people." She gazed at a watercolor print that echoed the peach-and-gold tones of the sofa.

"I can't help you much there. You just have to get out and meet people. Join a club or something."

"You're right, of course. It just sounds so easy when someone says it." She bent and ran her fingers over the fabric of the couch. Her tight skirt hugged her derriere as if it had been painted on.

Bryan looked away. "I'm afraid I'm not the one to help you. I've been gone, you know. Many of the people I knew have moved, and I haven't made many new friends myself. I wouldn't know what to suggest."

"It's so sweet of you, really, to even listen to me." Monica's voice sounded as if she were suppressing tears, but she kept her back to him. "Most people don't know this, but I'm so terribly lonely."

"Monica, I don't—"

"My marriage was a very unhappy one. Donald was a terribly cruel man. Not that he ever struck me—I don't mean that—but he was mentally and emotionally cruel."

Bryan wasn't sure what to say. He couldn't push her out of the house if she was actually on the verge of tears as she sounded, but he was terribly uncomfortable with the degree of intimacy she was assuming.

"When I moved here, I had money, but no self-esteem at all," she continued in a pitiful voice. "He had convinced me that I was unattractive and undesirable to any man." She turned to face Bryan so that he could see the tears in her eyes. "Can you imagine what that has done to me?"

"I find it hard to believe."

"Thank you, but it's true." Monica's fingertips delicately touched the corners of her eyes. "I find it almost impossible to trust men after Donald."

"Monica, you really ought not to be telling me all this. You'll wish you hadn't, I'm afraid."

"But don't you see, Bryan? You're different. I can trust you. God, do you know how long it's been since I said that to a man?" Monica's eyes brimmed, and tears coursed over the makeup on her cheeks.

"What you need is a glass of ice water." Bryan almost bolted from the room. How in the hell had he gotten into this, he demanded of himself as he threw a handful of ice cubes into the first glass he could find.

"I'm not a cold woman," Monica called from the next room. "I'm not. No matter what Donald said, I've got feelings just like anyone else."

"We all have feelings, Monica." Bryan shoved the glass under the tap and filled it with water. How was he going to get rid of her? He wished Lani were home.

"Do you think I'm unattractive, Bryan?" she called out.

He didn't answer. Was that the sound of a car pulling into the drive? He leaned forward and peered out the window as the fender of Lani's car passed by. Thank goodness she was home. Together they could get rid of Monica.

"Here's your water," he said cheerfully as he went back into the living room. When he saw Monica standing there in her bra and skirt, he stopped as if he had been turned to stone.

"I'm not an unattractive woman," Monica said earnestly as she whipped off her bra. "I could make you happy!"

Just then the front door opened, and Lani came in. "Is that Monica's car out front? I..." When Lani saw Monica and her bare breasts, her mouth dropped open.

Bryan hurried to his wife's side. "Lani, this isn't what it looks like. Monica brought a receipt by, and..."

"Lani!" Monica gasped at the same time. "I thought you had some errands to run!"

Lani felt as if her world had shattered. She saw Monica trying ineffectually to hide her breasts and Bryan standing there with a drink in his hand, but it hardly made sense. "Get dressed, Monica," she heard herself say.

"Lani," Bryan said with an edge of desperation in his voice. "I know what this looks like, but..."

"Don't make it worse, Bryan," Monica said as she scrambled into her bra and blouse. "She won't believe you."

"Lani, nothing was going on! Monica was telling me about her divorce and she started to cry, so I went to the kitchen to get her a glass of water and when I came back she was like that!"

Monica hastily buttoned her blouse and shoved her shirttail into the tight waist of her skirt. "I had no idea you'd be home so soon," she murmured.

Silently Lani went to Bryan and took the glass from him. She put it to her lips and tasted it. Water! All at once relief poured over her, and she felt incongruous laughter start to bubble past her lips. Suddenly the whole scene was so ludicrous that Lani burst out laughing.

"What's so funny!" Monica demanded. "Are you crazy? You caught me half naked with your husband, and you're laughing?"

Lani laughed harder. The look on Monica's face was ridiculous, and Bryan looked even funnier.

"Honey? Are you okay?" he asked in concern. "Lani?"

With an effort Lani brought herself under control. "Monica, get the hell out of our house," she said between laughs.

"Well!" Monica exclaimed. "I've heard of stupid women before, but you take the prize! You must have heard the rumors going around town!"

"What rumors?" Bryan demanded.

"Of course I have," Lani said as she dried her eyes, "but I don't believe them." She looked up at Bryan and slipped her arm around his waist. "You see, I love my husband, and you can't love someone—really love them—and not trust them. If Bryan says nothing was going on, then I believe him."

Monica grabbed her purse off the table and flounced to the door. "You're a foolish woman, Lani Cameron! The most foolish woman I've ever seen!"

Lani didn't look around. "I'll send someone in to pick up my pottery. Under the circumstances I don't care to sell my work through your stores."

Monica slammed the door so hard the windows rattled.

Bryan eyed his wife warily. "There really wasn't anything going on."

"I know."

"How do you know?"

"For the reasons I told her. If you could have seen the looks on your faces, you would have laughed, too."

"I doubt it. God, Lani! I've never been so scared in my life as when I came in here and saw her half naked, and knew you were coming through the door!"

Lani smiled and put down the glass so that she could put both arms around him. "You were vulnerable, Bryan."

He gazed down at her, his dark eyes searching her face. "Maybe a little."

"Maybe a lot?"

"I still don't understand why you aren't mad as hell."

"I am—at her. You were her victim."

"Most wives wouldn't see it that way."

"I know you, Bryan. If you were fooling around, it wouldn't be with a vampire like Monica Denton. And you wouldn't have a glass of ice water in your hand. And you would certainly be smarter than to fool around *here*. No, I believe you."

"You think you're pretty smart, don't you?" he asked as he relaxed a bit. A slow smile lifted his lips.

"I know I am."

"You realize, of course, this could have blown our marriage apart?"

"Yes." Lani smiled up at him. "I have to admit, before today I was becoming jealous of you and Monica. Helen Edwards has spread it all over town that you two are having an affair. When I first walked in, I was stunned."

"Then why would you believe me?"

Lani's smile disappeared. "Because if I hadn't believed you, our marriage would have been over."

"I love you, Lani. I've never wanted another woman and I never will."

She edged him down the hall toward their bedroom. "Prove it. Right now I need for you to make love with me."

Bryan grinned. "I'm just the man for that."

Chapter Thirteen

Lani was glad she had come to Houston in time to set up the waterfall exhibit. Ella Marset had understood the details of assembling the cascades, but she had not understood the subtly significant part the water was to play. Lani moved among her treasures, tilting a bowl here, leveling a shell there, until each had the sound and appearance she wanted.

"It's rather damp," Ms. Marset said with a sniff. "I hadn't expected so much humidity."

Lani nodded. "That's why I specified that no paintings or moisture-sensitive works were to be exhibited in the same area of your building until my show is over."

"Thank goodness it's not cold yet. We can run the air conditioner and take the humidity out of the air. My goodness, but it's damp in here!"

"One sculpture in a house will serve as a humidifier. Twenty-five makes it more like a steam bath."

"I'll see to the air conditioner," the woman said as she moved away.

Lani said to Bryan, "I tried to tell her all this when I was down here for the initial interview. I thought they understood the humidity problem."

"She'll cope," Bryan reassured her. "Ms. Marset looks as if she could cope with anything."

"I guess that's everything for tonight." Lani glanced around the spacious room. "How does it look?"

"Spectacular. Suggesting they bring in all those tall potted plants was an inspiration. It's like a civilized jungle."

"It does look rather nice at that. Oh, Bryan, I'm so nervous! What if nobody shows up? No one knows who I am."

"People will come. I saw the article in the newspaper, and it was a good write-up. Houstonians love their museums, according to Ms. Marset. You'll have a good crowd."

"Get me out of here before I start to rearrange it all over again."

As Bryan helped her turn off the pump motors on all the fountains, the splash and gurgle slowly ebbed from the room. Their footsteps seemed loud on the slate floor as they went to the back door. The night janitor let them out and secured the door behind them.

Although the hour was late, a steady stream of cars passed by the museum. Overhead a few brave stars penetrated the cloudy sky. After Laredo, Houston seemed like a different country.

"We're a long way from home," Bryan commented as he opened her car door.

"Whoever would have guessed that Lani Keyes would grow up to be Lani Cameron and have a sculpture exhibit in a Houston museum? I still can't quite believe it. This is a tremendous event in my career."

"Today the Museum of Cultures, tomorrow the Museum of Fine Arts."

"It may take me a little longer than that," she said with a laugh. "But I would like to go there for a visit while we're here."

"Let's take a couple of extra days and call it a vacation," Bryan suggested.

"Can we do that?"

"We're already here. Why not? Galveston is just an hour away. When was the last time you walked on a beach?"

She smiled. "It was on our honeymoon."

Bryan reached out and touched her smooth cheek. "That's what I thought," he said softly.

Lani slid into the car, and Bryan went around to the driver's side. He backed out of the museum parking lot onto the side street that fed into the busy thoroughfare. "How do people live with traffic all day, every day? I'd go crazy."

"I guess they get used to it. Our turnoff is at this next corner."

Their hotel was nearby—one of Houston's finest. It was older than the one that had awed her in Chicago, but nonetheless elegant. The lobby was paneled in golden oak, and thick Oriental rugs had been strategically placed over the marble floor to define several conversation areas. Palms and ficus benjamina trees lent a woodland setting to the informal dining area that spilled out into the back part of the huge lobby. Beyond she saw a formal dining room with candles and snowy white tablecloths.

Not only was the hotel's ambience gracious and friendly, but the staff was as well. Although Lani wore jeans and a pullover sweater, an outfit suitable for arranging sculptures, the concierge treated her as if she were attired in a ball gown. The bellhop respectfully nodded to them as they went to the elevator, and with a warm smile he held the brass doors open for them until they were safely inside. Lani felt truly welcome here.

The doors closed silently, and Lani leaned her head back with a sigh. "Just imagine being able to actually live like this!"

"You'd be homesick in a month."

"But what a month it would be!"

The elevator stopped at their floor, and they walked hand in hand down the hallway to their room at the far end, their steps muted by the plush delft-blue carpeting beneath their feet. "This is my favorite hotel," Lani whispered to Bryan, "but it must be costing the museum a small fortune for us to stay here."

"It is, but I found out they have a package deal for a longer stay that's terrific."

"You mean we're going to stay here? I assumed we would move to a less-expensive place."

"We're on vacation. We deserve to be pampered." He slid the magnetic key card into the door slot, and the electronic lock responded with a muffled click. Bryan pushed open the door and politely waited for Lani to enter first.

As was the lobby, their room had been decorated in shades of gold, ivory and blue. Two chairs that would have graced the living room of even the most discriminating of guests were arranged in front of the floor-to-ceiling window around a small antique oak table that was topped with a bouquet of silk flowers. Side tables of a similar style flanked the brass-appointed bed. Their maid had turned down the covers, exposing the pale blue sheets. A chocolate mint had been left on each pillow with a handwritten note from the maid wishing them a good night's sleep.

"How wonderful," Lani breathed. "We've been tucked in."

Bryan laughed and tossed her one of the mints. "All the comforts of home."

"I don't recall ever finding a mint on my pillow there," she countered. "And the bellhop was definitely missing."

"A small detail." Bryan walked toward her as he unwrapped his mint. "For the next few days, you don't own any dusty jeans, and I don't work on Jeeps." He fed her the mint that he held, and opened his mouth to accept the one he'd tossed to her.

"Just two happy-go-lucky millionaires out on the town?" she teased with love shining in her eyes.

"That's right. Since the museum is providing us this room, the staff seems to think you're a famous sculptress."

"Do you think so?"

"And that I'm just your gigolo."

Lani laughed. "Surely they think you're at least my chauffeur. You did drive me here, you know."

Bryan nuzzled the ticklish part of her neck, and although Lani laughed and squirmed as though she wanted him to stop, he didn't have much difficulty holding her still so he could continue. "Chauffeur, huh?"

"Okay, okay. You can be the gigolo," she panted with laughter. "Now stop that before we get thrown out of here!"

Bryan stopped tickling her, but he kept his arms around her. "I'm proud of you."

"What brought that on?"

"I was watching you while you set up the sculptures. You were so knowledgeable, so certain of what you wanted."

"My sculptures are my babies," she said, then paused. She had not yet told Bryan about her pregnancy. She had planned to wait until a doctor had confirmed it.

Almost wistfully, Bryan said, "You know, I wish we had had a baby right away." With his open palm, he stroked Lani's red-gold hair. "I know I was the one to say we should wait, but I was wrong."

"It's not too late."

"But now I know how uncertain life can be. Lani, it did something to me, being caught and caged like that. I always thought if a person stayed straight with the law, he was safe. I lost years for no reason at all. If it happened once, it could happen again, couldn't it?"

"I don't think writers are as subject to that as cargo pilots."

"No? What if I have to do some research that takes me into a troubled area? We lose war correspondents all the time."

"Then don't write about wars."

He shook his head. "You know what I mean. Life is so uncertain."

"It always has been. What are you trying to tell me?"

Bryan sat on the bed and drew Lani down onto his lap. "I want to start a family, but I'm afraid of the responsibility. I guess I'm trying to convince myself that it's better not to bring a baby into such a troubled world."

"You should have convinced yourself of that sooner," she said. "I think I'm pregnant."

Bryan stared at her as if he couldn't digest the words.

"The world is no more troubled now than it has been or will be. You just saw it at its worst."

"You're pregnant?"

"I think so."

"You shouldn't have been lifting those bowls for the waterfalls! What do you mean, you think so? Honey, are you all right?"

Lani laughed. "Of course I am. I haven't seen a doctor yet, but Debbie says she felt the same way I do."

"Why didn't you tell me?"

"I wanted to be sure first." She hesitated, then added, "And I wanted to be sure you'd be happy about it."

"Happy! Of course I'm happy! How could you think I would be otherwise?"

"Our marriage has been strained lately. At times I wasn't sure if you wanted it to continue—much less that you would welcome the complications of a baby."

Bryan stared at her. "You thought *I* wanted to end our marriage?"

"I want you to know that this baby isn't meant to patch up the marriage. Babies can't do that. If you aren't absolutely certain you want to stay married to me, you have to promise me that you won't stay just for the baby's sake. I'll let you see him as often as you wish and..."

"Will you shut up a minute? I don't want to leave you. It's the other way around."

"What? That's ridiculous. I love you."

"What about Jay? He called last week, incidentally, and left his new studio address. I threw it away."

"Why would you do a thing like that? How will I know where to write him?"

"That was what I had in mind."

Lani tried to stand up, but he pulled her back onto his lap. "You're crazy! Do you know that?"

"Maybe so, but I don't trust Harmond. If you need to communicate with him, I'll do it for you."

"He's afraid of you for some reason. We can't afford to alienate him until your book sells. Remember?"

Bryan refused to let his jealous thoughts or his anxiety over finances spoil the moment. Playfully he toppled her over onto the bed and leaned over her. "Are you really having our baby?"

She nodded, thoughts of Jay Harmond disappearing from her mind. "I'm almost certain."

He put his large hand on her slender waist and stroked her flat stomach. "Our baby." His voice was choked with emotion.

Lani covered his hand with hers. "Do you want a boy or a girl?"

"I don't care. I just want you to be okay. As soon as we go home, you're going to the doctor."

"All right."

"I'll move my office down to the back room. We should have the baby sleep close to us so we can hear him in the night. Or her. The walls need painting if we're going to use it as a nursery."

"I think that would be a good idea," she agreed, thinking of the vibrant blue Bryan had impulsively painted the walls when he decided to use it as his office.

"Or maybe the baby will like bright colors. There's no rule that says they have to have pastels everywhere, is there?" He thought for a minute. "I think I'll paint my new office green. What do you think? Something like the color of river moss."

"We have plenty of time to discuss it," she said with a smile.

"A baby," he repeated softly. "Say, are you feeling okay now? Maybe we should go home after the show opens tomorrow."

"And miss my second honeymoon? No way!"

Bryan smiled tenderly at her. "I love you, Lani." His hand stroked her middle. "And I love our baby-to-be."

"You know, this is one of the few times I've seen you so gentle since you came home. Maybe you aren't so different after all. Maybe I had blown you into such a paragon in my memory that you were never that way at all."

"No, honey, I have changed. Just as you have. But that doesn't have to be bad. Maybe this way is even better for us."

"I love you," she whispered.

"Is there any rule about not making love when you're pregnant?" he asked as his hand found her breast.

Lani shook her head. "Not yet. Not for months and months."

He lowered his head and claimed the willing sweetness of her lips.

Lani felt as if she were still glowing from Bryan's lovemaking as the museum's doors opened and the first viewers entered. She saw him across the room, attentive to her yet standing back so that she could bask in her limelight. A sensual smile tugged at her lips as she memorized the lean shape of his body and the way his navy suit made him look even more like a pirate traveling incognito.

Lani confidently mingled with the crowd, answering their questions as though she did this sort of thing all the time. No one knew she had started the day trembling like a leaf. Several patrons made discreet inquiries about purchasing her waterfalls after the show was over, and as she and Bryan had prearranged, she referred them all to Bryan, who was acting as her manager. She and Bryan had agreed on a basic price for each piece and that he would ask for more—if he thought he could get it. She had explained to him that the museum was conducting the exhibit for art's sake, not for profit, but Ms. Marset had given her permission to discuss potential sales with the museum's patrons as long as she didn't initiate the idea or allow any of the pieces to leave the museum before the show was over. She had been somewhat nervous about turning over the price negotiations to anyone, but her trust in Bryan's judgment was stronger by the end of the day. From the broad smile on his face, she was certain he had made several sales, and she was glad she had put her confidence in him. During a lull later in the afternoon, Lani drifted over to Bryan and whispered, "I was watching you from across the room, and you remind me of a man I made love with all last night."

"I thought you looked familiar!" he teased. "Are you busy later this evening?"

"If I'm lucky."

"You'd better not keep tempting me or we're going to disappear behind that potted palm and really give them something to see."

"Promises, promises," she said with the satisfied smile of a woman who is well loved. "I'm surprised how many have asked if the waterfalls are for sale."

"You're going to be even more surprised when you hear what I got for them." He pulled a notepad from the inside pocket of his coat and flipped it open to the back page where he was keeping a running total.

Lani's eyes widened. "You can't be serious. They must have thought you were joking."

"I also have checks and the addresses where they are to be delivered. We'll fly down and take care of that the day after the show closes."

Lani looked back at the notepad. "You've sold them for more than I've made in two years!"

"It's a museum show," he said with a shrug. "They didn't expect cut-rate prices."

"Bryan, do you realize what this means?" she asked in excitement. "If I can find a regular outlet where I can make money like this, I won't have to make pottery for shops like Monica's!"

"Or clay gods for Jay Harmond."

She smiled up at him. "Is that your ulterior motive?"

"Of course. That's why I quadrupled the basic price you set. And it worked."

"It's very tempting," Lani admitted, "but I have no guarantees that I can continue to sell at this rate."

"There are no guarantees in life at all. Remember? A wise woman once told me that."

"I have to go. Some more people are coming in. Keep up the good work."

He gave her a bedroom wink that made her blush. After taking a moment to regain her composure, she hurried back to greet the newcomers.

By closing time Bryan had sold a number of the sculptured waterfalls and had taken orders for several more.

"I should have had you as my manager all along," Lani marveled, when they were back at the hotel. "I never dreamed I would sell a single one, let alone half a dozen. And the prices people were willing to pay for them astounds me!"

"For those who placed orders, you'll have to work up sketches for their approval before those deals are finalized, but I wrote down the type of sculptures they preferred."

"You're magnificent!"

"It's hard for an artist to bargain over his own work. That's what has held you back. When you look at your adobe-style sculpture, for instance, you think of the vacation we took once to the pueblo ruins in Colorado and how it rained that day, and your memories get in the way of your business sense."

"You're right. As I've said before, the waterfalls are like my children. It's hard for me to price them."

"But it isn't for me. Also, I have this little gem as an added bonus." He presented her with a business card.

"Who? I never heard of him." Lani looked curiously up at Bryan.

He flipped the card over so that she could read the note scribbled on the back. "He owns a museum in Austin and would like to negotiate your having a show there in two months."

Lani gave a choked cry of excitement. "Another museum? In Austin? Oh, Bryan! We've made it!" She threw herself into his arms and squeezed him tightly. "We've really done it! Now we really can afford to stay here a couple of more nights!" she said with shining eyes. She waved the checks in the air. "It's not a fortune, but it looks like one to me!"

Bryan laughed softly and held her close. This was her moment of glory, yet she was saying "we." Before this show, he had never felt she wanted him to be a part of her work. He was glad to have found a way to be useful. Although Lani had the creative genius and had done all the work, he had seen to it that those who wanted her sculptures paid a fair price for them.

Although he was very proud of her success, a part of him was envious. After lunch, while Lani was powdering her nose, he had called his agent and learned that his book had had another rejection. But the result of the news hadn't been all bad, because his frustration had made him an even tougher negotiator for Lani that afternoon.

At the moment, however, the bruise to his ego was painfully sore.

"If I bomb out as a writer, I guess I can always hire on as your manager."

"You're going to be my manager even if you hit the bestseller list! Bomb out indeed. Just wait until you talk to Richard! I'll bet he's selling your book right this very minute."

Bryan smiled and didn't contradict her. Lani was happier than he had seen her since his return, and he didn't want to do anything to mar her joy.

The next day they headed for Galveston Island for a quiet stroll on the beach. As they had anticipated, most of the tourists had packed up and gone, but the sands were far from deserted. It appeared as though the majority of Houston's and Galveston's teenage population had permanently settled on the pale tan beaches.

However, at the west end of the island, they found a strip of sand without the blare of radios or the shrieking of teenagers. They parked on the firm sand and walked arm in arm along the damp crescents left by the receding waves.

"We ought to be thinking of a name," Bryan said seriously.

"For the baby? We have months yet. I don't even know if I'm really pregnant."

"You are."

"How do you know?"

"You feel different. Now that I know what to look for, I can tell the difference. And your nipples are darker. I've read that's a sign."

"I didn't know we were playing doctor last night."

Bryan laughed. "How about Cuthbert?"

"For our baby? Forget it!"

"I had an Uncle Cuthbert and I was very fond of him."

"Nope." She thought a minute. "How about Cassie? My best friend in high school was named Cassie."

"No, I knew a Cassie once who was stuck-up. What about Mellisande?"

"No one but you could spell it. How about Bryan, Junior?"

"Or Lani the Younger?"

"I see your point. The baby needs a name of his or her own." Lani looked out at the endlessly rolling sea and breathed in the tangy air. "I hope I'm really pregnant."

"If you aren't now, you will be." Bryan pulled her back against his chest and rested his cheek on the top of her head as he gazed out over the gray waters of the Gulf of Mexico. "I love the beach. It's a shame Laredo is so far inland."

"We could move."

"I love our farm, too. Maybe someday we'll have enough money for a beach house. Would you like that?"

Lani nodded. "It reminds me of our honeymoon. Remember? We were going to change the world and knew just how to accomplish it."

"We were so young. A lot has happened since then."

"Bryan, I've been thinking. Let's use some of the sculpture money for you to go back to college."

"After all this time? I couldn't do that." But his voice was wistful.

"You only have two years to go until you have your degree."

He was thoughtful. "You hear of people doing that. Going back and finishing, I mean. I might be able to."

"I know you could." She turned to face him. "Please, Bryan. I want this for you."

Bryan lovingly touched her face. "You're good to me, Lani."

"I love you."

"I've always regretted not getting my degree."

"I know."

A grin broke over his face. "I'll do it!"

"And when you finish, I'll start." Lani said with excitement. "I never told you, but I regret not getting a degree, too."

"We could both go at once."

She smiled. "One of us has to stay home and baby-sit."

His grin widened. "Oh, yeah. I forgot."

Lani felt as if she would explode from so much happiness.

"How about Hildegarde or Horatio?"

"Nope," she said happily as she matched her steps to his.

"Adolphis if it's a boy; Adolphia if it's a girl."

"Forget it, Bryan. I should never have brought up the subject of names." Lani pulled her lightweight sweater more closely around her shoulders against the air-conditioned chill of NASA's visitor center.

"I would have noticed, don't you think?" He peered into the display case that housed a collection of lunar rocks. "Just think, that came from the moon."

"It's hard to believe, isn't it?" She turned to look up at the Gemini spacecraft that was suspended from the ceiling and the cutaway of an Apollo spacecraft that revealed the cramped quarters the astronauts had had to endure on their trip to the moon and back. "We've actually sent men to explore the moon. Sometimes that's hard to believe."

"And there is talk of a cooperative venture between us and the Soviets to go to Mars. Maybe space exploration such as that will help in bringing the countries of the world closer together. Maybe our children will actually go to another planet."

"Or our grandchildren. It's like a fantasy, isn't it?"

"I wonder how Richard would like a book on space travel." Bryan looked at the black walls of the room as he pondered. "I would have to come here to research it, and that would be a great excuse for renting a beach house."

"Sounds good to me. Maybe you should call Richard and see if there has been any news."

Bryan turned away. "When we go back home, I'll call him."

"Is there something you're not telling me?"

Bryan gave her an innocent grin. "Of course not."

"Yes, there is!"

"All right, I talked to Richard the day your museum show opened. I've had another rejection."

"Oh. Well, that's not so bad. There are a lot of publishers. Richard will sell it. You'll see."

"Of course he will." Bryan wanted to dismiss the subject.

Lani put her hand in his, and they wandered down the hall lined with photos of Jupiter's moons, then to the room where a lunar-landing module sat. "Even if this book doesn't sell," she said carefully, "it doesn't mean the end of the world. Richard says you have a talent for writing. Maybe your idea about a book on Indians will be the one."

"You know how important it is to me for this book to sell, Lani."

"I know, honey, but you've given it your best shot."

Bryan opened the door for her, and they stepped out into the sultry air. "It's not just the book. I feel as if *I* am being rejected when it's turned down. It's as if all I went through isn't worth four dollars and fifty cents, or whatever the cover price is these days. Do you know how that makes me feel?"

"I know, but you're looking at it all wrong. They aren't rejecting you, only the book."

"This editor had the same complaint as the other one—weak ending. Hell! It's the only ending there is! That was my whole idea, to write something that will catch these smugglers. Also she wanted Richard to ask me why I never say for sure what was being smuggled. If I knew that, I might be able to catch them myself!"

Lani looped her arm through his as they sauntered toward a duck pond between the office buildings. "Don't be discouraged. You've started the Indian book, and now you have an idea for a space book. It will all work out."

Bryan looked down at her. "Do you really have that much confidence in me? Even when I don't?"

"I always have confidence in you. Just as you do in me."

"You're a good friend. You know that?"

Lani smiled and winked at him.

"You know, maybe we should stay on vacation forever. There are no Monicas ripping off blouses here or Harmonds trying to seduce you."

"Jay could no more seduce me than Monica could you."

Bryan was suddenly quiet, and Lani felt the barrier rising between them that had been absent for days. "Don't pull away just because I said his name. Don't you trust me at all?" Her voice took on a testy edge as she released Bryan's arm.

"You're the one who's pulling away, not me. And yes, I trust you. That business with Monica taught me a great deal about trusting the one you love. I just don't trust Harmond."

Lani turned her attention to the ducks on the pond. She didn't trust Jay Harmond, either. There had always been something backhanded about Jay, but she had attributed it to his blatant sexual innuendoes. Now she was wondering if there might not be more to it. His suggestion that she duplicate real artifacts had disturbed her. Was he up to no good?

No, she told herself firmly. Her imagination was running wild. Jay wanted her to duplicate artifacts for exactly the reason he had told her. And his studio must be on the level or he wouldn't have had a new address to give to Bryan. She only wished Bryan hadn't thrown it away. She wanted to drive by and see for herself that Jay had a bona fide place of business.

"What are you thinking about?" Bryan asked.

"Nothing."

"You looked pretty serious for it to be nothing."

"How about Zerdali if it's a girl and Zorya if it's a boy?"

"You're right. It was nothing."

Laughing softly, they went back to the car.

Chapter Fourteen

"I've enjoyed our honeymoon," Lani said as she and Bryan walked into the cavernous spaces of the Museum of Fine Arts. "I feel closer to you than I have been for a long time."

He put his arm around her under the disapproving eye of the museum guard. "I was just thinking the same thing. There's no reason our differences have to come between us." He took a brochure from a rack to read about the Museum's current exhibit. "We still love each other, and that has to take precedence over everything else."

"I agree. We shouldn't try to be something we aren't. Now that I've gotten used to your moodiness, I don't mind it at all." She winked at him to indicate she was teasing.

"And your bullheadedness isn't so bad now that I know to expect it." He squeezed her playfully.

"Don't press your luck, Cameron," she warned with a laugh.

The exhibit turned out to be one of a recent Mayan excavation. It was on loan from a Florida man named J. Montrose Bearde. "What luck," Lani said in the hushed tones the museum seemed to demand.

"What a name," Bryan said.

"We aren't naming our baby either Montrose or Bearde. But really, isn't it fortunate for us to find a Mayan exhibit? After spending so much time with the little fellows, this is like a class reunion."

"They still look squatty and childlike to me."

"That's part of their charm."

"I'll bet I could make one. Now, you take that fellow there," Bryan said as he gestured at a curly-snouted statue wearing beaded bracelets. "I could do that."

"That's an Ehecatl. A wind god. They are far more complicated than you seem to think."

"How do they know these are real and not the products of what's his name? Brigido Lara?"

"I guess they just know."

"Maybe I should ask that guard over there. We might be able to do them all a service and expose some fakes."

"You'll do no such thing," she said with a laugh. "If you don't behave, you're going to get us thrown out of here."

Bryan took her hand and led her into the adjoining room.

Lani leaned over to peer into a glass-topped display case. "Look at this pottery shard. What a lovely design."

"Breathtaking," said Bryan, who had already seen as many Mayan artifacts as he cared to see. "Hey, look over there. It looks just like your hearth god."

Lani looked up with an indulgent smile. "They all look alike to you." She followed his gaze, and suddenly her smile faded.

They went to the glassed-in display case and Bryan said, "It sure looks like it to me. See? There's a chip missing from the arm where you dropped it when you took it out of the fire."

"It *is* the same!" Lani reached up and jiggled the handle, but the case was locked.

"Here now!" a guard reproved sternly. "None of that!"

Lani turned to him. "This piece is in here by mistake. It isn't authentic."

"Nonsense. Of course it is."

"No, it really isn't," Lani insisted.

"She should know; she made it," Bryan added.

A gray-haired man in a dark blue suit walked briskly up to them from out of nowhere. "What seems to be the trouble?"

"This lady says that statue is a fake," the guard answered.

"It *is*," Lani insisted.

"I'll take care of this," the man in the suit said in dismissal of the guard. He gave Lani and Bryan a cold smile and said, "My name is Fred Burkhower, and I'm in charge here. I can assure you this piece is authentic, as are all the rest."

"I'm Lani Cameron, and this is my husband, Bryan. I don't know about all the others, but this one is here by mistake. I know because I made it myself. See, there's a chip missing from where I dropped it."

Burkhower again smiled frostily. "Most of the pieces are chipped and broken. After all, they are a thousand years old."

"Not this one."

"Ms. Cameron, if you insist upon causing a scene, I must ask that you leave."

"I don't want a scene. I just want you to know that this hearth god was made in my studio and fired in my back yard."

"I'm sure you're mistaken. Look at it more closely. See how the patina is darkened in some places and grayed in others? See the crazing in the helmet? These are things that occur with extreme age."

"They also occur when the clay is baked in a circle of burning twigs and painted with a glaze of cement, fresh lime and ammonia, and hot sugar water before the clay cools. The sealer is common glue made in Mexico. I just mixed it with a little dirt."

"That's ridiculous."

"I can prove it's mine. Open the case and look at the bottom of the statue. You'll see a tiny pyramid-shaped mark. I put it on all my pieces."

"I'll do no such thing! This is a priceless work of art!"

"My fingerprints must be on it! Call the police and have them check for imprints in the clay!"

"I'll do no such thing! Now I must insist that you leave!"

Lani made an effort to calm herself. "Look, we aren't trying to start trouble. This is a very prestigious museum, and I know you want to keep your credibility intact. Just remove my hearth god and put something else in its place. I'm sure it's an honest mistake."

"The Houston Museum of Fine Arts does not make mistakes," Burkhower said scathingly.

"Mr. Burkhower, I can understand your position," Bryan said, "but she really is right. I saw her drop this statue myself."

"Guard!" Burkhower said between clenched teeth.

"All you have to do is open the case and look for my pyramid mark," Lani protested. "If it's not there, then I'll apologize, and you'll never see me again."

"Guard, please escort these people out the nearest door," Burkhower commanded.

Lani jerked her chin haughtily. "That won't be necessary. We're leaving."

She and Bryan hastily beat a retreat. "Can you imagine?" Lani fumed when they were outside. "He didn't even believe me!"

"I can see why, can't you?"

"But I told him how I could prove it!" She glared back at the museum. "I think we should go to the police. How could such a mistake have happened?"

"I'm not so sure it was a mistake."

Lani looked up at Bryan's angry features. "What do you mean?"

"I think Harmond is selling your clay gods as the real thing."

Lani's mouth dropped open. "Bryan, that's the most despicable thing I've ever heard! Jay would never do that!"

"No? Then why does he insist that you take such pains to age them?"

"They are all my own creations!"

"So were Brigido Lara's, as I understand it."

"That's ridiculous! I can't believe you would accuse Jay of actually being dishonest!" She was so shocked by all this that her own recent doubts about Jay were forgotten. Defensively she crossed her arms over her chest. "I've refused to copy any artifacts!"

"He asked you to make copies? Doesn't that prove it?"

"It doesn't prove a thing!" she stormed defensively. "Only that you dislike Jay and would say anything against him!"

"Is that what you think?" Bryan demanded angrily.

"What else can I think? You know how you are!"

"I don't have to listen to this!"

"Neither do I!" Lani flounced away. With a loud whistle she flagged a cab and slid in.

"Lani! Damn it, don't you run away from me again!" It was too late; the cab was already gone.

Cursing under his breath, Bryan ran to their car. Why did she always have to end every argument by running away? He drove the few blocks to their hotel and walked briskly through the lobby. There was no sign of Lani, but he hoped to find her in their room. She wasn't likely to fly home without going back for her airplane ticket.

The room was empty. Bryan slammed the exhibit brochure down onto the dresser and again let loose a string of curses. Where in the hell could she be? She had had ample time to get here before he did.

A quick glance in the pocket of his suit coat told him both airline tickets were still there. As a precaution in case she had not arrived yet, Bryan put them in his wallet and slipped his wallet into his pants pocket. At least now she was likely to stay in Houston and not take off for Laredo.

He couldn't decide if he should stay there and wait for her to cool off and return or if he should go look for her. He had no idea where she could have gone.

His glance fell on the mirror, and something caught his eye. For a minute he wasn't sure what was out of place, then he leaned closer. The mirror reflected the name of the company that had acted as an agent for the Mayan showing. On the brochure the name was Atoi, Inc. In the mirror the word read "iotA," and IOTA was the name of the company that had hired him in Mexico City that fateful day.

Bryan grabbed the brochure and read the fine print. The show was put together from the J. Montrose Bearde collection, by James Herrington, owner of Atoi, Inc. Bryan's pulse leaped at the similarity of the initials of James Herrington and Jay Harmond—and neither Atoi or IOTA were common names for a company. He had assumed IOTA was an acronym for a more complicated name, but it could just as easily be Atoi spelled backward!

He read further, scanning the details of how J. Montrose Bearde had accumulated the most extensive collection of Mayan artifacts outside of Mexico. Bryan's attention riveted to the address of Atoi, Inc; 423 Court Drive was familiar to him. Monica had told Bryan that Jay Harmond lived there.

Suddenly Bryan knew where Lani had gone. He bolted from the room and ran for the elevators.

Lani was so angry as her cab pulled away from the museum that she was crying. Once she was away from Bryan and could think clearly, she knew he was right. Jay Harmond had all but told her he wanted to market forged artifacts, and she had let her stupid, overzealous loyalty blind her to the facts. There was no other reason at all for him to want copies of the real Mayan finds and no reason why an exact copy would sell for more than one of her originals. Unless, of course, he was selling them as originals.

No! She commanded herself to be reasonable. The exhibit belonged to J. Montrose Bearde from Florida. Bearde was the culprit! He was bilking the art world, and if Jay was innocent, he had to be told. That had to be it! Jay was as much a victim as she was!

In her confusion Lani gave the cabdriver the address where she had mailed all her correspondence to him for years. When he stopped at the address, Lani groaned to see the restaurant again. She racked her brain to recall if Bryan had given her the new address. He had not.

In her turmoil she almost couldn't remember Jay's home address. Court Drive, that was it! She told it to the cabbie and leaned back restlessly. When she found Jay Harmond, they could decide what to do about this crook, Bearde.

Anger boiled and fumed inside her, and she mentally urged the driver on. They seemed to hit every red light and traffic jam in Houston. Lani nursed her fury. She wanted Jay to hear everything that was on her mind about Bearde and for him to reassure her that he had nothing to do with it.

At last the driver delivered her to the seedy row of town houses. Lani paid the driver and sent him away. Her stride was jerky with anger, and when she reached the front door, she ignored the bell and banged on it with her fist.

From deep inside the house she heard a movement and she pounded the door again. The footsteps came nearer. Jay opened the door. "Lani! What—"

She pushed past him into the house. "I've seen the exhibit at the Museum of Fine Arts!"

Jay dumbly stared at her.

"You must have seen it! Don't tell me you haven't!"

"As a matter of fact, I have." He watched her with the wariness of a stalked animal.

"Then you saw my hearth god!"

"Listen, Lani, there is a perfectly simple explanation for that."

"Oh? I'd love to hear it!" She paced his dark living room, not noticing the lumpy couch and clutter of newspapers on the scarred coffee table.

"There was an... an opening for a statue just that size. One broke. Yes, one broke in shipping, and to help out the museum, I..."

"What? That's the most moronic explanation I ever heard!" She glared at him. "Didn't you tell the museum the statue was a fake?"

As Jay began to get himself under control, he gave her his most winning smile. "Lani, this is all so confusing. Sit down and start at the beginning. Can I get you a drink?"

"No!" Lani plopped down on the couch and frowned. A spring was poking her through the fabric. She finally noticed the worn material and strewn newspaper. Her frown deepened. What sort of interior decorator would let his own belongings deteriorate to this condition? She glanced around. The pictures on the wall were garish prints, and the walls themselves needed painting. The carpet was the color of dirty oatmeal, and mud was ground into a path from the front door toward the rear of the house. Apprehension began to replace her anger.

"No, as I was saying, there is an explanation for all this. I sold your hearth god to Bearde. I had no idea he would try to pass it off as authentic." Jay smiled again.

"Why didn't you tell me that when I first got here? What was all that about a broken sculpture and my hearth god statue being used as a replacement? The card beside it says it was found in Veracruz." She looked at the water circles on the top of the coffee table and the cheap glass ashtray mounded with cigarette butts.

"It does?" Jay said in a good imitation of surprise. "I had no idea. When you came in I was confused. I was talking about something entirely different." He laughed as he watched her closely. "You took me quite by surprise, you know."

"This is Tuesday," she said. "Why aren't you at work at your new office? Where are the painters and workmen who are doing your redecorating?"

"You certainly ask a lot of questions." His voice wasn't quite so friendly, and his smile didn't reach his eyes. "I gave the workers a day off."

"Jay, why are you lying to me?" Lani demanded bluntly. "There are no workers, and I can't believe an interior decorator of your reputation would have loose springs in his couch."

The smile disappeared. "What are you suggesting, Lani?"

"I think you've taken advantage of me. That you are selling my clay gods as authentic Mayan pieces."

"That's ridiculous." His voice was silky, but held a warning.

"Is it, Jay? It would be very easy to pass my designs off as the real thing. After all there has been relatively little study until recently on Mayan art and the Lara statues have confused what little we did know. My patinas would pass most examinations. My designs look as believable as the real thing."

"Be careful, Lani. You don't know what you're saying."

"Don't I?" Her voice rose as her anger again started to build. "I think you've taken advantage of me from the very beginning!"

She jumped to her feet, and Jay stepped menacingly toward her. Lani said, "I'm going to go to the police and tell them exactly what's happened!"

"No, you're not!"

Suddenly the door bell rang, followed immediately by a hard pounding. Lani and Jay both wheeled to face the door. Through the window Lani saw her car. "Bryan!" she called out.

Jay grabbed her and twisted her arm, yanking her into his grasp. One hand clapped over her mouth, but not before Lani screamed.

Bryan didn't hesitate. He kicked the door with force that was driven by his anger and jealousy. The lock gave way, and the door swung open, banging against the wall. In the next town house someone shouted something about calling the police.

Bryan crossed the room in two strides and aimed a punch at Jay's jaw, but missed his mark as Jay shoved Lani toward Bryan and reeled back to fumble at a drawer in the desk.

"It's a gun!" Lani cried out as she fell.

Jay tried to aim the weapon as he turned, but Bryan was already on top of him. For a minute they struggled, the gun caught between them. Then there was a loud report, and Jay dropped to one knee. He groaned and clutched at the red stain spreading over his thigh, and Bryan backed away, still holding the gun pointed at him.

Lani couldn't move. She could hear the neighbor yelling over and over that she had called the police, but none of it made any sense. She could only stare at Bryan and at the blood pooling beneath Jay's leg.

"Okay," Bryan said as he tried to catch his breath. "Let's hear about IOTA."

Jay glared at him.

"The police are on their way," Bryan snapped. "It's going to all come out. IOTA and Atoi are both the same company, aren't they!"

Miserably, Jay nodded.

"And I wasn't hired to smuggle drugs at all, was I! It was Mexican art treasures!"

"You have no proof of that!" Jay snarled. "I know my rights! You came in here and shot me! I'll see you in prison for this!"

"No, you won't. Your neighbor can tell the police that I broke in here to protect my wife. Once the police look around, I suspect they will find enough evidence to put you away for quite a while!"

Unsteadily Lani got to her feet. "Jay set you up?"

Jay glared at her. "It was an accident, damn it! The villagers found out what we were doing and tried to stop us.

If they had left well enough alone, you would have flown out and no one would have been hurt!"

"But people were hurt!" Bryan countered. "I saw people getting shot, and I was in jail for five years!"

"It's illegal to ship artifacts out of a country," Lani said, as the wail of sirens from the arriving police cars came through the open door. "You set Bryan up!"

Jay scowled at her and didn't answer.

Bryan readily turned Jay over to the police. As he told the officers what had happened, Jay's half-hysterical neighbor appeared, swearing over and over that she was positive Jay was trying to kill the woman when the woman's husband intervened.

One of the policemen called an ambulance for Jay, although his leg had almost stopped bleeding. The other policeman wrote down the disjointed story from the neighbor and even got a confession from Jay.

"Are you sure you're okay?" Bryan asked as he put his arm around Lani.

"Yes. Just scared half out of my wits and shaken up a bit. Are you?"

Bryan nodded. He watched as the policeman wrote down everything that Jay was saying. "Looks like you're out of the clay god business."

"You bet I am," she agreed fervently.

Epilogue

The porous surface of the dish, which had already gone through the bisque firing stage, soaked up the gray glaze as fast as Lani could sweep it on. After the second firing the dish would be an aquatic swirl of blue, green and lavender and would be assembled on the brass spiral of Lani's newest waterfall.

"How is it coming along?" Bryan asked as he entered the studio.

"Terrific. I'm almost finished. Are you through for the day?"

"Yep. This Indian book is coming along pretty well. It's hard to find written documentation, but everybody in town seems to have a story to tell me about the tribe."

Lani smiled. She knew Bryan was enjoying talking to so many people, all under the guise of research. He always had been fascinated with people and the stories they could tell.

"Aren't you going to ask if we got any mail?" he queried, as he eased one hip nonchalantly onto the edge of the cleaner of her two worktables.

"Okay. I'll bite. Did we get any mail?" She finished applying the glaze, being careful not to get any on the base so the dish wouldn't stick to the rack in the kiln.

"Just this." He handed her an opened envelope from the Richard Sinclair Agency.

Lani looked at him questioningly, but he gave her no clue. She pulled out the enclosed check, and her eyes widened. Quickly she lifted her eyes to meet Bryan's. "Your first royalty payment! I never expected this much!"

"Neither did I. I even called Richard to see if he put the decimal in the right place. He says he did. It seems everyone wants to buy the book now that it has an ending and we discovered what exactly was being smuggled."

"It still seems funny to see our names in print."

"It does to me, too," he admitted, "but you were part of the story, thanks to your clay gods."

"A woman I don't even know stopped me in the grocery store this morning and asked when Jay will get out of prison. Can you imagine?"

"Whenever he gets out will be too soon to suit me."

She smiled up at him. "Don't tell me you're still jealous!"

Bryan shifted self-consciously. "Maybe a little. After all he was putting the make on you."

Lani laughed. "You writers have such a colorful way of expressing yourselves." With a sideways glance she added, "Your Monica has finished moving."

"She isn't *my* Monica. I know, I saw the realtor sign on her lawn. Maybe she will find Oklahoma City more to her liking. I don't think she was ever happy here in Laredo."

"Her happiness isn't a big item with me."

"If I didn't know you to be such a paragon, I would suspect that was a trace of jealousy. Naturally that's impossible. Right?"

Lani grimaced at him. "Okay, so I'm human. Is the baby awake?"

"She sure is. She helped me type most of the last page."

"You know you're spoiling her rotten," Lani said with a happy grin.

"I know, but she looks so much like you that I can't help it." He watched her clean the glaze from her brushes. "Debbie called and she is bringing Little Frank over this evening to play."

"Good. To watch him, you'd never know Frank had ever wanted a girl in the first place, would you?"

"I don't think Frank even remembers his Think Pink campaign."

Lani put away the brushes and finished cleaning up her day's work. "Will you help me straighten the living room before the Goldmans get here?"

"It's already done."

"I thought you said you two were in there typing."

"A little typing, a little playing, a little housecleaning. I want our daughter to be a well-rounded individual."

"With the name we picked, she will have to be," Lani said with a laugh.

"You're right," he agreed with a grin, "but surely artistic parents such as ourselves are allowed a bit of poetic license."

Lani put her arms around him. "I love you. I'm glad we were able to work out our problems."

He kissed her lightly. "So am I. And I'm glad you finally quit running off every time you get mad."

"I never did that!" she objected.

"Yes, you did."

"I did not!"

They were still bickering good-naturedly as they went into the house.

1989
IS THE YEAR OF THE MAN!

What makes a romance? A special man, of course, and Silhouette Desire celebrates that fact with *twelve* of them! From Mr. January to Mr. December, every month spotlights the Silhouette Desire hero—our **MAN OF THE MONTH**.

Sexy, macho, charming, irritating...irresistible! Nothing can stop these men from sweeping you away. Created by some of your favorite authors, each man is custom-made for pleasure—*reading* pleasure—so don't miss a single one.

Diana Palmer kicks off the new year, and you can look forward to magnificent men from **Joan Hohl**, **Jennifer Greene** and many, many more. So get out there and find your man!

Silhouette Desire's
MAN OF THE MONTH...

ATTRACTIVE, SPACE SAVING BOOK RACK

Display your most prized novels on this handsome and sturdy book rack. The hand-rubbed walnut finish will blend into your library decor with quiet elegance, providing a practical organizer for your favorite hard-or soft-covered books.

Only $9.95

Approximately 16" x 8" when assembled

Assembles in seconds!

To order, rush your name, address and zip code, along with a check or money order for $10.70* ($9.95 plus 75¢ postage and handling) payable to *Silhouette Books*.

Silhouette Books
Book Rack Offer
901 Fuhrmann Blvd.
P.O. Box 1396
Buffalo, NY 14269-1396

Offer not available in Canada.

*New York and Iowa residents add appropriate sales tax.

Silhouette Special Edition

COMING NEXT MONTH

#505 SUMMER'S PROMISE—Bay Matthews
Burdened with grief, Joanna felt empty, old, weary of living. But when her estranged husband, Chase, appeared on her doorstep, need and desire took hold... and a new life began.

#506 GRADY'S LADY—Bevlyn Marshall
Ladies' man Ryan Grady had tangled with Blythe Peyton's type before—blond, beautiful, deadly. He had to protect his brother from her poison, no matter how sweet it tasted....

#507 THE RECKONING—Joleen Daniels
Once, Cal Sinclair had offered her an ultimatum. Laura Wright had chosen college over marriage... and Cal had chosen Laura's sister. Could heated passion ever sear away burning regrets?

#508 CAST A TALL SHADOW—Diana Whitney
Juvenile investigator Kristin Price was gutsy, but a harrowing stint on Nathan Brodie's ranch for delinquents truly tested her courage. Even for love's sake, could she confront her most intimate terrors?

#509 NO RIGHT OR WRONG—Katherine Granger
Single mother Anne Emerson didn't need another man—or another scandal—messing up her life, and her best friend's ex-husband was a candidate for both. Somehow, though, being wrong had never felt so right.

#510 ASK NOT OF ME, LOVE—Phyllis Halldorson
Was Caleb's past too dangerous to speak of—even to his love? What terrible secret had made him dodge Nancy's questions and desert her in a time of need?

AVAILABLE THIS MONTH:

#499 LOVING JACK
Nora Roberts

#500 COMPROMISING POSITIONS
Carole Halston

#501 LABOR OF LOVE
Madelyn Dohrn

#502 SHADES AND SHADOWS
Victoria Pade

#503 A FINE SPRING RAIN
Celeste Hamilton

#504 LIKE STRANGERS
Lynda Trent